The General's Notorious Widow

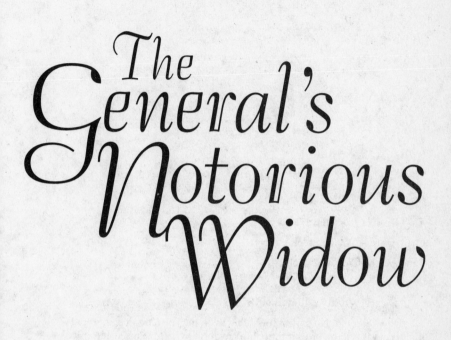

The General's Notorious Widow

STEPHEN BLY

CROSSWAY BOOKS

A DIVISION OF
GOOD NEWS PUBLISHERS
WHEATON, ILLINOIS

The General's Notorious Widow

Copyright © 2001 by Stephen Bly

Published by Crossway Books
        a division of Good News Publishers
        1300 Crescent Street
        Wheaton, Illinois 60187

Cover design: Cindy Kiple

Cover illustration: James Griffin

First printing 2001

Printed in the United States of America

Library of Congress Cataloging-in-Publication Data
Bly, Stephen A., 1944-
   The general's notorious widow / Stephen Bly.
      p. cm. — (The belles of Lordsburg; bk. 2)
    ISBN 1-58134-280-2 (alk. paper)
    1. Women pioneers—Fiction. 2. New Mexico—Fiction. 3. Widows—
Fiction. I. Title.
PS3552.L93 G4   2001
813'.54—dc21
                                       2001002091

BP		13	12	11	10	09	08	07	06	05	04
15	14	13	12	11	10	9	8	7	6	5	4	3

for
Jutti West

The LORD will destroy the house of the proud:
but he will establish the border of the widow.

PROVERBS 15:25 (KJV)

One

Lordsburg, New Mexico Territory . . . August 1, 1884

When Elizabeth Miller stabbed the asparagus spear, the big man flinched. Pink lips pursed tightly exhaled each word like bubbles released under deep water. "Do you make a habit of harassing women who dine alone? Or is there some purpose to this intrusion?"

The heavy-set man took a step backward. His jowls and his shoulders drooped. "Harassing? Intrusion? Mrs. Miller, I thought I was being charming."

The setting sun cast long New Mexico shadows in the street and through the window. Lixie Miller dropped her fork on the china plate. "'I reckon a widow gal your age is sick and tired of eating alone' is about as charming as finding a half-eaten cockroach in your salad."

He drew out a white cotton handkerchief and wiped his forehead, leaving a red dirt streak. "I, eh, wasn't expecting you to sit right here by the window. You caught me by surprise."

"With my back to the door and face to the window, just how is it I caught you by surprise?"

He pulled off his bowler and revealed thick, curly dark hair. "It was jist small talk. I was pontificating off the top of my head."

"That doesn't say too much for your quick wit, mister." Lixie stared out the window at two dogs running toward the railroad tracks across the street. "Nor your courtesy. I don't believe you even introduced yourself." She glanced up at him. "That way I'll know who to avoid next time."

His ample chest swelled, and his buttoned shirt collar pinched as his face grew even redder. "Oh, I thought you recognized me." The loud reply silenced the half-filled restaurant. "I'm none other than Charles P. Noble of Philadelphia, Pennsylvania."

Lixie Miller retrieved her fork and knife and sliced off a bite of roast. "Should I call you None? Or None Other?"

Noble glanced around as if waiting for someone to translate. "What?"

"I see satire is not your strong suit. Good day, Mr. Noble. Thirty years as an army wife taught me much about dining alone." Lixie forked a bite of slightly pink roast into her mouth and chewed as she gazed out the window at a pig and a white duck trotting side by side toward the tracks. "At times I rather enjoy dining alone." She wiped her mouth on the burgundy linen napkin. "This is one of those times."

"But, Mrs. Miller, I'm Charles Noble!"

"I'm sure that means a great deal to your mother, but it means nothing to me. I've had a rather depressing day, Mr. Noble. . . . Good day." *Okay, Lord . . . a depressing week, month, year, and decade, but I wasn't going to tell him that.*

He placed his hands on the back of the chair next to hers. "But you don't understand. I'm a famous writer!"

"That's nice. I'm quite happy for you. Today it would not matter if you were Charles Dickens. Why don't you go somewhere famous and write?"

"Mrs. Miller!" The voice was young, breathless. "Mrs. Miller!"

A hatless, barefoot boy in a white shirt and denim jeans sprinted into the dining room.

She put her arm around the young boy's thin shoulders. "Paco, seeing your smiling face cheers me up. What can I do for you?"

His round brown eyes sparkled. "Have you seen Buddy and Sylvia?"

She brushed his bangs out of his eyes. "They just loped across the tracks."

Noble stared out at Railroad Avenue.

"Buddy's a pig, Mr. Noble, and Sylvia's a large, fat duck. They terrorize the town's dogs," Lixie reported. "Perhaps you would like to write a novel about them." She turned to the boy. "Would you like to eat with me?"

He licked his lips and leaned back on his heels. "Nah, I promised I'd get Buddy home to Mrs. Sinclair before supper time. She said he's been getting into more and more trouble since he started hanging around with that duck."

A grin crept across her face. "Yes, one must be careful of the companions one chooses."

Paco stared at the big man holding the crisp brown bowler.

"I'm Charles Noble, the writer," he mumbled to the boy.

"And I'm Paco Ortiz, the future governor of New Mexico. Someday I may let you write about me. Good-bye, Mrs. Miller. Perhaps I will eat supper with you tomorrow." Paco sprinted back toward the hotel lobby.

"Anytime, Paco," she called out. She turned back to face the window and ran her fork through cold and curdled brown gravy.

Noble plopped his hat brim on the table. "Perhaps this interview would go better if I sat down and jotted a few notes while you dine. I particularly wanted you to describe the hotel room where you found your husband and that . . . other woman." He began to slide the oak chair back.

She reached over and caught the chair. "Please don't. Mr. Noble, do you see this asparagus on my fork?"

He leaned over the table. "Eh, yes."

She snapped off a bite with such force she heard her teeth click. "It was hot and tender when you walked up. Now it has become cold and stringy. I would appreciate it if you did not ruin any more of my meal. I have absolutely nothing to say to you. I will live with the consequences of my past and my husband's past until the day I die. But I will not *relive* them. Nor will I allow them to be put in a book for others to read. Please leave."

He jammed on his hat and stepped back from the chair. The bags under his eyes hung down toward his thick, drooping mustache. "I don't think I've ever been treated so rudely."

A train pulled up at the station across the street. "If this is the way you treat all of us 'old widows' and have thus far never been treated this rudely, then you do indeed live a charmed life, Mr. Charles Noble. Good day."

He didn't budge. "But what about my book?"

Lixie Miller slammed her elbows on the table and rested her chin in her hands. *Dear Lord, if You are testing me with Mr. Noble, then I'm afraid I fail. Could I just admit defeat and go on to the next step? I don't know how to get rid of this man.*

"I can put your story in every home and barbershop in America."

"Do you carry a gun, Mr. Noble?"

"A gun? Heavens no. My wife wouldn't approve of it."

"That's unfortunate. I don't have one either." She turned around in her chair. At the back wall two men in leather vests and dirty hats sat eating huge beef chops. "Excuse me, could one of you gentlemen lend me a hand?"

"Yes, ma'am," the taller one said. "What can we do for you?"

"Perhaps one of you would be so kind as to shoot Mr. Nibble for me."

"That's Noble," the writer insisted.

"What's noble?" the dark-haired cowboy asked.

"Are you joshin' us, ma'am?" the first man called back.

"My name is Charles Noble—not Nibble."

She sighed. "Yes, I'm kidding." She turned her back to the men.

Her coffee tasted lukewarm, bitter. "Mr. Noble, if I paid you, would you leave me alone?"

He rubbed his puffy lips. "What?"

"May I buy you supper at the Matador?" she offered.

"This is the Sonoran," he replied.

"I know."

"Lixie Miller, what a surprise! Evenin', ma'am."

Lixie spun in her chair and spied a tall uniformed man approaching her table. His black campaign hat was tilted to the right. Both the hat and the yellow worsted hat cord were frosted with red dirt. Charles Noble backed up several steps.

Lixie's hands flew to her cheeks. "Captain Parker? Congratulations, Monty! I do believe it was second lieutenant last time I saw you. How delightful! Are you stationed near here?"

He pulled his hat off his neatly combed dark brown hair. "Not too far, ma'am. I'm with General Crook over in Arizona. Just came in on the train. There's been a delay, so I thought I'd get somethin' to eat. I didn't know you were in Lordsburg."

"It's quite a surprise to me as well." She reached out and took the captain's strong, callused hand. "I presume you get along well with Georgie."

"General Crook? Yeah, he's sort of different. Just like you told me that time we got stuck in the Dakota snowstorm. Do you remember that?"

"Yes, I do."

"But the general took a likin' to me, and I'm doin' fine."

She reached over to pick a short tan string off his navy blue coat. "General Crook is a very fine judge of character. If Georgie likes you, you deserve it. Congratulations."

Captain Parker shoved his hat back. "Nobody calls him Georgie but you and Mrs. Crook."

"How is Mary doing?"

"He doesn't confide in me much."

"He still writes to her incessantly?"

"Yes, ma'am." He glanced over at Charles Noble. "Am I interruptin' somethin'?"

"Mr. Charles Noble, this is Captain Montgomery Parker, one of our finest young officers."

"I'm not all that young, Mrs. Miller."

"You will always be young to me, Captain Parker. Mr. Noble, Monty once carried me blanket-wrapped three miles through a blizzard. Now there's a story for you to write. But you were just leaving."

Charles Noble inched back closer to the table. "Actually, I wanted to interview Mrs. Miller . . ."

"Captain Parker, will you be in Lordsburg long?" she asked.

"We're just takin' the train back to the fort after a trip to Washington. There's a mechanical delay of some sort."

Noble continued to mumble, "I'm writing a book about her."

Lixie Miller completely ignored the big man and focused on the captain. "Did you say 'we'? Is General Crook with you?"

"No, not hardly," Parker laughed. "I'm traveling with Colonel Banks."

Lixie Miller stood up and gazed around the room. "Strat Banks is here?"

Charles Noble pulled a small notebook from his coat pocket and began to write with a short pencil. "Is that Colonel Stratford 'Iron-Jaw' Banks?"

She rubbed her chin and stared back at the wide door leading to the lobby. "I can assure you, Mr. Noble, more than Strat's jaw is as strong as iron," she murmured as she sat back down.

"Well, now, this is quite fortuitous," Noble blustered. "This will make another exciting chapter in my book." He laid his notebook on the table across from Lixie and pulled back the chair.

This time she couldn't reach the chair. "I did not invite you to join me, Mr. Noble," she snapped. "I think I've said that as clearly as possible."

Noble paused at the back of the chair. "Well, I assumed—"

"Monty, on the other hand, is an invited guest. I do hope Strat is able to join us. I don't miss army life, but I certainly do miss my army friends."

Captain Parker held his hat in his hand. "The colonel went to talk to the sheriff and then was to join me here if the train is not repaired."

She pointed to the chair next to her. "Well, by all means, please sit down. We really need to get caught up."

Noble looped his thumbs in the pockets of his light brown vest. "I'm calling the book *The General's Notorious Widow!*" he blurted out.

"Where would you like me to sit?" Captain Parker asked.

"Mr. Noble, you will not write a book about me!"

Parker dragged a chair across the painted wooden floor. "Would this be all right?"

"Eh, yes, Monty, that's fine. You sit on my right side, and Strat can be on my left."

"Perhaps I should sit across the table," Noble offered.

"Perhaps you should get on a train and leave town."

"Mrs. Miller, you can't stop me from writing a book about you."

"I will not cooperate with you in any way."

"Then I'll make it all up."

"And I'll sue."

"It's a fiction book, Mrs. Miller. You can't sue me for a piece of fiction."

A tall, thin, white-aproned waiter scooted over to her table. "Mrs. Miller, Mr. Elsworth from the CS Ranch wishes to have a word with you."

Lixie glanced around the room. "Where is he?"

"He's in the lobby."

"Tell him to come in and join the party."

"I beg your pardon?" the waiter replied.

"Tell him if he wants to talk to me, I'm here in the dining room, but I will not leave my supper to talk to some man in the lobby." She spun around to face the now-seated Charles Noble. "Mr. Fiction Writer, I do not want you at my table. You are not invited. Would you please leave? Where may you be reached?"

"I'm staying in Shakespeare. Do you want the room number?"

"Not at all. I merely wanted to know where my attorney could contact you."

"Attorney?"

"You write about me, and there will be a lawsuit. Now out with you."

Noble pushed to his feet. "I didn't know you'd get so irate about a dime novel."

"Irate? Captain Parker, I believe you have seen me irate."

"Yes, ma'am, I reckon I did."

"Am I acting irate now?"

Parker laughed. "No, ma'am, you aren't throwin' silverware, nor have you discharged a weapon in his direction."

"Hmmm . . ." Noble jotted down a few words in his notebook. "Fiery, violent temper . . . yes, that's good."

"Did you hear me, mister? I want you to leave!" she shouted.

The approaching Langford Elsworth jumped straight back. "My word, Mrs. Miller, are you addressing that remark to me?"

Lixie traced her fingertips across her temples and could feel her heart beating. "No," she replied softly, "I was addressing Mr. Charles Noble. But you did surprise me, Mr. Elsworth. I thought you would still be in Santa Fe. I heard you were testifying at Ramona Hawk's trial."

The Englishman pulled off his gold wire-framed spectacles and rubbed the bridge of his nose. "Yes, well, the trial was cut short. She escaped."

"Escaped?" Lixie gasped.

"Ramona Hawk escaped?" Charles Noble flipped a page on his notebook.

Elsworth pulled out a gold pocket watch and glanced at it. "Yes, it seems that she and two of the courthouse guards are missing."

Captain Montgomery Parker stood up. "I'll need to inform the colonel."

"What about Gracie and Colt?" Lixie questioned.

"They are in no danger as far as I know. We didn't chat much," Elsworth replied.

"Gracie? You mean, Senator Denison's other daughter?" Noble sputtered. "You know Grace Denison?"

"Grace Denison Parnell," Lixie corrected.

"Oh, splendid, I'll do two books!" Noble licked the lead tip of the pencil and continued to scribble. "No . . . three books . . . one about Ramona Hawk and her two amours!"

"Knowing Miss Hawk's reputation, I imagine they have both been murdered by now," Lixie commented.

"Splendid! Even better," Noble mumbled.

"I say," Elsworth huffed, "who is this man?"

"He claims to be a writer," Lixie explained. "I've never seen his work, but he has mastered rudeness and audacity."

The voice sounded like a man commanding a thousand

mounted troops. "Mrs. Miller—surrounded by men, of course. Lixie, how are you?" The officer strolled across the restaurant. All conversation in the room hushed.

"Strat! It's so good to see you!"

The colonel removed his hat and gave her a brief hug. "Monica will be quite put out that she wasn't here."

Oh, Lord, how I miss the hug of a handsome man in uniform. "I trust she and the boys are doing well?" *To tell You the truth, Lord, I miss any kind of hug. Or touch.*

"Lixie, there are only two perfect army wives. I married one. You're the other."

"Strat, there has only been one perfect army wife, and that's your Monica!" She turned to the Englishman. "Mr. Elsworth, do you know Colonel Banks?"

Elsworth shook the colonel's hand. "Only by reputation."

"That's Colonel 'Iron-jaw' Banks?" Charles Noble blustered. "But he's not even as big as me."

Lord, this man is like a curse that won't go away. "None other than Mr. Charles Noble of Philadelphia, Pennsylvania, was just leaving, Strat."

The colonel nodded. "Yes, well, I thought we might grab a quick meal while the train is being repaired. Ethan told me you lived in town."

"At the moment I live in their guest room. Where did you see Captain Holden?" she asked.

"At the marshal's office. I think he's going to swing by here."

"Sit down, Strat. Let's visit over supper," she insisted. "What did you need to tell the marshal about?"

The colonel lowered his voice and leaned so close Lixie could smell his shaving tonic. "A band of Apaches have fled the San Carlos Reservation. We think they're headed this way, according to the report of a couple of prospectors up in the Mogollon Mountains."

"My word," Noble sputtered, "I trust you're sending troops after them."

"This is a wild land, Mr. Fiction Writer. Nothing but time is going to change that," Lixie lectured.

Captain Parker held his coffee cup up for the waiter. "Well said, Mrs. Miller."

"None of that 'Mrs. Miller' stuff, Monty Parker. Mr. Noble has already commented on my age. I was hoping you would make me feel young by calling me Lixie," she insisted.

The colonel inspected the writer as if selecting a beef cow for slaughter. "Old? Obviously, Mr. Noble has never seen you dance."

"Speaking of dancing," Elsworth interrupted, "Mrs. Miller, I wondered if there's any chance you'd be so kind as to—"

She smiled at him. "I'm sorry, Langford. I simply must finish my meal before I dance with you."

"Well, yes. I didn't mean now," Elsworth said. "There's no music!"

"That never stopped Lixie Miller before," Colonel Banks laughed.

She reached over and squeezed the colonel's hand. "Mr. Elsworth doesn't know me well . . . yet."

Langford Elsworth tugged at his black tie. "Mrs. Miller—"

"Lixie."

"Lixie, I need to speak to you for a moment in private," he insisted.

"Langford, I'm afraid nothing will be private about this supper. Perhaps we could meet tomorrow."

Elsworth stared out at the darkening shadows on Railroad Avenue. "I simply must get back to the CS and tell the boys about the Apaches headed this way. I'll send them out in twos and threes."

"If a band is on the prowl, you'd better send your men out in tens and twenties," Banks roared.

"Yes, but there are limits to our manpower," Elsworth mumbled.

Miller could feel her neck start to cramp from staring up at the standing men. "Tell them about Ramona Hawk as well. She's a vengeful woman, and Tommy Avila did work for the CS. Maybe she won't be satisfied with just killing him. I urge you all to be careful."

Elsworth cleared his throat and peered at the men in uniform. "Lixie, what I wanted to ask concerns next Friday and Saturday."

"Don't mind us," Colonel Banks urged. "We'll just sip our coffee and hope the waiter brings out a plate of chops soon."

Elsworth cleared his throat again. "I say, Lixie, Lord and Lady Fletcher will be coming through to spend a couple of days on the ranch. You know how rough things can be with no women up there, so . . . well, I know this must sound quite forward, but I've stewed over this for weeks . . ."

Lixie's brown eyes sparkled as she batted her long eyelashes. "You wanted me to come cook and clean?"

"My word, no!" Elsworth roared. "I would never think of such a thing. I wondered if you would join us for the weekend and play the hostess. I really need help to pull things together."

Lixie giggled. "My goodness, a social invitation. I'll have to check my calendar." *Elizabeth Miller, you haven't giggled since Grace and Colton got married. This is good. This is very good.*

"Ethan and Mary Ruth Holden are coming up Saturday, but I was hoping to have someone with style to be there and entertain Lady Fletcher. I'm afraid hunting javelinas in the brush will not be quite proper."

"Lady Fletcher is an American, isn't she?" Lixie asked.

"Yes, quite," Elsworth replied.

"Well, Langford, that's quite an honor you have afforded me."

"You would be doing me a sincere favor. I would be quite indebted," Elsworth said.

With bowler in hand, Noble scooted closer to the table. "Say, isn't Fletcher the one who partnered with Stuart Brannon over in Arizona?"

"I believe it was Colorado," Lixie corrected him.

The colonel surveyed the fat man with sagging beard. "Who is this gent, Lixie?"

"Colonel Banks, this is Charles Nibble."

"Noble!"

"He writes dime novels."

"Historical fiction."

"He specializes in dredging up the past."

"Merely discovering the reader's interest."

Banks reached across the table to the standing man. "Well, any friend of Lixie's is a—"

"I assure you, Strat, he's no friend of mine."

Noble shook the officer's hand. "I'm goin' to write a book called *The General's Notorious Widow*."

"My word," Elsworth huffed, "he's actually writing a book about you?"

"I'm debating whether to shoot him or just tie him to a Joshua tree and let the buzzards peck away," Lixie said.

Colonel Banks yanked a .45 army Colt from his holster. He shoved it, grip first, in her direction. "Be my guest."

Noble backed away, using his notebook to shield his chest. "Don't encourage her!" he roared.

"Mr. Elsworth, you'll need supper somewhere. Why don't you join us before you return to the ranch?" she offered.

"Then you will come to the CS and be hostess?"

"I believe I will."

"Splendid!" Elsworth beamed. "I'll send one of the boys down with a carriage for you on Friday."

"Send a couple of the boys, well-armed," she requested.

"Yes, of course. You're quite right."

Noble scribbled in his notebook. "The Apaches wouldn't come this close to a town, would they?" He faced the incredulous stares of those at the table.

Colonel Banks took a slow sip of coffee. "Well, Lixie, you have a party to plan. That sounds like old times. When you and Monica got together to plan a social event, it was the party of the year." He glanced out the window. "I don't know why some things have to change. Those were good days, weren't they?"

For a moment Lixie closed her eyes and relaxed her forehead. "Yes, they were, Strat." *A room full of tall uniformed men with West Point posture and well-dressed ladies . . . Lord, those were good days. Very good days.*

"What do you normally do on weekends?"

She opened her eyes and laced her hands in her lap. "I sit on the Holdens' patio and read."

His posture as straight as his oak chair, the colonel took another sip. "Lordsburg is quite a tranquil place, I presume."

"Oh, yes," she said. "As Mr. Noble so aptly put it, 'I reckon a widow gal your age is sick and tired of eating alone.'"

Colonel Banks banged down his coffee cup. "He said that?"

Charles Noble tugged on his tight shirt collar. "Well, I was just making small talk."

Lixie laid her hand on Captain Parker's sleeve. "I believe that's reason for court-martial, isn't it, Monty?"

He squeezed her fingers. "He's a civilian, Lixie."

"I suppose the best we can do is send him before the firing squad," Colonel Banks boomed.

"You boys are gettin' a bit touchy, aren't you?" Noble mumbled. "It wasn't anything personal."

"It was certainly personal to me," Lixie said.

Colonel Stratford Banks stared out the window. "Lixie, why is that little Mexican boy leading a pig and a duck?"

"That's my friend, Paco."

"Which one?" Banks prodded.

"The boy!" she laughed.

A tall, stately man with a pipe came up to the group. "My goodness, Lixie, this looks like a crowd."

"Ethan! Did you come to rescue me?"

Ethan Holden looped his thumb in the gold watch chain that dangled from his wool vest. "Rescue you? I came to rescue the United States Army."

Elizabeth Miller folded her thin arms across her chest and laughed. "This *is* quite a gathering. I don't think I've had this much attention since the Sixth Cavalry found out I was the only woman in southeast Montana."

"I remember that time." Captain Parker grinned.

"So do I," she murmured. *My husband assigned me to assist Dr. Conner, and 75 percent of the men reported in sick. The general was livid. Of course, I was younger then. Much younger.*

Ethan Holden moved behind her chair. "I stopped by to let you know that Mary Ruth and I will be driving out along the line this evening. The telegraph signal has been poor all day. I wanted a visual check of the wire, and Mary Ruth wanted to get out a little in the cooler part of the evening."

"I hear Apaches are roaming north of here," Lixie cautioned.

"Yes, I know. I fully intend to stay on the telegraph road and will certainly be back to town before dark."

"Well, you must be Mrs. Miller!" The man who strolled toward the crowded table had gray hair at the temples, a thick mustache, and short, straight sideburns. His three-day beard was gray and black with a tinge of red. Deep wrinkles framing his eyes told of hard years; a sly smile teased of energy and mystery. A long-barreled Colt was strapped to his hip. His spurs made a faint sound, like distant bells.

"Have we met?" she asked.

He pulled off his black beaver felt hat. The mostly gray hair was creased by the hat band. "No, ma'am. I'm Jefferson Carter."

"Mr. Carter, you need a shave and a haircut. Yes, I'm Lixie Miller. Just how did you deduce that?"

"I need a bath, too, Mrs. Miller, but I don't usually have folks tell me so. At least, not on the first meeting. I have a message to deliver to you. Mrs. Parnell said you'd be easy to spot. You would be surrounded by men."

"Gracie Parnell? You've been with Gracie?"

He seemed to be surveying everyone but Elizabeth Miller. "Yes, ma'am. I met them at the trial. Grace and I have some mutual friends in the U.S. marshal's office in Washington."

"Are you a marshal?"

"Nowadays I'm an attorney. I was one of those prosecuting Ramona Hawk."

Lixie peered intently at his eyes. "You're a lawyer, Mr. Carter?"

"Yes, ma'am. Does that surprise you?"

"No . . . well, yes, I suppose in some way," she admitted. *A dusty, gun-packing lawyer? Only in the West. Only in New Mexico.*

"Most of my cases seem to involve disputed Spanish and

Mexican land grants. But I assisted in the Ramona Hawk case . . . that is, until she disappeared."

"When are Gracie and Colt and my darling little Ruthie-girl coming back to town?" Lixie asked.

"They took the train to Iowa to see some of her kin," Carter reported.

"With little Ruthie?" Lixie glanced up at Ethan Holden. "Now won't that be interesting? I wonder how the senator will respond?" she murmured.

"Now that he's dropped out of the race for the presidency, I don't suppose it will be so touchy," Holden replied.

"I don't understand," Carter said.

"I don't suppose you do. Is there anything else they wanted to tell me?"

He brushed off the sleeve of his white shirt. Red dust fogged the air. "They asked if you would be willing to house-sit for them until they return in a couple weeks."

"House-sit? How charming. You see, Mr. Nibble, my life is not totally boring. I get to look after an empty house."

"My name is Noble," the big man grumbled.

She turned to Holden. "What do you think, Ethan? Can you and Mary Ruth survive without your permanent boarder?"

"We will miss you, of course. Rob will miss you the most."

"Rob? Who's Rob?" Elsworth asked.

"The Holdens' college-age son. He's adopted me as his aunt."

"I assure you, Lixie, 'aunt' is not exactly the category in which he has placed you."

She studied the tall man who stood with hat in hand. "Mr. Carter, I will be delighted to house-sit for the Parnells. Thank you very much for bringing me the message. I presume you had other business in our area?"

His thumbs were looped in his bullet belt. "No, I just came to tell you about that."

"You traveled all the way from Santa Fe to deliver that message?" *The brass casings of the bullets have started to turn green from being in the belt so long. I would guess you have not had to use that gun too often recently.*

"Mrs. Miller, you're surprised at me again."

"I assumed someone who was once a telegrapher, like Gracie, would have merely sent me a telegram, not a handsome barrister, with her message." *Did I just call this total stranger handsome? Lixie, control yourself.*

"Grace mentioned a telegram. But I wanted to . . . It just seemed like a good opportunity to . . ."

Lixie laughed and clapped her hands. "To come check out the general's notorious widow?"

The tall man rocked back on the heels of his boots. "I reckon that's about it."

I would narrow my eyes, but it only shows the lines more. Elizabeth Miller, you are a vain woman. "Well, Mr. Carter, what is your opinion?"

He blushed. "Of you?"

"You did say you came to Lordsburg to check me out, didn't you?"

Colonel Banks signaled for the waiter to bring more coffee. "Good heavens, Carter, don't let us intimidate you. We've all acted the fool around Elizabeth Miller! Isn't that right, Lixie?"

She stared at the six men seated at and surrounding her table. "Yes, you have. And some on more than one occasion."

The colonel sat straight up as if at attention. "Well, no reason to get personal." Then he relaxed his shoulders and grinned. "And that, Mrs. Miller, was before any of us got married."

"So come on, Mr. Carter. Tell us your opinion of the notorious Mrs. Miller," Ethan Holden insisted.

The lawyer studied her before he spoke. "I believe she is exactly what I was expecting."

I have no idea in the world if he is happy or disappointed. "Oh, even the crow's-feet around my eyes and the gray streaks in my hair?"

"Yep. I was expecting that too."

"Mr. Carter, I'm happy I could live up to your expectations. You're a surprise to me."

He scratched the back of his neck as he stared down at his brown boots. "I am?"

"I don't believe I've ever met a lawyer who wasn't wearing a suit and tie. She glanced at Colonel Banks and Captain Parker. "Or at least a military uniform."

"I do have a suit and tie," he said. "Didn't figure it was needed in Lordsburg."

"You're quite right," she said. "And you came all the way here to see the general's widow?"

"And to trace a couple leads on little Charley McComas."

"You think he's still alive. It's been over a year."

"I promised the family I'd check it out."

"Did you know Judge and Juniata McComas?"

"No, ma'am. I didn't."

"My word, Lixie, you are certainly grilling this man," Ethan said.

"But she didn't ask him the hundred-dollar question yet," Colonel Banks jibed.

"The hundred-dollar question?" Carter puzzled.

"Are you a married man, Mr. Jefferson Carter?" Colonel Banks boomed.

"What?" Carter gasped.

"Now, Strat," she asserted, "that was totally uncalled for. I happen to know that Mr. Carter is not married."

"How could you tell that?" Carter asked.

"Because you traveled all the way from Santa Fe to get a glimpse of the general's notorious widow. No wife would let her husband do that," she reported. "Besides, you blushed way too much for a married man. In fact, I would venture that you have never been married. Am I right?"

"I reckon you've got me pegged. I thought I was a fairly complicated man."

"I trust you don't blush this easily in court," she said.

"I didn't think you'd notice."

"Mr. Carter, I not only noticed the blush, but I noticed the wrinkle in your right eyebrow where you were undoubtedly creased with the barrel of a revolver at one time. I noticed how you favor your right hip, and I figure it was either broken or shot. I noticed your Missouri drawl. I noticed how you stared me up and down when I was talking with someone else, thinking I didn't see you."

"Good grief, Lixie," Colonel Banks cautioned, "don't embarrass the poor man."

"And I notice that he's searching for the doorway, trying to figure out how to exit quickly at this very moment," she concluded.

Jefferson Carter shook his head. "I've never met a woman quite as blunt as you before, Mrs. Miller."

"Welcome to the club," Captain Parker added.

"Ethan, the colonel and the captain know I was an army wife for thirty years. I survived such a life by being forthright and candid. Some would say brusque, curt . . . even harsh."

"But we wouldn't say it to her face," Colonel Banks hooted.

The waiter slipped in beside her. "Mrs. Miller, would you like to adjourn to a larger table where your entire entourage could join you for supper?"

"Did you hear that? I have an entourage! How delightful for a widow gal my age, eh, Mr. Noble?"

"I do look forward to interviewing you," Noble said.

"And I look forward to avoiding you," she countered.

"Don't set a place for me," Holden insisted as he turned to the lobby. "Mary Ruth is waiting for me in the carriage."

Langford Elsworth shoved on his hat and straightened his tie. "Yes, well, I really should get back to the CS Ranch tonight. I want to warn my drovers that the Apaches are on a rampage again."

"What exactly constitutes a rampage?" Lixie asked. "I suppose it must be a matter of semantics. Does one death make a rampage? And how is a rampage different from a murder?"

"Colonel Banks!" someone behind her shouted.

Lixie spun around. A short, barrel-chested sergeant with a dark mustache marched across the dining room. "Colonel Banks, the train is repaired. We'll be leaving in ten minutes. They're asking the passengers to reboard."

Colonel Stratford Banks stood. "Well, Lixie, it looks like Captain Parker and I can't stay for supper after all."

"I'm disappointed." She held out her hand to the colonel. "Do give my regards to Monica, Strat. You don't know how much I would love to see her. If she comes out, please have her stop for a few days in Lordsburg. We can visit and tell old army lies. Actually," she grinned, "most of the stories about Lixie Miller are true." She turned to the waiter. "I don't think we'll need another table. I believe most are leaving, but don't take it personal. I'm sure it has nothing to do with the bill of fare. Except perhaps the asparagus."

The waiter scurried off to the kitchen.

Lixie glanced at the two men who were left. "Mr. Carter, you've traveled a long way. Would you care to join me for dinner?"

"Maybe we both will do that," Noble blurted out.

"Mr. Carter, would you usher this great American writer to the door?"

Jefferson Carter nodded slowly. "Do you always give orders to men who are perfect strangers?"

"Mr. Carter, I find you neither perfect nor strange," she snapped. "And, yes, I suppose I do give orders to men."

Carter brushed his hand across his nose, and for the first time Lixie noticed that it was a little crooked. "I presume none of them refuse to obey you?" he challenged.

"Only one."

"Oh, and where is this lucky fellow?"

"Dead," she declared.

"Now that, Mrs. Miller, is a very convincing argument. I will usher this man to the door." Carter motioned toward Noble.

She sat back down at her table. "Will you come back and join me for supper?"

"How come he gets an invite for supper, and I don't?" Charles Noble complained. "Why, you've known me longer than you've known him."

"That's exactly why you don't get invited. I know too much about you."

Jefferson Carter tipped his hat. "I reckon I better pass too while I still remember who I am. Mrs. Miller, you kind of overwhelmed me."

"Will you be leaving soon to return to Santa Fe, Mr. Carter?"

"I reckon that depends."

"Upon what, Mr. Carter?"

"On whether I have the nerve to talk to you again."

"Oh, come now, surely an attorney is not so easily flustered."

"Mrs. Miller, if you ever take up the legal profession, the rest of us might as well retire."

"There's no chance of that, Mr. Carter. I live a very quiet life."

"A table surrounded by men panting like hounds after the fox is hardly a quiet life."

"Why, Mr. Carter, were you panting like a hound after the fox?"

"I reckon that was obvious enough. And a good reason to excuse myself." He turned to Charles Noble. "Come on, mister. It's time for us to exit."

"I believe I'll just stay here and eat at this table next to Mrs. Miller's."

Jefferson Carter's hand slammed down on the man's shoulder.

"On second thought," Noble declared, "perhaps it *is* time to go."

Like a dust storm that finally settles, Lixie's table was clear, and she could once again see the patrons in the dining room. The waiter straightened the other chairs at her table and toted off the used coffee cups.

Lixie stared down at her plate.

Well, Mrs. Miller, that was rather like a tornado blowing through. I can hardly remember where I was when the storm hit. I was either contemplating my future . . . or the asparagus. Lord, Mr. Noble was correct, of course. I'm just a sad, old woman eating supper by myself. And the saddest part is, it will be that way for a long, long time.

The bite of asparagus was cold and sour.

She took a sip of tepid coffee. It was strong and bitter as it slinked down her throat and into her stomach.

Perhaps this is a capsule of my life—a very small island of activity in a sea of loneliness. I have always eaten alone. Mother was always sick in bed, and dear Daddy much too busy at work. So I ate alone. Or sneaked into the kitchen to eat with Helena and Dalton.

She scraped the cold brown gravy off a wedge of beef chop and took a bite of it. The meat was cold, tough, and stringy.

Then I became an army wife. I would travel. I would meet people. I would raise a family.

But a barren womb.

A barren marriage.

She broke off a hunk of sourdough bread and nibbled on it. It was crusty, dry, stale.

Of course, I didn't know it was a barren marriage. He was just busy. Always moving up in the ranks. Always taking troops somewhere I couldn't go. Always needing to check in with the War Department in Washington, D.C. So I would stay at the fort and plan a big gala for his return. Little did I know that every time I planned a big affair, he was having one.

She dipped the small wedge of bread into the cold gravy, stared at it, and then dropped it back on the bread plate.

Twenty-seven difficult years, always believing that things were going to get better. Finally I traveled to Washington to surprise him on his birthday. I can't believe I was so naive that I carried a wrapped present in my hand.

That pair of birthday cuff links had more covering than she did.

She grabbed a blanket.

He clutched his heart.

And died on the spot.

She retrieved the napkin and reached up to brush her lips. She wiped her eyes instead.

Lord, I died that day too. All my hopes. All my childhood dreams. All my teenage fantasies. All my longings for a life together.

Dead.

Hollow.

She stabbed a small, round purple grape with her fork and held it up as she surveyed Railroad Avenue out beyond her window.

With moments of life breathed into me—moments like this one this evening.

Bless you, Mr. Elsworth. I have no idea why you think I should host Lord and Lady Fletcher, but it gives me a reason to survive another week.

She chewed on the grape, puncturing a bitter seed, which she swallowed quickly, and laid down her fork. Her hands dropped to her napkin-covered lap.

Gracie was a brief respite—a beautiful fragrant flower to remind me how to giggle and plot and plan. Then she married. I cried at their wedding. I cried for me.

She watched an elderly, shawl-covered Mexican woman shuffle down the sidewalk, using a hand-carved cane.

It's depressing, Lord.

I attract the likes of Charles Noble and scare off the ones like Jefferson Carter. Why is that?

And why, at my age, does it even matter to me?

She held out her hands in front of her and examined both sides carefully.

Age spots have replaced a wedding ring. I put up with so much because those retirement years would come. I'm much too young for the golden years and way too alone to enjoy them.

But Monty and Strat made me laugh this evening.

I am an army wife. But I can never go back. Too much pain. Too many glances. Too many whispers.

The waiter came up to her table. "May I warm up your supper for you?"

"It's fine. I'm just not very hungry."

"Would you like anything else?"

I'd like Mr. Jefferson Carter to come back. Or Captain Parker. Or Strat Banks. Or Langford Elsworth. Or even Charles Noble. "Could you warm my coffee?"

"Yes, ma'am."

Perhaps not Mr. Noble. He was too brutally honest. I'm just a lonely old widow eating alone. I'll hide in the desert town of Lordsburg and die a slow death. Interrupted by momentary delights.

"I don't think I'll serve asparagus to Lord and Lady Fletcher," she blurted out. Then she realized no one was there to listen.

This is not an abundant life, Lord. What possibly could be Your purpose for having me here? I waited so long, and now my days seem wasted.

Lord, if You don't have anything for me to do down here on earth, maybe it's time for me to move on up to heaven. There's just got to be more for me than relaxing and reading and on rare occasions being surrounded by a horde of men.

"Well, at least," she mumbled aloud, "there has to be more than relaxing and reading."

Two

Elizabeth Miller strolled by Alfredo's Saddle Shop, refusing to glance in the window. From the corners of her eyes, she could see the reflection of a black-and-gray-haired, five-foot-two-inch woman with good posture and a slightly tilted hat, but she knew if she looked closer, all the wrinkles, creases, and unconcealable signs of middle age would leap back at her.

She looped the parasol handle over her arm and tugged on the beige fingerless gloves that almost reached her elbows. *Perhaps I will wear gloves like these the rest of my life. My fingers look rather nice. It's the backs of my hands that I dread.* She stared at her left hand and then let it drop to her side. Her right hand slowly twirled the dusty green parasol that now rested on her shoulder.

Lord, I know that many widows wear their wedding ring for the rest of their lives, but there is something about having your husband die in another woman's bed. He was not mine on that day. Nor is he mine now. Perhaps he never was.

She paused at the corner of a raised boardwalk as half a dozen dusty cowboys rode slowly past her. Their horses plodded with the determined steps of a long ride almost over.

That's not true, Lord. He was mine. There were times. Sweet times. Wonderful times. Times when all our life was before us. His career waited. My children waited.

His dreams came true.

Mine didn't.

He never said anything, but he blamed me. I know he did. Each year

*the eyes hardened. The touch became more callous. He stayed up later
and got up earlier until we hardly touched at all.*

The cowboys tied up to the rail in front of the saddle shop
behind her.

*I can't believe I'm reliving all this. Lord, do You see what I'm doing?
Absolutely nothing! Other than rescue little Ruthie from the Omaha
orphanage, I have accomplished nothing during my time in New Mexico.
I sit in the Holdens' patio and feel sorry for myself. I have relived every
moment of my life so many times I could scream.*

As she stepped out into the dirt street, a cowboy's words floated
her way. "See, what did I tell you? There are purdy señoritas in
Lordsburg!"

She peeked around the parasol. All six men stared her way.
Lixie quickly looked away.

"Don't mind ol' Pat, ma'am. He just blurts out what's on his
mind without thinkin'. No offense intended," one of them shouted.

She never looked back but walked on with a spring in her step.

*The Lord bless you, Pat, whichever dirty, weak-eyed drover you
are. It doesn't matter. I needed that. And today I'll take praise from
wherever it comes.*

*Lixie, did you just wiggle your backside? No, I just sort of caught
my heel on a rock.*

She turned north and out of the corners of her eyes noticed
that the cowboys entered the saddle shop.

*Of course, if the attention happened to come from a certain broad-
shouldered, gray-haired Santa Fe lawyer, that would be . . . nice.
Elizabeth Miller, you chased the man off, and now you want him to
appear and compliment you?*

*I think I'll go to California. I always did like it there. Martina
Hackett keeps asking me to come visit. But I won't go right away. Not
before Langford Elsworth's party at the CS or before Gracie and Colt
return. I did promise to watch their place. Maybe I'll go to California
for Christmas.*

A barefoot, brown-skinned boy jogged up to her. "Hi, Mrs.
Miller. Are you through supper?"

"Hello again, Mr. Paco. Yes, I'm finished. Did you eat at Mrs. Sinclair's boardinghouse?"

"Nah." He jammed his hands in his pockets. "I didn't like the menu."

"What was the bill of fare?"

"Roast duck."

Lixie's hand flew to her mouth. "She cooked Sylvia?"

"No, it was one of them almond-stuffed ducks from Lin Fee's Market. She threatened to cook Sylvia though. Buddy's hiding under the house and won't come out. Mrs. Sinclair said she'd bribe him with a piece of warm apple pie." Paco walked alongside Lixie Miller.

"Why do you think she spoils that pig so?"

"I reckon she loves him." He reached up and took her hand as they walked. "Aunt Julianna says that love is giving someone better than they deserve."

"Your aunt is very wise."

"Thank you."

His palm felt warm and sweaty. Lixie squeezed it as they walked.

"You have beautiful fingers just like Miss Gracie," he announced.

"Oh, you are a charmer, Paco Ortiz!"

"Oh, no. You are the charming one. That man said so."

She glanced down at the young boy. "What man?"

"Oh, you know. The one at the hotel."

"Mr. Carter?" she pressed.

"Yes, I guess so. I don't remember his name."

She looked back over her shoulder toward downtown. "When did you see him?"

"At the water trough in front of the Matador. Buddy and Sylvia wanted to swim before we went home, and he walked by. He said, 'Young man, could you tell me where the charming Mrs. Miller lives?'"

He asked about me? "What did you tell him?"

"I told him you are a very good friend of mine, and I would not divulge your dwelling place."

"You did?"

"I didn't think you wanted strange men calling on you."

"You're quite right. Of course, Mr. Carter is not exactly strange."

"You mean, it's all right if I tell him where you live?"

"I think that would be all right. However, I do appreciate your warning me first."

He let go of her hand. "I will go and tell him."

Lixie tried to grab his shoulder but missed. "Don't run, Paco."

"Why not?"

"I don't want you to hurt yourself. Besides, I wouldn't want Mr. Carter to think I'm in a hurry to get him the message."

"Aren't you?"

"Paco, trust me. Walk slowly. If you happen to see him, just say, 'Oh, by the way, Mrs. Miller lives with the Holdens on Fourth Street.'"

"But I can't run?"

"Absolutely not."

"Do you want to see him or not?"

"Perhaps."

"Ayeee. I still do not understand women."

"How old are you, Paco?"

"Nine years old."

"You are quite smart for being only nine."

"But I am too short."

"Too short for what?"

"To dance with you or Miss Grace."

"I don't think that matters to me."

"Really?"

"Certainly not." Lixie folded her parasol and draped the hooked handle over her arm. "Would you like to dance now?"

"Out here in the street?"

"Why, yes."

"In front of the whole world?"

She glanced around at the empty street. "Just who are we in front of, young man?"

"Eh . . . I better go tell that man you want to see him."

"Tell him where I live. That's all. It's up to him to decide to call on me or not. And don't run."

"No, ma'am. Is it okay if I saunter?"

Lixie restrained a laugh. "Yes, by all means. You can saunter."

He sprinted off south, then spun back. "I don't know how to dance very good."

"Do you want me to teach you sometime?"

"Yes. Miss Grace was going to teach me, but she got married. You aren't goin' to get married on me, are you?"

"I don't think you have to worry about that."

"Good!" he shouted. He ran toward Railroad Avenue.

I'm not at all sure what Paco is going to say to Mr. Jefferson Carter, and somehow it just doesn't matter. The worst that can happen is that the man gets on the train and goes back to Santa Fe. The best that could happen . . .

She pushed open the heavy, weathered wooden door to the Holden patio and strolled inside.

Just exactly what would be the best thing that could happen? Mrs. Elizabeth Miller, you met the man an hour ago, talked to him for five minutes in a group of other men, and then chased him off. What do you think will come of this?

She strolled over to the raised circular pool of water in the center of the patio.

Frankly, anything will be better than the last few weeks. Perhaps I should find a Protestant convent.

She sat on the rock bench that surrounded the pool and dipped her fingertips in the cool water, let out a deep breath, and surveyed the shaded patio.

Perhaps I have found that convent already.

"Lixie, have you seen my father?"

She turned to twenty-year-old Rob Holden. His white cotton shirt was buttoned at the collar, but the sleeves were rolled up above his elbows. "Your father said he and Mary Ruth were going for a ride out along the telegraph line. Didn't they mention it to you?"

"Mother said something about going somewhere, but I didn't pay much attention," he mumbled.

Lixie noticed he hadn't shaved in a day or two. Maybe longer. "I think they plan on returning before dark. Ethan wanted to inspect the telegraph line, I believe."

Rob Holden jammed his fingers in his back pockets. "I guess that means it's just you and me for supper. Would you like to eat at the Sonoran?" he suggested. "They have a nice spread. Of course, I'm a little short on funds."

"Perhaps you have enough for yourself. I just ate there, Rob, thank you. Why don't you go on and eat?"

"You had supper already?"

"Yes."

"All by yourself?"

"Now that is a matter of opinion. But, yes, I think I could say I dined alone." Lixie continued to let her hand drift in the pool of water.

"But—but—why didn't you ask me? No woman should have to eat alone," he protested.

"I believe I've heard that more than once this evening. I was downtown shopping and then decided to eat."

"I guess I can just fix myself something here."

"Why don't you go on to the Sonoran? The food, when hot, really is quite tasty."

He folded his arms across his thin chest. "By myself? That sounds boring."

"You'll probably find someone you know."

"Yes . . . but I wouldn't want to leave you all alone."

"Oh, that's very kind, Rob, but don't worry. I believe some company might stop by, so I won't be alone."

Holden strolled over and parked his brown bull-hide boot on the rock step beside her and leaned on his knee. "Anyone I know?"

"Probably not. He just arrived in town."

Holden stood at attention. "A gentleman? Perhaps I should stay here, you know, to be chaperon."

Lixie laughed.

"What's so funny?"

"You flatter me, Rob, to assume that a lady my age and station has to worry about a chaperon. That's quite a compliment."

"You aren't all that old. You know I think you're a very smart-looking lady."

"Thank you, Rob. You're kind."

He laid his hand on hers. "It's the truth."

She raised up and plopped the parasol over her shoulder. "The truth is, I am six months older than your mother."

He shifted his weight from one foot to the other. "That doesn't seem like such a big gap, does it?"

"You know, Rob, if that's true, then according to your earlier statement, you and I should always have a chaperon here, shouldn't we?"

His neck and shoulders stiffened. "That's not necessary."

"I completely agree." Lixie strolled toward a big wooden patio chair.

He followed her. "Is someone really coming over?"

"I don't know for sure." She didn't turn back and face him but continued to stroll. "There's a possibility."

"Don't worry about me, Lixie. I'll stay out of the way. I'll just rummage in the kitchen and find me something to eat."

"Certainly."

"Are you sure there's nothing I can do to help you?"

She hung her parasol on the back of the wooden chair. "There are a couple things. That is, if you have time."

He hurried to her. "I've got time."

"After you eat, could you bring my large trunk from the storage room and place it in my bedroom?"

"Are you leavin' with this man?" he gasped.

Lixie stared at the young man. Then she ironed the wrinkles off her forehead with her fingers. "I will allow that insulting remark because of your youthful enthusiasm. No, I most certainly am not going off with any man."

"I'm sorry, Lixie. That did sound coarse."

"Yes, it did. Grace and Colt Parnell will be gone a couple more weeks and have asked me if I could house-sit for them. I'll be moving over to their place. That's all."

"You're movin' out?"

She eased down on the edge of the chair and plucked up a book from the little black iron table. "I'll be four blocks away for a couple of weeks."

"But—but—"

"And the other favor—perhaps you could find me a wagon and tote that big trunk over to the Parnells'."

"Tonight?"

"Well, yes. I believe they were counting on my overseeing things right away. Of course, I'll spend the weekend at the CS Ranch."

He backed up toward the doorway to the corridor. "What am I supposed to do for the next two weeks?"

"I believe you should find a job, since you decided not to return to college."

"Now you're sounding like my mother," he muttered.

"I could sound like your father if you'd like."

He stared at her, then grinned. "I reckon you could, couldn't you? I'll move the trunk and get a wagon."

"Thanks, Rob."

"After I eat."

"Naturally."

He paused at the archway and peered back. "I guess I sounded the fool."

"That's all right. I enjoy your enthusiasm."

"You do?"

"Yes, it makes me feel younger."

"You see, I told you age doesn't matter."

"Oh, it matters. I didn't say I felt young . . . just younger."

"Are you going to wait for him out here, or do you want to come fix me something to eat?"

"I believe I'll wait out here," she replied.

Rob Holden ambled toward the kitchen.

Lixie leaned back in the wooden chair and plucked up a tablet of paper from under a stack of books. *I probably don't need to move everything to the Parnells'. The one trunk will be sufficient. I can always stop by and pick up anything else.*

She jotted some words down on the paper and then glanced at the gate.

Jefferson Carter? Why did I write down that name? This is all quite silly, but it feels good anyway. Daydreams are often much better than reality.

He had ducking pants, spurs, and a holstered gun. Why would he wear spurs on the train? No one wears spurs there. Maybe he rode horseback over from Deming. Maybe he rode horseback all the way. No, that would take too long. It's a question I'll ask him. When and if I see him, I'll say, "Hello, handsome Mr. Carter. Nice of you to visit the needy widow lady. Why do you wear spurs on the train?"

A rap on the front patio gate caused her to drop the notebook on the tile floor. She leapt to her feet.

Well, Mr. Carter, you did come! I'm surprised. Well . . . maybe not too surprised.

Lixie Miller waited for the knocking to intensify and then sauntered across the patio toward the front gate. She stopped a few feet short of it to brush her bangs to the side. She felt to make sure her hair was still pinned up.

I should have checked in a mirror. If I owned this home, I'd have a small mirror by this front gate. Lord, that is so vain. What am I doing? It's just a man coming to visit for the first time . . . albeit a very good-looking, broad-shouldered, square-jawed, brown-eyed man.

"Yes, just a moment," she called. Lixie grabbed the cool black iron handle of the gate. The squeak of the large hinges sang out a greeting. "Why, isn't this a . . ." When she caught sight of the man, her voice trailed off to a whisper. ". . . surprise?"

The big, rotund man rocked back on his heels. "You aren't nearly as surprised as I was."

"Mr. Noble, what on earth are *you* doing here?" Lixie stepped through the gate and glanced up and down the dirt street.

"What kind of question is that?" he boomed.

"I think it's fairly obvious." She continued to gaze down the street toward Railroad Avenue. "I believe I made myself clear at the restaurant that I did not want to talk to you."

"But you sent for me," he protested.

"I most certainly did not!"

Noble tugged off his round hat and ran his fingers through his thin brown hair. "You mean that little Mexican boy is a liar?"

"Paco?"

"I don't know his name. Anyway, I asked him after supper where you were staying, and he wouldn't tell me. Then not more than ten minutes ago, he ran up and said you were here at the Holdens and wanted to see me real bad. What's goin' on here?"

"Paco said that? That I wanted to see you?"

"The brown-skinned lad you had your arm draped around at the Sonoran."

No, Paco, not Charles Noble! You said it was Jefferson Carter, didn't you? I can't believe this! Lord, I acted presumptuously and fool-ishly, and You are making me pay for it. Of all the people in this town, this is the one I absolutely did not want to see.

"Aren't you going to invite me in?" Noble asked.

Lixie's shoulders slumped. She shook her head. "Mr. Noble . . ."

"My friends call me Chuck."

If I send him away, he'll say that Paco is a liar. I just assumed . . . Why did I assume it was Jefferson Carter? "Mr. Noble . . . I didn't— eh, I didn't expect you to . . ."

"To come over so quickly? A writer is always ready to listen to a good story, Mrs. Miller. Do you mind if I call you Lixie?"

"I would prefer to be called Mrs. Miller."

He pulled a notebook from his pocket and jotted down a few words. "That was a very good line. I like the way you said it. I just might use it for the opening line in the book. . . . Yes, I think so . . ." He waved his hands in front of him as if conducting an orchestra. "I prefer to be called Mrs. Miller," he mimicked. "Wonderful!"

Lixie stared at the rotund man.

"But I really think we need to sit down to do the interview." He strolled past her and into the patio. "It's gettin' dark in here. I might need a lantern after a while."

"Mr. Noble, I'm afraid there's been a mistake. I think . . ."

"Now, don't worry, eh, Mrs. Miller. I find everyone is a little self-conscious and nervous when having a story written about them." He marched across the arcade. "Oh, what a lovely patio. Its description should go into the introduction. I'll have you leave the tranquil setting of a Spanish hacienda and be thrust into that lurid scene at the Washington hotel."

"What? I—I was living in a Virginia farmhouse at the time."

"Yes . . . well, a little artistic license, you know. That's what we writers do."

Lixie ran her hand across the back of her neck. "Mr. Noble, I have a confession to make—"

"Don't say another word," he interrupted. "It happens to me all the time."

"It does?"

"Yes. Women seem to be overcome in the presence of a famous writer. Why, some of the stories I could tell you . . . I mean, not that I would, of course."

She stared at the large, overweight man with sagging jowls. *You've been writing fiction way too long. I believe you no longer can recognize reality.* "Mr. Noble, I would appreciate it if you wouldn't put words in my mouth. I have personally met the likes of Generals Sheridan, Sherman, and Lee, as well as President and Mrs. Grant, not to mention Mr. Melville and Mr. Twain. I do not get flustered in front of a dime novelist."

"That's all right, Lixie. No need to apologize," he blustered.

"This is him?"

Lixie spun around to see Rob Holden standing in the archway.

"Who is this young man?" Noble asked. "Is he your son? You don't have a son, do you?"

"No, this is not my son!" she snapped. Then she turned to Holden. "No, Rob, this is not the man I mentioned."

"Who is he then?"

"I'm Charles Noble."

Rob Holden's eyes widened. "The famous writer?"

Noble's back straightened, and his chin raised. "Yes. You've heard of me?"

"I read your books about Stuart Brannon!"

"Well, actually . . . I didn't write the books about Brannon. That was Hawthorne Miller." He turned toward Lixie. "No relative of yours, I presume."

"Not hardly."

"Oh, I know! You wrote the Pecos Williams series," Holden remembered. "And the Panhandle Tex series."

"Why, yes!" Noble strolled over toward the twenty-year-old.

"I read them all ten times when I was a kid."

"My word, a true fan!"

"I even wrote to you once," Holden said.

"You did?"

"I told you there was an error in one of the books."

"Did I write back?"

"Yes, you said you would see that it got changed in subsequent editions. Did you do that?"

"Well, I, eh . . . I actually don't recall. That was years ago," Noble mumbled.

Lixie scooted toward the archway. "Rob, did you move my trunk to my room?"

"Eh, yeah."

"Good, I'll just leave you two to visit while I pack."

"But what about the interview?" Noble quizzed.

"Now, Charles, I wouldn't dream of standing between you and your adoring fans."

"Humph, well, yes. I should . . . I mean, keeping fans happy is a part of what I need to do."

"Exactly. Now if you'll excuse me, I have to pack."

"Are you moving?"

"Yes," she replied.

"Where?"

"Charles, a widow lady has to be discreet about giving out her address. With your fame, you probably have the same dilemma."

"Well, actually . . . yes, I believe I know what you mean," he murmured.

"Did Ranger Williams really shoot six comancheros with only four bullets?" Rob Holden asked.

"Quite so," Noble boasted. "He's a remarkable man."

Rob Holden rubbed his slightly fuzzy chin. "How is that possible?"

"Well, you see, son, the evening sun was low on the horizon, about like it is today, creating long shadows. Well, the ranger could tell . . ."

Lixie hurried out of the patio and down the long corridor. *Thank you, Mr. Rob Holden. I owe you a favor. A big favor. But I don't think I should tell you that.*

With her clothes, jewelry, and personal items packed in the large trunk, Lixie crept back out to the tile corridor. She peeked into the patio. *They're gone? They just left? They didn't say anything to me about leaving.*

Lixie lit the lantern near the fountain pool and meandered across the shadowy patio to the front gate. *How can they just leave? Rob hovers around me like a lost puppy, and Charles Noble has hounded me for hours. Now they just walk away without a word?*

The street lamps cast a dull light on the dirt street. Two men rode by in an open-top carriage.

"Evenin', ma'am," one called.

"Good evening!" she called. Then she stepped back into the patio, leaving the gate open.

Rob was going to help me get a wagon and move my trunk to the Parnells' house. Now I'll have to find a hack myself. Well, Mrs. Miller, you are a widow lady. There's no man in your life to carry your bags.

She hiked back to the pool.

There's no man in your life to do anything.

After retrieving her black straw hat, Lixie stepped out into the shadows of early evening. She hiked about twenty steps and then stopped at the sound of a familiar grunt. A quite rotund pig came into view.

"Buddy, what are you doing out this late at night?"

The pig ambled past her.

"Where are you going?"

The pig kept waddling toward Railroad Avenue.

"Buddy, if you see Paco, tell him I want to see him right now," she called out.

The pig's head twisted around.

"You heard me. Find Paco and send him over here."

Buddy let out a snort as he trotted toward the tracks.

I can't believe I've just been talking to a pig. Elizabeth Cartouche Miller, you really must do something with your life. This is horrible, Lord. Give me something to do—something better than fleeing boring men and talking to barnyard animals.

She spied a man holding the lead lines of a two-horse buckboard.

"T-Bang, is that you?" she called.

"Evenin', Mrs. Miller. It's finally coolin' off a little, ain't it?"

"I think it is. Is that your rig, T-Bang?"

"The Berry sisters rented it. I'm just drivin' them around. They hate to shop when it's hot. Did you need a lift?"

"I need my trunk moved over to the Parnells'."

"Are you movin' in with them?"

"Just going to house-sit until they return."

"Shoot, I can help you. It beats waitin' here."

"I don't want you to leave the Berry sisters stranded."

"They went into Millie's to try on hats. I don't reckon they'll come out for an hour. Hold these horses. I'll go tell them I'm movin' your trunk." He crawled down out of the buckboard.

"Thank you, T-Bang."

Lixie clutched the headstall of the lead horse and stroked the horse's neck as T-Bang slipped into Millie's Fine Dresses and Hats. She moved around between the two horse's heads.

"Well, you two, you both look sleepy. One of you has a back hoof cocked up and eyes sagging. But at least you have a purpose in life."

It was so dark that she could not recognize the cowboys riding down the center of Railroad Avenue only a few feet away. Just beyond her one of them shouted. There was an explosion and a long flash of flame from a revolver.

The team reared up, lifting her off the ground. Then they bolted straight forward. She held onto both harnesses and dragged her feet. "Stop it right now!" she screamed.

Both horses pulled up and danced in place. Lixie regained her footing and tried to catch her breath.

"Sorry, ma'am," one rider called out. "I was just showing ol' Jack my new pistol. Didn't see you there."

She straightened her hat. "Please be more careful. You almost caused me to be run over."

"Sorry, we didn't reckon no regular women was out here."

"You are a regular woman, ain't ya?" the other cowboy asked.

She brushed her hair back over her ear and then rubbed the horse's necks. "Yes, I believe you could say that."

"Would you like to go dancin'? Me and ol' Jack would make it up to you."

"I ain't that old," the other one said.

"Boys, that's the best offer I've had in quite a while, but never invite a woman to dance that you haven't seen face to face," she called back.

She clutched the horse's harnesses as the two men rode closer. One struck a sulfur match and leaned out of the saddle, holding it in front of her.

"Just as purdy as she can be, Jack. I kin pick 'em, cain't I?"

Mister, if the alcohol on your breath catches that flame, you will explode. What exactly does "pretty as she can be" mean? And am I sure it's a compliment?

"Wheweeee, Teddy boy. Maybe she's got a sister."

Lixie Miller began to laugh. "Boys, thank you for your attention, but I was older than both of you when they fired on Ft. Sumter."

The one with the match sat up. "You are one well-preserved lady, and I'd be pleased to take you to the dance."

"Thank you, Teddy boy, I'll remember that if I change my mind," Lixie said.

"I'll be at the Matador until we go broke or get thrown in jail."

"Or both," Jack added. "Evenin', ma'am." He tipped his hat.

"Good night, boys. Be good and have fun."

"You know, that's what my mama always told me. For the life of me, I never could figure out how to do that."

"What's the team doin' up here?" T-Bang called as he stomped out.

"They bolted forward a little."

"You don't say. What spooked them?"

"Just some noise in the street."

"The Berry sisters said for me to help you 'cause there is only one hat they like in the store, and they are arguin' over who should have it, and it will take a good hour to decide."

Lixie climbed up into the buckboard. "Poor Millie."

"Nah, she went home."

"What?"

"She just lets them look around and take what they want and pay for it tomorrow. Let's go get you moved."

T-Bang circled the buckboard west and turned the corner south on Fourth Street. A young boy ran out from under the streetlight.

"Mrs. Miller!"

T-Bang stopped the wagon.

"Paco, it's getting late for you to be out," she scolded.

"It's getting late for *you* to be out," he replied.

"Yes, you're right. T-Bang is helping me move my things over to Gracie and Colt's place. Why don't you come ride with us?" she called.

He jumped up beside her before she finished the sentence.

"I want to talk about that man you sent over to see me tonight," she said.

"Mr. Carter?"

"You did not send Mr. Carter. That was Charles Noble who came over."

"It was? I must have gotten the names mixed up. Which one is Mr. Carter?"

"He's rather tall, broad-shouldered, with a square chin, brown eyes—looks similar to Colt Parnell, only older and with more gray in his hair."

"I don't know him, but I can look around town if you want."

"No, I do not want you to. You need to go home. Your Aunt Julianna will be worried."

"Yes, you are right. She might have to go to El Paso this weekend. I think my uncle is in jail again. Anyway, she is going to bring me another notebook. I am writing a book, you know."

"You are? I'm afraid to ask what it's about."

"I'm calling it *The Boy Governor of New Mexico*."

"It's autobiographical, I presume."

"No, it's about me," he replied.

"Looks like a commotion at the Holdens'!" T-Bang called out.

"No one was home when I left," she murmured.

Marshal Yager loomed next to the lantern at the front gate of the patio. Several other men crowded inside. Paco leaped off the rolling buckboard and then held up his hand for Elizabeth.

"Ethan, what's wrong?" she called.

Holden stepped over to the buckboard. "Someone shot at us, Lixie."

"Oh, no! Is Mary Ruth . . ."

"Neither horse nor human was injured, but two of the four shots tore into the canopy of the carriage."

She could not see much past the clay pipe in his mouth. "Who was it?"

"I have no idea. I drove a little too far down the line. Someone had shot our insulators. I wanted to know how many were damaged. We were on the way back, near the broken walls of the old Kennett place, when the shots rang out."

"Do you think it was Apaches?" she asked.

Marshal Yager stepped up to the carriage. "I never knew Apaches to waste bullets like that."

"I'm tryin' to dissuade him from riding out there tonight," Holden added. "It would accomplish nothing and jeopardize the deputies."

"Colonel Banks asked that we investigate every claim of Apache movement. We're to telegraph him in Arizona if we find any traces of them. Of course," the marshal said, "if those are Apaches, by mornin' there will be no trace."

"Marshal Yager, as one resident of Lordsburg, I would feel much safer if you and the deputies were in town all night rather than out on the desert," Lixie said.

"Well put, Lixie," Holden chimed in.

The gray-haired marshal looped his thumbs in the pockets of his leather vest. "I don't like people takin' shots at our folks and gettin' away with it."

"No one was injured," Holden reminded him.

"I suppose I'll ponder on it a spell," the marshal added. "I can't figure out why they were shootin' at you."

"How's Mary Ruth?" Lixie asked.

"She went to the kitchen. Lixie, would you check on her?"

"What about your trunk?" T-Bang called out from the buckboard.

"Could you deliver it to the Parnells' and just set it in the hallway, T-Bang? I'll go over later."

"I'm goin' home," Paco called out. "Do you want me to find that handsome man and send him to the Parnells'?"

"I most certainly do not!" Lixie snapped.

"You don't want me to look for him at all?"

"Not tonight. But if you happen to find out tomorrow where he's staying, I'd be curious to find out. But don't tell him I said so. Is that clear?"

"I never make the same mistake twice, Mrs. Miller."

"I know, Paco. Thank you."

Mary Ruth Holden was pouring hot water into a china cup when Lixie entered the room.

"How are you doing, Mary Ruth?"

The woman spun around. "Oh, Lixie, did you hear about our adventure?"

"Adventure? I heard someone tried to kill you."

"Kill us? Oh, no, I don't think so. They were merely shooting at us."

"Listen to you, Mary Ruth. They were shooting at you. Bullets kill."

"I suppose." Mary Ruth dipped a tea strainer into the hot water. She pulled down another cup. "It was rather exciting. Like bees buzzing at our heads. Have you ever been shot at?"

"Once when there was an Indian attack on Ft. Grant, but it was over before I realized they were bullets."

"Then Ethan raced the team back to town—the wind in our faces, the shouts, clutching each other. Oh, my, it was quite exciting." She handed Lixie a cup of black tea.

"I can't believe this. I was expecting you to be shaking and in tears over this horrible ordeal, and you enjoyed it." Lixie took a sip of the tea and felt it scald the tip of her tongue.

"Oh, no, I didn't enjoy it. I was scared to death." A sly smile crept across Mary Ruth's narrow face. "I just enjoy memories of surviving it. It must be the way the men felt after a big battle when they came out alive. Remember how they would come home and bounce around the house for days with such enthusiasm?"

Lixie stared across the long, narrow kitchen. "Yes, I do remember that."

"As you are well aware, my life in Lordsburg is so routine I could be unconscious and complete my rounds."

"Your life? What about mine, Mary Ruth? I don't even have a household to oversee."

"Perhaps you should drive out along the tracks," Mary Ruth murmured. "No, I didn't mean that. It's just . . . well, it seems to me there are certain risks in life. It's a part of being human, and sometimes we work our whole lives to eliminate those risks. And if we're really successful, we can end up with an incredibly boring life. Oh dear, now I'm beginning to sound as philosophical as my son. Where is Rob?"

"The last I saw him he was with Charles Noble."

"The writer? He's here in town?"

"You've actually heard of him?"

"Oh, yes. Rob was quite a fan when he was about twelve or thirteen."

"Yes, well . . . Mr. Noble thinks he wants to write a story about the general's notorious widow."

Mary Ruth clapped her hands. "Oh, how delightful! I mean . . . what do you think about it?"

"I don't want any part of it."

"You're right, of course. There's no reason to relive those painful scenes in public. I was merely thinking of the adventure of having a book written about you."

"Adventure?"

"Lixie, someday, mark my words, there will be a book written about our Gracie Denison Parnell. Wouldn't you agree?"

"No doubt."

"And I believe someday there will be a book about Lixie Miller, no matter what the title. But, honey, there will never ever be a book written about Mary Ruth Holden. So I will have to enjoy notoriety vicariously through my friends."

"And get a thrill when someone shoots at you?"

"It all sounds rather silly to someone like you, I suppose."

"Mary Ruth, you are making more sense every day."

"Are you still going over to the Parnells' tonight?"

"Yes, I am."

"But it's after dark."

"It will be an adventure."

"Oh, yes. Quite right." Mary Ruth allowed the tea to steam her face but didn't sip any. "Do you need Rob to bring some things over for you?"

"T-Bang loaded up my case."

"You know, if you ever need him to, I'm sure Rob would stay over to keep you company."

Oh, that would be an adventure, all right, Mama. The last thing I need in my house is an overenthusiastic twenty-year-old. "I'll be fine. I'll spend the weekend at Langford Elsworth's ranch. Are you and Ethan still planning on coming up on Saturday?"

"Oh, yes. I've never met the Fletchers. Have you?"

"No, I haven't. You two be careful, what with trouble hanging around the outskirts of town."

Mary Ruth set her cup down and clapped the palms of her hands together. "Oh, yes, and Ethan said he would let me carry the shotgun!"

Lixie laughed. "Mary Ruth, look at us—two middle-aged ladies looking forward to fast rides with dangerous curves in the road."

"Well, Lixie dear, the only dangerous curves around me any-more are the ones in the road!"

The sun had just peeked over the eastern desert hills when Lixie strolled out onto the front porch of the Parnells' white clapboard house. She sipped hot green tea as a huge duck waddled down the street.

"Good morning, Sylvia," she called out.

Lixie brushed her white canvas apron down over her plum gingham dress and sat down on the top wooden step. A small boy several blocks away sprinted up the slope toward her. The duck cut down an alley before meeting the boy. The lad slowed to a skip.

"Good morning, Mrs. Miller!" he called out as he approached. "I saw you come out on the porch when I was all the way down on Railroad Avenue. It looked like you were talking to Sylvia."

"I did say hello to her."

"What kind of mood was she in?" Paco asked.

"Actually, Paco, I don't speak duck. Now what are you doing up so early?"

"I helped my Aunt Julianna pack for her trip. Then I went to find Mr. Jefferson Carter for you."

Lixie took a sip of tea and watched the barefoot boy cross the yard. "You needn't do that so early."

"I wanted to find him for you."

"Did you have any luck?"

"Yes and no."

"What kind of report is that?"

He plopped down on the step next to her. "Mr. Jefferson Carter stayed last night at the Hornaby Hotel, room 103."

"My, you did investigate. Thank you very much."

"But he's not there now."

"Where is he?"

"I don't know."

"Paco, what are you talking about?"

"Bobsy Larkin—he works at the stable—said Mr. Carter left town."

"You mean, he went for a ride?"

"Nope. Bobsy said he tied on his satchel and everything to his buckskin horse and rode out."

"But he—he came here just to see me. He wouldn't leave without saying good-bye," she stammered. "Or something."

"Well, he just did."

"He'll be back by nightfall," she insisted.

"Not when he took his bedroll and satchel."

"But—but . . . this isn't the way it's supposed to be," she stammered.

"Listen." He jumped to his feet.

She leaned forward, and in the distance a bell rang. After the final ring he spun around and plopped down beside her again. "That was Grace."

"How can you tell which bell is ringing?"

"They have different voices. They are pretty bells, aren't they?"

"Yes."

"Aunt Julianna says that bells always signal a beginning or an ending. Which do you suppose it is? Is this the end or the beginning?" Paco asked.

The thought of a gray-haired, strong-shouldered Santa Fe lawyer riding north out of Lordsburg teased her mind. "That, Mr. Paco, is what I've been sitting here trying to decide."

Three

꧁❧꧂

"My name is Elizabeth Miller, but I would prefer that you call me Lixie." The straw hat shaded her eyes. She hoped it hid the creases.

"Lixie? That's a mighty fine name, ma'am," replied the grinning cowboy at the reins of the faded green ranch wagon. "I'm Johnny White, and this here hombre is Mean Mike Mason."

Lixie glanced at the tall, extremely thin cowboy wearing a brand-new hat and contagious dimpled grin. "Nice to meet you boys. Mean Mike, how did a young man with such a delightful smile ever get that name?"

He tugged on the navy blue bandanna that hung loose around his neck. "The boys gave me that name, ma'am. Said I was too friendly. They said if I didn't sound tough, no one would listen to me."

"That ain't all true," Johnny White joshed as he helped Lixie up into the wagon, his hand callused, his grip strong. "If you ever play whist with ol' Mason, you'll know how mean he can get—mighty mean."

"We brung you this here corduroy pilla, ma'am," Mean Mike said.

She took the dusty brown pillow and fluffed it up. "I appreciate your coming down for me. Johnny, aren't you the cowboy who saved Grace Parnell from that runaway team?"

The cowboy dropped his gaze to the floorboards. "She was Miss Grace Denison then," he murmured.

Lixie sat down between the two cowboys and patted White's

arm. "I surmise you and every other cowboy in the district are a little disappointed that Gracie's married."

"Ain't that the truth," Mean Mike added. He had a distinct
aroma of spice tonic on his clean-shaven face.

Johnny drove the wagon north over the tracks along the Silver
City road. "Don't get us wrong," Johnny replied. "Us CS cowboys
have a lot of respect for Colt Parnell for the way he handled things
after Tommy got killed. We probably got a whole lot more respect
for him than the ol' man does."

"Oh dear, does Mr. Elsworth still hold a grudge?" Lixie posi-
tioned her parasol to keep herself in the shade.

"He don't mention it or nothin'. But he's very protective of us
cowboys, and when it looked like Parnell was in on Tommy Avila's
death, well, naturally he took issue with that."

"That's behind us." She slipped a hand in Johnny's arm. "Now
we have to go entertain Lord and Lady Fletcher." Johnny sat up
straight, shoulders back, chin out.

"I don't rightly know how to treat a lord and lady. Are you goin'
to give me and the boys some lessons?" he asked.

She hugged his arm a little tighter. "What kind of lessons are
you going to need?"

Lixie watched Johnny's Adam's apple as he swallowed hard.
"Ma'am, are we supposed to bow, walk backwards out of the room,
and not speak until they speak to us?"

"Horace Mack says you got to walk backwards in the presence
of royalty," Mean Mike Mason blurted out.

She released her grip on Johnny's arm. Her left hand fell to her
lap. "Well, boys, just relax. You don't have to do anything different from normal. I'd suggest all of you clean up and wear your best
shirts. Other than that, be yourselves."

"This is my best shirt," Mean Mike mumbled.

"It's beautiful on you. What's that color?"

"I call it my red shirt," he answered.

"I think it's carmine red."

"No foolin'? I figured it was just faded."

"You think them Fletchers will talk funny like Mr. Elsworth

does sometimes?" Johnny White slapped the lead lines across the horse's rump and picked up speed.

"Edwin Fletcher certainly will have some British accent, but he's been in the States a long time, so I hear. I would imagine it's not too pronounced."

"I heard he was a pard to ol' Stuart Brannon," Mean Mike said.

"Yes, I've heard that too," she replied. "Have you boys ever met Mr. Brannon?"

"Is he still alive? I thought he got shot," Mean Mike said.

"I believe he's still living on his Arizona ranch," Lixie said. "Lady Fletcher is an American. She was a friend of Brannon's, and that's how she met Mr. Fletcher."

"She's an American?" Johnny White asked.

"From Prescott, I believe."

Mean Mike pulled off his hat and spun it in his hands. "You don't say? Well, shoot, I didn't need to buy a new hat for no American lady."

"You needed a new hat. Ever since that cow made a deposit on your old one during the spring branding, it's smelled pretty rank," Johnny said.

Lixie watched the dirt roadway ahead of the rolling, jostling rig. *Remind me, Lord, never to enter a bunkhouse. Oh my, what aromas must be there.* She patted the '73 Winchester carbine lying across Mean Mike's lap. "I see you're prepared for trouble."

"There's Apaches on the move," Mason replied.

Both men surveyed the desert wilderness that stretched ahead into rolling barren hills.

"Have you seen any Indians around the ranch?" she asked.

Johnny White rubbed the sweat off his upper lip with the back of his hand and smeared a little dirt across his cheek. "Ain't seen um, ma'am, but they're there. Three yearlin' steers got butchered last week up at Single Tree Canyon. We moved the cattle down to Big Burro Springs and haven't lost any more."

"So far," Mean Mike added.

Lixie found that if she sat up straight, the jarring ride was more tolerable. "What is Mr. Elsworth going to do about the loss of the cattle?"

Johnny kept the team at a slow trot. "Nothin', as long as it don't get worse. When we rode out there where the steers were killed, we found a lot of little footprints."

Lixie frowned. "Children?"

"That's what we figure. They are movin' their families somewhere. Mr. Elsworth just shrugged and said, 'I don't blame a man for wanting to feed his children.'"

"Mr. Elsworth said that?" Lixie twirled her parasol in her right hand. "Well, good for him."

"But don't you worry, ma'am. Me and Johnny will protect you if there's a problem," Mean Mike offered.

"Thank you. How many guns are you protecting me with?"

"I've got my carbine and my Colt," Mean Mike announced.

"And I've got my .45, and there's a shotgun under the seat," White added.

Lixie swung her knees to one side and peered under the seat. "Good. I'll use the shotgun."

"You, ma'am? You know how to shoot?" Mean Mike asked.

"Not only can I shoot, but I can reload my own shells, take the gun apart, clean it, and reassemble it. Mean Mike, my husband was a general in the army."

"Yes, ma'am, I reckon ever'one has heard about your husband."

"I suppose you have," she sighed. *Lord, is there any place in this country that hasn't heard about me?* "I've been stationed at forts all over the east and west. Often there isn't much to do at a fort, so I would do some target shooting."

"No foolin'? You just don't seem the type," Johnny said.

"Oh, just what does that mean?"

"You just seem mighty purdy and fancy . . . a fine lady, you know, for a gal your age."

"Boy, oh boy, you are a smooth talker, Johnny White," Mean Mike hooted.

"Shoot, you know what I mean. Don't you, Lixie?"

"I will accept it as a compliment, Johnny."

She laid her parasol in the back of the wagon, reached under the seat, and pulled out the double-barreled shotgun. Drawing a linen handkerchief from the cuff of her dress sleeve, she wiped off the dusty receiver. She held it up to the bright New Mexico sun. "Janssen Sons & Co.? I've never heard of this gun maker."

"It's been with this wagon since day one. I don't reckon any of us knows where it came from," Mean Mike reported.

Lixie shoved the release lever to the right and let the barrels pivot open. She pulled out the two twelve-gauge shells, inspected them, and then shoved them back in and snapped the shotgun closed. Pushing her hat back, Lixie lifted the gun to her shoulder and tracked imaginary geese across the cloudless morning sky.

"Do you really know how use that gun?" Johnny said.

"Try me."

"What do you mean by that?" he countered.

She clutched the cold steel receiver with her right hand and let her index finger slide onto the front trigger. "Toss up a target for me and I'll show you. I trust you have more than two shells."

"Oh, yeah, there's another dozen in that gunny sack under the seat," Mean Mike reported.

"Then toss me up a target."

Johnny White glanced at Mean Mike and mumbled, "You're kiddin' us."

"Do I look like I'm joking?" she challenged.

"You really want to shoot that thing?" Johnny asked.

"Yes."

"Why?"

Lixie jammed the brass butt plate into her shoulder and let her left hand slide down the forearm wood. "Because neither of you think I can."

"Well, I ain't got no glass target ball to toss," Mean Mike declared.

"A rock will do."

"Stop the wagon, Johnny. Let's see if this lady can shoot."

White pulled the buckboard off the roadway and parked it by a cluster of yucca plants. Mean Mike hopped off while the wagon was still rolling and began to scout for a rock. Lixie stood, cocked the two stiff hammers, and held the shotgun in front of her.

"Maybe you ought to shoot from the ground. It might be a little safer. I'll help you down, ma'am," Johnny White offered.

"Here's one!" Mean Mike shouted from the somewhere off to the east. He slung a rock high into the air out in front of the wagon.

Lixie yanked up the short-barreled shotgun, tracked the rock, and pulled the stiff trigger. The shotgun blasted in her ear like dynamite as the butt stock slammed into her shoulder.

The horses reared in unison.

She lost her balance and grabbed his shoulder.

Johnny White reached over to steady her.

The horses bolted forward.

Lixie tumbled to the back of the wagon.

Johnny White fell with her.

The frightened horses galloped across the desert.

Fragments of the shattered rock rained granite silt into the air.

Lixie's hat blew off, and her hair came unpinned. She dropped the shotgun. Her shoulder ached. Her skirt blew up to her knees. She climbed over Johnny White and crawled across the wagon seat, ripping her dress as she dove for the lead lines. She snatched them with her left hand, climbed up in the seat, and yanked back on the lines with both hands.

"Whoa!" she screamed. "Whoa, horses! Whoa!"

Lixie yanked the lead horse to the left. The wagon took a long circle to the west. By the second loop, the horses calmed down, and Johnny White had climbed up to the wagon seat beside her. They raced back to where Mean Mike stood by the yucca.

"Wheweee!" he hollered as they approached. "I ain't never seen nothin' like that!"

Lixie thought about tumbling back with her skirt up to her knees. "Like what?" she challenged.

"Ma'am, you know how to shoot and drive horses. I ain't never know'd a woman like you at any age."

"You weren't supposed to toss the rock until she got down," Johnny White shouted.

"Nobody told me that," Mean Mike mumbled.

Lixie rubbed her right shoulder and glanced down at her torn dress. "I hit it, didn't I?"

"You shattered that sucker, Lixie."

"I knew I could."

"You shouldn't have done that, Mean Mike. Lixie could have gotten hurt."

"I'm all right," she laughed. "My shoulder will be black and blue for a month. I ripped my dress. I lost my hat and my combs and totally embarrassed myself, but other than that, it was quite fun."

"Hey, here comes someone!" Mean Mike called out as he climbed back into the wagon.

"I do hope I don't have to shoot him," she grinned. "My shoulder couldn't take another shot." She handed the lead lines to Johnny White and brushed down her skirt. She didn't look up until she heard the voice of the approaching rider.

"Is everything okay here? Are you all right, Mrs. Miller?"

"Mr. Carter?" she gasped.

"I heard a shot and figured there was trouble," Carter reported.

His carbine lay across the saddle horn. He seemed to be staring at her from head to toe. She tried to brush her hair back.

Why did he show up now? Why? This isn't funny, Lord. This is humiliating! "I was just doing a little target practice, Mr. Carter."

"You're the one who fired the shot?"

"Yes, the twelve-gauge shotgun."

"I can't believe you shot the gun," he mumbled.

"I'm not sure why that seems to surprise all of you. Well, the horses bolted, and I seem to have lost my hat."

"And your hair got messed up, your dress is torn, and you have blood on your hands."

"I do?" Lixie glanced down at her fingerless gloves to see red streaked across her fingertips.

"That ain't her blood; it's my blood," Johnny White announced.

"It is?" Lixie looked over and spotted scratch marks on Johnny White's neck.

"She scratched me when she climbed over me."

"She did what?" Carter blurted out.

"I fell back on top of her, and she climbed over me and grabbed the lead lines and turned this rig around when the horses bolted."

"Yeah," Mean Mike reported. "Lixie is a cracker with a shotgun! You want to see her shoot?"

"No more," she insisted. "My shoulder won't take it."

"Are you okay then, Mrs. Miller?" Carter asked again.

"I'm just fine. What are you doing out on the desert alone, Mr. Carter? It could be dangerous."

He stood in the stirrups and stretched his legs. "I'm looking for the Apaches."

"Why on earth? One man can't capture a whole band," she challenged.

"I don't want to capture them. I just want to talk to them."

"How do you intend to do that?" Johnny White questioned. "They'd shoot you on sight or roast you over a fire first."

Carter pulled off his sweaty felt hat. "I believe they're the only ones who know what happened to little Charley McComas when the Judge and Mrs. McComas were murdered."

"You're crazy," Mean Mike insisted. "Them savages will kill you. Don't you have somethin' better to do?"

Jefferson Carter glanced at Lixie, who immediately tried to gather her disheveled hair back into her combs. "As a matter of fact, I don't have anything better to do."

"Mr. Mason, could you hand me my hat?" Lixie said. "Mr. Carter, I believe it would be helpful in your quest for information about the missing lad if you were to visit General Crook in Arizona. I could provide you with a letter of introduction if that would be helpful."

"You know General Crook?"

"George and Mary have been friends for a very long time."

"You seem to know a lot of officers."

"My husband was a career officer. Just what do you find unusual about my knowing officers?" she snapped.

He let the hammer down on his carbine. "Sorry, ma'am. Didn't mean to imply anything."

"Here's your hat, Lixie." Mason climbed back into the wagon. "Looks like it got run over by a wagon wheel. But don't worry, you look mighty purdy with your hair down."

She grabbed the hat. "Mr. Carter, why don't you ride along with us toward the CS Ranch? They might have more news of the Apaches. The boys say that Indians were on the ranch a few days ago."

"Where's the headquarters?" Carter asked.

"About twenty miles north of here near the Gila River," Johnny White said.

"I guess I'll ride on up by myself."

"There's safety in numbers," she suggested.

"Looks like you're safe enough." He spurred his horse and galloped on up ahead.

"He ain't that gunman from El Paso, is he?" Mean Mike asked.

"The one that roped the front gate of the Mexican jail so his buddies could escape," White added.

"I believe he's an attorney from Santa Fe." Lixie sat down and tried to straighten out her crunched straw hat.

"He don't look like a lawyer," Mason said. "He looks more like a gunman."

"He don't act like a lawyer," White said. "He acts like a sheriff."

"Whoever he is, I seem to have the ability to chase him off." She retrieved the shotgun from the back of the wagon.

"What are you going to do?" Johnny White asked.

"Replace the shell, of course. A half-loaded gun is of little value."

"You ain't goin' to shoot again, are you?" Mean Mike groaned.

"No, I believe I've already shot myself in the foot as it is."

"Did you get hurt?"

She stared ahead at the trail of dust left by Jefferson Carter. "Nothing I haven't experienced before."

By the time they reached the three-mile driveway from the Gila River up to the headquarters of the CS Ranch, the sun was half past straight overhead, and the rip in Lixie's dress had been mended. Hornet Creek, and the ribbon of cottonwood trees that traced it, skirted the rimrock to the south and turned north, splitting the headquarters into two sections. Three large fenced corrals lined the western side of the creek. Each covered more than five acres. On the east a garden, tool sheds, and a cookhouse paralleled the creek. Running straight north, a 190-foot barn stood like a fortress. One end of it was the bunkhouse. Back against the rimrock was a small wood-framed guesthouse that sported fresh white paint and two dormer windows.

The dominant building at the CS headquarters was the big house next to the guesthouse, a fifty-foot-square two-story building with wide covered veranda stretching out on all four sides. Lixie counted six stone chimneys. Only one belched a thin column of gray smoke.

"This has the feel of a small town," she said.

"What kind of town doesn't have any women?" Johnny White complained.

Lixie studied the buildings. "Then perhaps it has the feel of a fort. That's something I'm more familiar with." *How on earth did they get this many freight wagons of sawn lumber to this remote canyon?*

As they passed the barn, half a dozen cowboys huddled at the huge open door. She glanced at the crates in the back of the wagon. "What are they looking at? Did you bring the mail?"

"Nope. I reckon they're starin' at the female," Mean Mike explained.

A blacksmith and a teenage boy also drifted out to watch.

"I feel like I'm on parade. I don't know if I'm supposed to wave or what. How long has it been since a woman was out at the CS Ranch?"

"Don't know," Johnny White replied. "'Course, this is just my fourth year here."

"My, this is a real privilege." *Elizabeth Miller, you must remember to visit more all-male ranches. Lonely men overlook a multitude of flaws. I really have no idea what a house that has not seen a woman in years will be like. I did tell Langford that I wouldn't clean the house, didn't I?*

The yard between the garden and the big house was packed dirt. Chickens scurried in front of the wagon as it rolled up to the faded green wooden steps.

Langford Elsworth hurried out the front door and down the steps to meet her. He was dressed in suit and tie, and his full mustache was neatly trimmed. "Mrs. Miller, how relieved I am that you are here. I trust there was no excitement on your journey."

"None that I didn't generate myself," she replied. She took Mean Mike's hand as he helped her out of the carriage.

"You ought to see Lixie shoot, Mr. Elsworth," Johnny called out. "She's a sure shot, all right."

"Shoot?" Elsworth tugged at his tie. "Was there trouble?"

Lixie folded her parasol. "Just target practice."

"Oh, good. I have everything waiting for you. Michael, would you pack Mrs. Miller's things to the room at the top of the stairs?"

"Did you know that Mrs. Miller once had supper with old Sittin' Bull himself?" Mean Mike blurted out. "And she and Mrs. Custer are just like that." He pinched his fingers together.

Langford Elsworth held out his arm. "I take it you had a long visit with the boys."

"I enjoyed it." She took his arm as they climbed the steps.

Elsworth held the door open for her. The big room was lit with daylight streaming through the open shutters of the windows. Lixie admired the huge brown leather chairs and sofas, as well as a rock fireplace that stood six feet tall, which was only halfway to the ceiling. What caught her immediate attention was the immaculate condition of the house.

She waltzed out into the middle of the room. "Langford, this is beautiful!"

He trailed along behind her. "Eh, yes. To be honest, I merely copied my grandfather's hunting lodge up in the Scottish highlands."

"It's very comfortable, richly furnished, and . . ." Lixie rubbed her fingerless glove along the side table and examined her palm.

"And clean?" he said.

"Yes!"

"For that you can thank my dear mother. She was a stickler for keeping things tidy. I've never outgrown the habit."

"A very commendable trait."

They stood at the base of the stairs as Mean Mike toted the trunk up.

"If you don't mind, I've put you in the big house with me and the Mendozas. The Holdens will be with us tomorrow," Elsworth said.

Lixie scouted the room. "The Mendozas?"

"Emile and his son Tony do the cooking, gardening, and cleaning. Their rooms are at the back of the house."

"And the Fletchers?"

"I'm putting them in the guesthouse. It has a little more privacy and isn't so noisy."

The only thing Lixie could hear was a pendulum clock ticking. "Langford, what would you like me to do first?"

"Oh, my word, by all means, relax and get settled. I have a list on the dining room table of possible meal selections and activities. I'd like you to decide on everything. Just take charge."

"You have great confidence in me."

"Elizabeth, I'm a needy man. I want to do things properly but feel overwhelmed. I've been in New Mexico twelve years, never once returning to the East, let alone going back to England."

"Have you known the Fletchers long?"

"Edwin and I went to school together. I haven't seen him since. I've never met Lady Fletcher."

"We'll just treat them to some New Mexico hospitality. We don't have to compete with England," she assured him.

"Yes, you're right. I need to go check the facilities next door. Please make yourself at home. For these next three days, you're in charge, Mrs. Miller."

"Thank you. I think it will feel good to stretch my legs and walk a bit after that long ride. I did have one question."

"Yes?"

"We came across a Mr. Jefferson Carter, a Santa Fe attorney, who was riding up this way. Has he stopped by the ranch yet?"

"Not to my knowledge, but you might ask the boys. Mr. Whetlock is my foreman. He'll be in the barn with the horses or in the blacksmith shop. He knows everything that happens within a hundred miles. He'll know if your Mr. Carter has been around."

Lixie took the stairs slowly. *He's not "my" Mr. Carter. At least, not yet.*

After washing her face and neck, recombing and pinning her hair, Lixie strolled out to the veranda. As she surveyed the yard, she saw activity at the barn. Someone squatted in front of a huge tub at the bunkhouse.

She glanced down at a neatly written list of proposed menus and activities in her hand. *Why does an English gentleman come to this remote region of southwest New Mexico and never go home? It sounds terribly lonely to leave all familiar things behind to be out here. What am I saying? It is terribly lonely. I should know.*

A well-worn footpath separated the garden from the creek. She strolled in the shade of the cottonwoods. A teenage boy was yanking carrots out of the ground as she neared the tool shed.

"Afternoon, ma'am. I reckon you're Mrs. Miller," he called out.

"Now that's a very good guess since I seem to be the only woman here. What's your name?"

"Tony Mendoza."

"Is your father the chef?"

"No, he, eh, cooks for the place. Would you like a fresh carrot?" the boy called out. "They're real sweet and tender. I can wash it for you."

"Thank you, Tony. I think I would, but I'll wash it."

He handed her a plump eight-inch carrot. The green top tickled her hand.

"Say, some of us have been wonderin', how long are you goin' to stay at the ranch?" he asked.

"Until Monday."

"This Monday?" he murmured. "That ain't very long."

"Those are the plans at this point. Did you hear something different?"

"We was hopin' you might just move up here."

"You mean, permanently?"

Tony's dark bangs hung down into his eyes. "It was just a thought. Do you have any idea what a difference a woman makes around a place like this?"

"Oh?"

"First of all, every last cowboy has had a bath, haircut, and shave in the last week. That alone is a miracle. We all walk taller, talk better, and dress with our nobbiest shirts, just because you're here!"

"I'm flattered, but I suppose it's mainly for Lord and Lady Fletcher."

"No, ma'am. I guarantee they'd do the same if it were just you. Are you sure you don't want me to wash that carrot?"

"No, you go on with your work. I'll take care of it."

Lixie strolled beside the creek behind the blacksmith shop and tool shed. She stooped down to rinse her hand in the cool, meandering stream. The water looked about six inches deep and perhaps six feet across.

She washed the dirt off the carrot and left it submerged to cool. *I was wrong about Lordsburg being perched at the edge of the world. This ranch is even more remote. A half-day's ride from Silver City. Even farther to Lordsburg. It's a little world all its own. At times, a peaceful world. If Apaches come calling, a violent world. But either way, a world separate from all others. No wonder Mr. Elsworth is used to taking the law into his own hands. It's the only law available.*

Lixie patted the carrot dry with her linen handkerchief and took a bite. *Oh my, this is sweet and tasty.* She circled around in front of the cook shack. A man with drooping mustache and sandy-blond hair crouched behind a tub of potatoes.

"Afternoon, ma'am," he said.

"Hello. It looks like you get the potato-peeling job."

"Yes, ma'am. We played poker for chores last night. I didn't do too good. I'm stuck with potatoes and midnight gate-watchin'."

"Gate-watching?" She took another bite of carrot.

"The ol' man wants a guard posted night and day while them

English folks are here. Meanwhile I'm peelin' potatoes instead of punchin' cattle."

I assume he doesn't know he has a potato peeling stuck to his fore-head. "I trust it's just temporary, and I appreciate your work. What's your name?"

"Bard McAllen. You must be Mrs. Miller."

"I really enjoy being called Lixie."

"Yes, ma'am. Them carrots is good, ain't they, Lixie?"

"Yes, they are, Bard. Listen, I'm a little thirsty. I wonder if I could get a drink of water in the kitchen?"

"Sure. Emile is in there. You got to be careful what water you drink around here."

"Oh?"

"Take the creek, for instance. You don't want to drink from there."

She thought about washing the carrot in the creek. "Why is that?"

"Shoot, Mrs. Miller, there's thirteen hundred head of cattle upstream that's drinkin' out of it and doin' who knows what, if you catch my drift. No, ma'am, don't go drinkin' out of that creek."

The taste of carrot grew bitter in her mouth as she pushed open the door to the cookhouse.

When Lixie finished planning the weekend menus with Emile Mendoza, she strolled across the dirt yard to the bunkhouse. Johnny White perched on the wooden step. "When do you think they'll get here?" he called out.

"Langford expects them right before sundown." She plopped down beside the cowboy.

"Nobody here calls the ol' man Langford. We all call him Mr. Elsworth."

"Perhaps I should change what I call him. Maybe I'll call him Langy."

"To his face?"

"Why not?" Lixie laughed. "But I don't believe he teases well.

Johnny, did any of the others see Mr. Carter? Remember, he said he was going to ride ahead to the ranch."

"Maybe he changed his mind."

"Why would he do that?"

"Perhaps he found the Apaches."

The distant report of two rapid gunshots brought both Lixie and Johnny White to their feet. They stared north down the long drive.

"Is that a gunfight?" she asked.

"It's a signal. They're comin'!" Johnny White pulled off his hat, slicked back his hair, and jammed his hat back on. "How do I look?"

"Like a New Mexico drover."

"Really?"

"How do you want to look?" she asked.

"I guess that's okay. What do I call them?"

"Mr. and Mrs. Fletcher will be just fine."

"And I don't have to bow?"

"You don't even have to curtsy."

Johnny's mouth dropped. "What?"

She patted him on the sleeve. "Never mind."

Cowboys now tumbled out of every building and corral. Most perched on stumps, broken chairs, corral rails, and steps. She counted twenty-six, but she did not see Langford Elsworth.

"Johnny, how many men work on the CS?" she asked.

"We got some day hands that have been added just to get the place cleaned up. There's only one man who knows the total ever' day."

"Mr. Elsworth?"

"Nope. Mr. Whetlock." Johnny hollered to the muscular man in front of the blacksmith shop. The man wore a leather apron and had arm muscles that seemed ready to split his shirt. "How many boys is workin' today?"

"Countin' those drivin' the carriage and those down at the South Fork, we got thirty-four. But most ain't workin' much!" The man stalked back inside the blacksmith shop and pumped the bellows.

Lixie pulled off her straw hat to fan herself. "That's Mr. Whetlock, the foreman?"

"Yep. You were expectin' someone different?"

"Well, he's so . . . so . . ."

"Strong?"

"Yes."

"I ain't never seen anyone stronger," Johnny said. "He can pick up that 120-pound anvil with one hand and toss it across the room. I've seen him do it."

"I'll remember that."

She stared down the driveway but couldn't see a carriage. "I suppose Langy-dear wants me up at the big house."

"Mrs. Miller, I'd give a month's wages to hear you call the ol' man that."

"How much do you make a month, Johnny?"

"Thirty-four dollars, plus room, board, mounts, and bullets."

"Well, don't go wasting it. You'll hear me call him that, but it won't cost you a penny."

"You're a peach, Mrs. Miller. I don't care what them others say—I don't think you're too old."

"Thank you, Johnny." She strolled across the dirt yard toward the big house. *I won't ask him what I'm too old for. I don't think I want to know.*

Langford Elsworth stood at the front door, wearing a long black coat and a charcoal-gray silk vest with gold brocade. His black tie was neatly tied under his chin.

"Langford," she called out as she approached, "I didn't know you were going to dress formally. Perhaps I should change."

"Yes, yes, quite so. It will be several minutes before they arrive."

Lixie scurried to the room at the top of the stairs and tugged off her travel dress. *I was saying that just to be polite. You're supposed to say, "You look lovely just as you are, my dear."*

Her reception dress was a light beige Sicilienne trimmed with golden brown velvet. A large velvet bow defined the back. French silk roses softened the scooped neckline. She pinned two matching silk roses in her hair.

She took a quick glance in the mirror. *Well, ol' girl, it's like the old days.* "The inspector general is here for a surprise visit. Hurry and put on something decent!" *For the life of me, I never figured out what was so indecent about my previous attire.*

By the time she reached the front porch, a column of dust trailed a carriage about a quarter of a mile from the headquarters. Langford Elsworth stood in the same place as before. He glanced down at her. "My word, Mrs. Miller, you look . . . eh, rather dashing."

"Thank you, Langford." *At my age "rather dashing" is about as high a compliment as I can receive from a sober man.* She straightened the elbow-length, loose-fitting ecru undressed kid gloves.

As the carriage pulled into the yard, the cowboys trailed behind it, hats in hand as it circled up to the steps of the big house. In the front seats were two carbine-carrying cowboys. In the back sat a man wearing a floppy, wide-brimmed hat and gray suit and vest, but he had no tie on his buttoned-at-the-top white shirt. The woman beside him wore a small straw hat. Her dress was cream-white flannelette with turquoise blue wool inlaid in small pleats. A thin layer of red dust covered the carriage and everything in it, including the tarp that covered the baggage behind the seat.

"My word, Langford, it's been years!" the tall man shouted as he climbed down and offered his hand to the woman.

Elsworth descended the steps. Lixie remained on the porch. "Yes, quite so, Edwin. Sorry to hear about your father."

The men shook hands vigorously as the cowboys crowded to the back of the carriage.

"Well, yes, but the ol' boy lived a full life and was ready to meet his Lord. I suppose that's all any of us can hope for."

"Quite right, quite right," Elsworth mumbled.

"Mr. Langford Elsworth, this is my wife, Harriet."

The woman's smile lit her vibrant blue eyes as she held out a smooth-skinned hand.

"Lady Fletcher." Elsworth took her gloved hand.

"Mr. Elsworth, I am only called Lady Fletcher by the newspapers in America. As you are well aware, that title is not recognized in England."

"We aren't in England . . . Lady Fletcher," Elsworth insisted.

"Thank you, Langford, I greatly appreciate that. But I am the former Harriet Reid from Prescott, Arizona, so please call me Harriet."

She smiled at Lixie, who had started down the steps. *I like this woman. And I feel horribly overdressed.*

Elsworth swept his hand toward her. "And let me introduce Mrs. Elizabeth Miller, a kind widow from Lordsburg who graciously agreed to come up and hostess the weekend for me."

Lixie shook hands with Lord and Lady Fletcher. "Langy-dear was quite convinced that it would be a frightful experience for you to be surrounded by thirty-four handsome cowboys and no other women for miles." Out of the corner of her eye, she saw a grin break across Johnny White's face.

Lady Fletcher glanced out at the huddle of cowboys. "Yes, men have strange notions at times. I'm delighted you're here. That's a beautiful dress. I feel quite boring and ordinary."

"This is my official Washington reception dress, a little out of place for New Mexico. But since I've abandoned Washington society, it might as well be worn somewhere."

"Mrs. Miller, you were in the capital?" Edwin Fletcher asked.

Lixie clutched her hands in front of her waist. "From time to time."

"Mrs. Miller's husband was, eh . . ." Elsworth paused.

"General Rockford Miller," Lixie supplied.

Harriet Fletcher gave her husband a glance.

"Yes, *that* General Miller. But, please, don't give it another thought. I didn't come to New Mexico to hide from the past." *Not successfully anyway.*

Langford Elsworth swept his giant hand toward the freshly painted small house. "The guest cottage is yours. There is hot water on the stove, and we'll give you a chance to clean up before a tour of the place. Edwin, you can't imagine how good it is to see someone from Eton after all these years."

Fletcher pulled off his long coat. Lixie noticed that he wore a bullet belt and holstered Colt revolver. "I spent so many years with

Brannon that I had almost lost my accent until my father's death brought me back to England."

"Edwin, we must take care of the girl first," Lady Fletcher insisted.

Edwin stepped to the back of the wagon. "Oh, my word, yes!"

"Girl?" Elsworth pressed.

Edwin Fletcher yanked back the dust-covered canvas tarp. Lying on a lap quilt wearing a man's long-sleeved shirt was a brown-skinned girl with matted black hair. She didn't move. Her eyes were closed.

"Is she dead?" one of the huddled cowboys called out.

"She's Apache!" another announced.

Elsworth scooted to the back of the wagon. "My word, Edwin, what's the meaning of this?"

"About five miles east of here we came through a narrow, rocky pass. This girl bolted in front of the rig, and the horses reared. She was struck in the head by flailing hooves."

"We felt in some way responsible," Harriet said.

"But she's Apache!" Elsworth protested.

"What difference does that make?" Harriet Fletcher insisted.

"We searched the area and found no traces of family," Edwin added.

"Of course you didn't. They're Apache." Elsworth stewed as he marched around the carriage. Exclamations rippled through the gathered cowboys.

"So naturally we brought her here." Fletcher laid his palm on the forehead of the unconscious girl. "It was our horse that injured her."

"But she can't stay here," Elsworth boomed. "Apaches are roaming the area. If we kidnap one of their own, there will be trouble at the CS for sure."

"We didn't kidnap her," Edwin Fletcher said.

"I wasn't going to abandon an injured girl along a deserted road," Harriet Fletcher replied.

Elsworth rubbed his chin. "We'll have to take her back."

"Take her back where?" Harriet Fletcher crossed her arms across her chest. "There is no one there to take her back to."

"They are there . . . and probably headed this way," Johnny White called out. Then he blended back into the crowd of cowboys.

"For heaven's sake, wait until she comes to. We can send her back with some gifts or something," Edwin Fletcher suggested.

"Yes, quite so." Elsworth turned to the huddled cowboys. "A couple of you boys tote the girl to the barn and lay her on the hay. When she comes to, I'll have Masley and Carpenter haul her back to Siesta Pass."

"I ain't ridin' into Apaches with a kidnapped girl," Limp Masley replied. There was a similar mumble from the other cowboys.

"Oh, posh. It's my situation. I'll drive her back," Lady Fletcher insisted.

"And I'll ride shotgun," Lixie added.

"You'll do nothing of the kind. My word, I'll do it myself before I let the ladies go out," Elsworth blustered.

"We'll all go out there together," Johnny White offered. "We just didn't want to go one or two at a time."

"We'll make that decision later," Elsworth said. "After the child wakes up."

"If she wakes us," Limp Masley mumbled. "She's been out a long time."

"I intend to stay with her until she does," Lady Fletcher said.

"I say, we did have a tour of the ranch planned before supper," Elsworth informed them.

"Why don't you and Lord Fletcher take the tour. Harriet and I will sit with the girl," Lixie suggested.

Elsworth hesitated.

"I'm really too tired of riding to travel much more," Lady Fletcher added.

"Very well. We will unload your things in the guesthouse and take a jaunt around the ranch." Elsworth turned to his foreman. "Mr. Whetlock, saddle the two black geldings for us."

"How many men are you takin' with you?" Whetlock pressed.

"Do you think we'll need assistance?"

"As long as you have that Indian girl, you will," Whetlock replied.

"Then how about you and five others?"

"How about six others, and I stay here?" Whetlock replied. "I think we should set up a guard around the headquarters."

Elsworth faced his foreman. "Aren't you exaggerating the threat?"

Whetlock leaned closer. "What extremes would you pursue to get your daughter back if the situation were reversed?"

"We don't know who she is," Elsworth murmured.

"That's not the point. She's someone's daughter."

Elsworth rubbed his chin. "Yes, indeed. Mr. Whetlock, set some boys on the perimeter of the headquarters."

Lixie motioned to the cowboys. "Bring this little darling up to the big house. It's too hot and stuffy inside; we'll put her on the veranda."

"I say," Elsworth huffed, "you aren't suggesting that I—"

"I'm suggesting that animals are kept in barns," Lixie shot back. "People are kept in houses."

"She stinks like a pig," Limp Masley said and immediately faced the scowl of Lixie Miller. "But I reckon on any other day but today, so do the rest of us."

The ranch tour contingent rode out the driveway as the declining sun cast long shadows east. The Indian girl was stretched out on a pallet made of several quilts. Lady Fletcher and Lixie sat on either side of the unconscious girl. A plate of cheese, apples, and biscuits had been placed nearby, covered by a dark green linen napkin.

Lady Harriet Fletcher sipped tea from a delicate hand-painted porcelain cup. "I'm afraid I stirred up trouble by insisting on bringing this girl to the ranch."

"What else could you do?" Lixie replied from behind a similar teacup.

"The drivers said to just leave her alongside the road. There was no way on earth I could do that."

"That's good advice for animals, but not for a little girl." Lixie gazed down the driveway and could no longer see the column of dust from the departing riders. "Do you speak Apache, Harriet?"

"French, Spanish, and a little German," she replied, "but no Apache. And you?"

"Most of my life's been spent in army housing at various forts. I've learned many choice words in dozens of languages, most of which should never be repeated," Lixie said. "That hardly represents knowing a foreign language. . . . Poor little thing. I believe she will wake screaming, don't you?"

"I don't think so. I think perhaps she will just stare."

Lixie Miller took another sip of tea. "Why do you say that?"

Harriet pointed her teacup toward the reclining brown-skinned girl. "Because her eyes are open right now. She's been listening to our every word."

Four

~~~

Lixie studied the swollen forehead and big brown eyes of the small girl lying between them. "Hello, sweetheart. . . . It's okay. You got hurt, but we'll take care of you."

The frightened girl pushed herself up on one elbow.

"Don't try to move," Harriet cautioned. "You need to . . ."

The girl coughed once and then repeatedly vomited down the front of her shirt. She began to cry.

Lixie dropped to her knees and cradled the girl's head and shoulders. "Oh dear, Harriet, go get some hot water and towels to wash her up." She plucked up the linen napkin that had covered the food and wiped the crying girl's face. "It's all right, honey. It's all right. I know your head hurts."

"I need some help up here!" she shouted to some cowboys loitering in front of the barn.

Three bowlegged men in boots came running.

"Is she dead?" one called out.

"One of you go tell Emile we need some of that ice he brought up from Silver City. Break it with a hammer and bring it here in a cotton sack. Hurry. We've got to get this swelling down."

"Her head surely looks like a pumpkin," another one mumbled.

"Do any of you have a small pair of trousers and a shirt that might fit her? Are there any children's clothes at this ranch?"

Mean Mike shoved his hands in his belt. "I got a little ready-made dress. I'm goin' home come November, and I bought a present for my little sis last time I was in Magdalena."

"Do you think it would fit her?"

"I reckon so."

"Can I buy it from you?" Lixie asked, still rocking the whimpering girl. "I'll see that you get one to replace it."

"I reckon it's the Christian thing to do. But it surely is a purdy dress for an Indian."

One glance from Lixie, and he sprinted back to the bunkhouse.

She still cradled the girl when Harriet returned with a basin of steaming water and two cotton towels. "What next?" Harriet asked.

"One of us should steady her head and hold the icepack when it gets here, and the other can strip off these soiled garments and bathe her."

"I don't think I can clean the vomit without losing everything in my stomach," Harriet admitted.

"All those years of helping doctor soldiers should count for something. I'll clean her. You take her head. Don't let her turn it to the left or right."

The girl whimpered and clung to both their arms. The putrid stench of vomit caused Lixie to hold her breath and clench her teeth as she pulled off the long shirt. It was the girl's only clothing.

Harriet Fletcher turned aside and took a deep breath.

The girl looked about ten or eleven. She was thin, and yet she had a round stomach. Her matted black hair hung down to her elbows. Dirt was caked in places on her body.

Harriet Fletcher held the ice to the girl's forehead as Lixie washed the little body with slow, gentle, circular rubs. The girl continued to whimper.

"I'm surprised she isn't trying to resist or escape," Harriet whispered.

"I think she's in too much pain."

"Did you see her tummy? I would say she hadn't eaten in a while and then stuffed herself with CS steer meat a day or two ago."

"I think you're right," Lixie said.

"Mrs. Miller," Mean Mike called out, "here's the dress. But I don't have any bloomers to go with it."

"Thank you, Michael. You're a very generous man."

"I reckon bein' hurt serious and separated from your family is about as bad off as a kid can get."

"A family who might be looking for her right now," Harriet added.

Tony Mendoza sprinted toward them. "Daddy dug up an old pair of my duckings that might fit her, but if you have a dress, I reckon you don't need them."

"They will be wonderful. She can use them for bloomers under the dress."

The girl lay still as Harriet cradled her head and stroked her soft brown cheek. The ice bag was propped on the highest part of the swell.

"Tony, take these soiled clothes out and bury them," Lixie instructed. "No one should have to wear them again."

Tony gawked at the pile of pungent clothing. "Can I go get a pitchfork?"

"By all means."

After the girl's brown skin was rubbed pink in places, Lixie raised her little arms one at a time and tugged on the dress. The girl's eyes widened, and she stopped crying as she watched Lixie dress her. When the trousers were pulled up and buttoned and the dress smoothed down, the girl reached over and clasped Lixie's fingers.

"You look very pretty, darling." Lixie stroked the girl's cheek. "We need to wash your hair. I suppose we should wait for the swelling to subside. But one does worry about the lice."

Harriet Fletcher pulled her hands away from the girl's head. "Oh dear, I hadn't considered lice."

"I'll hold her head for a while. Go get some clean warm water and some lye soap. I'm sure there must be some somewhere."

"To wash the hair?"

"I have to try."

"Should I bring a little perfume?"

"That would be nice. I trust it won't cause her to vomit again."

The girl chewed on a wet rag as Lixie and Harriet scrubbed her hair.

"Leave the lye soap lathered for a few minutes," Miller advised. "We want to make sure we take care of all the varmints."

"You seem to know a lot about such matters."

"Lady Fletcher, you can't imagine the condition of some of the western forts and camps. The walls are literally alive."

Harriet dried her hands on a flour-sack tea towel. "You're getting lye soap all over your beautiful dress."

"I've debated for years why I keep this dress. I've had no occasion to wear it since my army days in Washington. It's out of place in southern New Mexico. It's time I toss it anyway."

Harriet strolled over next to Lixie. "Do you plan to stay in New Mexico permanently?"

Lixie eased her soapy hands into the basin of fresh water. "That's a very good question."

"Do you have an answer?"

"I have an answer for it every day. It's just not the same answer."

"Where is your family?"

Lixie paused and glanced out across the dirt yard toward the garden and the row of cottonwood trees along the creek.

"I'm sorry," Harriet added. "I'm getting too personal. I'm very aware that people come west to avoid some situations, and I have no business digging them up."

"No, it's quite all right. The questions you ask are the same that I ask myself. That's why I pause. I suppose I'll stay in this area until the Lord gives me some direction. For several years life has seemed without much purpose. Maybe it's the curse of being a widow."

"A young widow."

"A scorned widow." Lixie felt the girl's hand clutch her fingers. "Anyway, enough of that." She began to rinse the lye soap out of the girl's hair. "Lady Fletcher, what are we really going to do with this little darling?"

"Maybe we will all have to go find the Apaches so that we may return her, like the men mentioned."

Lixie combed her fingers through the thick, matted hair. "I suppose if she runs off, we should just let her go."

"Yes, I suppose," Harriet murmured. "I still can't believe there was no one around when she got hurt."

"Perhaps she was lost."

"Do Indians get lost?"

"Little children get lost," Lixie replied.

"Very true."

Lixie held the girl's hair at the roots with one hand and began to gently comb it with the other. With ice still perched on her forehead, the young girl flinched with each stroke, but made no protest. She stared with wide dark brown eyes at Lixie as she chewed on the wet rag.

"Darling, do you know any English? Do you understand what I'm saying?"

The girl reached up and touched Lixie's lips with her fingertips. "You know I'm talkin' about you, don't you?"

The girl blinked her eyes shut.

"I'm still shocked she's not trying to get away," Lixie remarked.

"Perhaps she's exhausted as well as injured. She obviously likes the care you show her," Harriet added.

"I wish we knew her name."

"She's a cute girl. Beautiful thick hair, brown skin, almost black eyes, and little round nose. Lixie, did you ever wonder why we take such pains to stay lily-white when there are so many beautiful brown-skinned women in the world?"

Lixie laid the palm of her hand on the girl's soft, warm cheek. "We should call her Little Beauty."

Tony Mendoza meandered back up to the porch. "Is there anything else I can do? Daddy wants to know if you need anything from the cookhouse."

"Perhaps a piece of plain bread," Lixie suggested. "I hate to put anything else in that little bloated tummy."

"How about another icepack? This one is melting through to poor Lixie's dress," Harriet added.

"Yes, ma'am." He nodded.

"Tony, do you know any Apache words?" Lixie queried.

"No, ma'am, but Mr. Whetlock knows a few, I think. And

maybe one or two of the boys, but that might be just all brag and no show. None of us ever want to get close enough to talk to them. I'm afraid all I know is a little Mexican."

"What is Spanish for Little Beauty?" Lixie asked.

"Bonita," he replied.

"Bonita? That's it, Harriet! We will call her Bonita!" Lixie exclaimed as she continued to comb the girl's hair.

Harriet adjourned to the guesthouse to unpack. Lixie sat on the quilts on the floor of the porch with the young girl's head on her lap. The sun barely hovered above the distant, treeless western mountains.

After several minutes Lixie carefully slid the girl's head onto a folded quilt. "Sleep, little Bonita. When you wake up, perhaps your head will be clear."

Lixie stood and tried to straighten her cramped legs. She meandered from one end of the veranda to the other, keeping the Indian girl in sight. Lady Fletcher emerged from the guesthouse wearing a light green dress and no hat. "How is our little Bonita?" she called out as she came across the dirt yard.

"Sleeping."

"Let me stay with her. It's your turn to freshen up," Harriet offered.

"I look and smell quite the mess."

"I still say, you ruined that dress."

"Harriet, the most cherished moments in my life are when I feel needed."

"Like with Bonita?"

"Precisely, and I would trade every dress in my wardrobe for the opportunity to be of use."

"You're absolutely right." Harriet hugged Lixie's waist. "Now go on and clean up."

Lixie eyed the soiled beige dress that had once been the focal point of her wardrobe, the party dress that turned the heads of generals and privates, now heaped on the floor of the guest room at the top of the stairs. *I know I could clean it. Sooner or later the stench would be gone. It would not have the same luster and shine, and yet it would be a very fine dress. But it belongs to another era, another time in my life. I'm no longer the general's wife. I'm not the queen of the fort's annual dance. I'm not sure who I am, but I know who I'm not.*

She pulled on her navy blue faille dress, striped with light yellow and blue and trimmed with fringe colors to match. The sleeves had striped cuffs slashed on the top in the form of a chevron and finished with a double row of small half-spherical pearl buttons.

Lixie glanced in the mirror. *It looks rather dated. But I can still wear it, and a remote ranch in New Mexico is not exactly a fashion corner. I'm the same size as when I was young. That's about the only comparison.*

Lord, I only seem to be happy when someone needs me. Gracie . . . or Paco . . . or little Bonita. But what does that mean? I was married for more than twenty-five years to a man who, it turns out, didn't need me.

I don't know if anyone in Lordsburg really needs me, but I know that no one else needs me.

One day at a time, Lord. Langford Elsworth needs me this weekend. Little Bonita needs me right now. I'll worry about Monday on Monday.

When she returned to the front porch, half a dozen cowboys loitered on the steps near Bonita.

"I see you're surrounded by handsome men, Lady Fletcher," Lixie teased.

"Yes, it's delightful to be the only two females for a hundred miles, isn't it?"

"Three females." Lixie pointed to the sleeping Indian girl.

"Well taken," Harriet concurred.

"Did you know Lord Fletcher partnered with ol' Stuart Brannon himself over in Arizony?" Mean Mike exclaimed.

"I did hear something about that." Lixie turned to Lady Fletcher. "Has Mr. Brannon ever remarried?"

"Oh!" Harriet's hand flew to her mouth. "I didn't think of it until now. You are perfect for him! Oh, my, I'll have to introduce you and . . ."

Lixie held up her hand. "That's not why I was asking."

"Of course it was."

"I'm sure Mr. Brannon is many years younger than I."

"I'm not sure of that. But I can guarantee you he looks older than you, Lixie."

The cowboys leaned closer to the ladies. When Lixie turned to them, they pulled back. "Thank you very much. Even the daydream is quite exciting, but how could I ever leave New Mexico? There are just too many handsome men right here."

Heads came up.

Shoulders back.

Chins squared.

Smiles crept across the cowboy faces.

A wide, easy smile broke across Harriet Fletcher's face. "You are a charmer, Lixie Miller."

"That's me, the general's charming widow."

Mean Mike stood by the porch post, looking down the driveway. "Looks like they're coming back."

"I better go tell Daddy," Tony Mendoza called out as he sprinted to the cookhouse.

When the party reached the yard, the men dismounted at the barn. Lord Fletcher and Langford Elsworth hiked up to the big house.

"How is the little girl?" Edwin Fletcher called out.

Lady Fletcher stepped down to the dirt yard and waited as the men approached. "She woke for a while and we bathed her."

"You did?" her husband inquired.

"Actually, Lixie did. I was the helper."

"My word, you didn't have to scrub and clothe the little savage," Elsworth mumbled.

"I most certainly did," Lixie snapped.

"You changed your dress too," Fletcher commented.

"She vomited a lot. Neither of us looked or smelled very fetching. We've named her Bonita."

"Since she's doing better, I'll have a couple of the boys carry her to the barn now," Elsworth announced.

"You'll do no such thing!" Lixie stood and faced him. "She should not be moved."

"But I can't leave her on my front step!"

"Why not?"

"Well . . . well, we're entertaining company and—"

"Lord and Lady Fletcher, does it offend you to have Bonita sleeping on the veranda?" Lixie questioned.

"Of course not!" Harriet Fletcher replied.

"Then I'll stay with her until she recovers," Lixie announced.

"W-what? You're joking, I trust," Elsworth stammered. "I need you inside."

"Oh, don't worry," Harriet soothed. "I will spell her."

"But—but—this is not what I had planned."

"Plans change, Langford. I have an idea. Let's string lanterns in the yard, set up tables out here, and have a picnic tonight," Lixie suggested.

"You mean all of us?" Johnny White called out.

"Yes. Wouldn't that be delightful?"

White's brown eyes widened and danced. He yanked off his hat and grinned. "Yes, ma'am, I reckon it would."

"Mrs. Miller, I believe this is still my ranch, and I make the plans!"

"Oh, I'm sorry, Mr. Elsworth. I thought you asked me to come up and take charge of things. Perhaps you had some other intentions in inviting me here."

One of the cowboys in the back let out a loud whistle.

A red-faced Langford Elsworth stammered, "Of course not. I . . . eh, of course you are in charge, Mrs. Miller. But I'm not sure we can arrange something like that so quickly."

"Me and the boys will set up tables and benches," Johnny White called out.

"I'll take charge of the lanterns," Whetlock offered.

"If a few of you will come with me," Tony Mendoza said, "we'll get the food ready to tote outdoors."

Lixie sidled over to Langford Elsworth and squeezed his arm. "Thank you, Langy-dear. I really think this will be a delight."

"Hmmph. Three hours at the ranch, and she has the crew eating out of her hand."

Harriet Fletcher scooted up to his other side. "Now, Mr. Elsworth, look at Lixie. Can you blame them? Your crew has very good taste in women."

"Older women, at least," Lixie laughed.

"It's just not what I had in mind," he pouted. "My word, Edwin, you've stood right there and never said a word."

Lord Fletcher rubbed his chin. "One time Brannon and I were caught in the brush by about fifty well-armed Ute Indians riding up the trail. I asked him, 'When do we open fire?' He said, 'Never.' He said to fire a gun would guarantee our death. That's how I feel at the moment. Only thirty men facing two strong-willed women? We don't have a chance in the world."

Lixie laughed. "You're a very wise man, Lord Fletcher."

"Don't just stand there," Elsworth told the crew. "You heard Mrs. Miller's instructions. There's work to do."

"Yes, sir!" Johnny White called out as he and the others scampered back toward the cookhouse and the barn.

Langford Elsworth stared down at the sleeping girl. "This is quite extraordinary. Right here on my porch."

"We've been wondering about her family. Did you see any traces of the Apaches?" Harriet Fletcher asked.

"We cut across an Indian trail down near the river. It was quite confusing. Couldn't tell if they were coming or going," Elsworth said.

"Or both," Lord Fletcher said.

Lixie stood at the rail and gazed out at the driveway. "Did you happen to see Mr. Jefferson Carter? He said he was coming to the ranch, and it's almost dark."

"We didn't see anything of him."

"And just who is this Mr. Carter?" Lady Fletcher quizzed.

"He's an attorney from Santa Fe. He was on the trail alone, and I was concerned, what with Indians in the vicinity," Lixie explained. "I believe his plans included a stop at the CS Ranch."

"He could have changed his mind and gone to Silver City," Elsworth suggested.

Why would he want to do that? He knew I was coming here. He rode all this way from Santa Fe to see me . . . which sounds terribly vain and conceited. Forgive me, Lord.

"Yes, that's true. He could have gone elsewhere. I just worry about his being alone on that road."

"How long has it been since the McComas massacre?" Lord Fletcher asked.

"Just over a year ago. It still makes southwest New Mexico panic every time another band leaves the San Carlos reservation," Elsworth said.

"No talk of massacres," Harriet Fletcher asserted. "Let's discuss supper outside so we can watch the stars."

Elsworth cleared his throat. "Yes, and I will make sure Mr. Whetlock has posted guards to watch more than the stars."

Bonita woke up just as Lixie came back to her side with a plate of food. The yard bustled with hungry men. They talked of danger and escapes as each man tried to leave an impressive oral testimony of daring and courage. Dual lanterns on the porch posts illuminated the front of the house with soft yellow hues. The air had cooled a little, and yet without a breeze, Lixie's dress felt stifling.

"Hello, sweet Bonita," she said. "Are you hungry?"

The Indian girl propped herself up on her elbows. The ice had melted into a puddle near her feet. She peered out between the porch railings at the lanterns and men, most of whom wore their guns on their belts.

"It's okay, darling," Lixie cooed. "Don't be afraid."

The girl touched the swollen lump on her forehead.

"Does it hurt?" Lixie asked.

When the girl glanced up, tears rolled down her cheeks. She looked as if she were about to speak but then bit her lip.

Lixie reached out her hand.

The girl hesitated, then reached back.

Lixie gave the warm sweaty palm a squeeze, and the girl clutched her fingers.

"I brought you some food, but I don't want you to get sick again. This is the only dress we have for you." She straightened the collar of the blue calico dress.

Bonita jerked back.

"No, darling, I'm not going to take it. It belongs to you."

The girl mumbled something.

"What did you say? Say it again, please."

She pointed to the dress and murmured, "*Bonita.*"

"Oh my, you know a little Spanish. Yes, the dress is very *bonita.*" Then Lixie pointed at her. "You are *bonita.*"

The girl grabbed her finger and pushed it down to her dress. "*Bonita,*" she said again.

Lixie placed her hand gently on the girl's face. "You are *bonita.* You are very pretty."

The girl's eyes widened, and for the first time a wide, white-toothed smile broke across her face.

"You do have a beautiful smile, young lady!"

The girl pointed to Lixie's dress. "*Bonita.*"

"Thank you. I think it's a pretty dress."

Then the tips of the girl's fingers brushed Lixie's cheek. "*Bonita,*" she added.

"Sweetheart, you will never know how good your words make me feel."

The girl reached up and touched one of Lixie's tears.

"I know, Bonita, that's silly, isn't it? I'm sorry. Perhaps you should try to eat. I brought you some boring plain mashed potatoes to try. I'm just not sure what would set right on your little stomach."

She scooped a small spoonful of mashed potatoes and held them up in front of the girl. "Would you like to try these?"

Bonita scooped the potatoes off the spoon with two fingers and jammed them into her mouth.

"Yes, that's one way to do it. But I think you might like to use a spoon."

Lixie spooned another bite of potatoes and ate them herself, demonstrating the procedure.

Bonita watched closely. Then she scooped potatoes off her plate with her fingers.

"I do believe you have your mind made up. I just can't imagine you've never used a utensil of some sort."

Bonita extended the wad of potatoes to Lixie.

"Actually, darling, I do like to use a spoon."

Just as she finished speaking, the girl shoved the potatoes into Lixie's mouth.

Finger-fed mashed potatoes from a little girl off whom I tried to wash the vomit and dirt just a couple hours ago? Oh, well.

Bonita broke into a smile and started to giggle. Then she picked up the spoon and began to eat the potatoes.

Lixie swallowed the potatoes. "You rascal! You tease! You did that just to get me to eat with my fingers! Or your fingers!" Lixie began to laugh. "I can't believe you did that to me!"

The girl reached over and touched Lixie's teeth with her finger. "*Bonita,*" she announced.

Lixie reached over and laid her fingers on the girl's. "*Bonita.*"

Bonita grinned and then shoved another spoonful of mashed potatoes into her mouth.

"What do we have here?" Harriet Fletcher called out as she approached.

"A mutual appreciation association. We have both decided that the other is very *bonita.*"

"She speaks Spanish?" Harriet asked.

"She knows the word *bonita.*"

"May I join you ladies? Edwin is spellbinding them with hunting tales from India. If I have to sit through that rogue white Bengal tiger story another time, I will pull my hair and scream." Harriet plopped down in a woven willow chair and balanced a plate of food on her lap. "Did you try these carrots? They have a very unusual flavor."

"No, I decided to skip them." Lixie glanced out at the men. "Is Lord Fletcher always this outgoing?"

"Heavens, no. Edwin never complains about being in the States, but when he meets an old chum from England, he seems to let age and worry melt away."

"How about you, Harriet? Are you able to relax?"

"I'm more relaxed here on a ranch than at some embassy banquet or ball. I always assume they wonder why Edwin married an American schoolteacher."

"And why did Lord Fletcher marry such a pretty lass?" Lixie watched Bonita continue to eat mashed potatoes.

"At the time he was not Lord Fletcher. He married me because he couldn't bear spending the rest of his life without me. At least, that's what he told me."

"He seems to be a very nice man."

"He's totally predictable and quite dull."

"Oh dear," Lixie murmured.

"And I love it, Lixie. He's absolutely perfect for me. He's like a rock foundation for every day of my life. He's God's special gift to me. I suppose that's the way every wife feels."

Lixie bit her lip and slowly closed her eyes. "Not every wife," she murmured.

They flew open when Harriet's arm circled her shoulder. "Oh, Lixie, how absolutely cruel of me. I'm so sorry. I had no desire to cause you such pain."

"I do know what you mean. I was madly in love with Rockford most of my married life. The rest of the time, I guess I was just mad. Certainly those first years were a special gift. At the end the marriage felt like a cruel, horrible joke. All the innuendos. The public ridicule. I have asked the Lord a thousand times what I did to deserve it."

"Did He answer?"

"Yes, He always seems to say, 'My ways are not your ways.' But I am such a weak-faithed woman that I'm not satisfied with the answer."

"Why don't I sit with Bonita? You go visit a spell with the men. They very much want to talk with you."

"They don't want to visit with Lixie Miller. They want to visit with the general's notorious widow," Lixie corrected. "There is a sensual air of mystery about that, I suppose."

"I heard nothing of the kind."

"Of course you didn't, Harriet. But men are not that difficult to read. Ignore most of what they say and study their presentation."

"That, Lixie Miller, is probably true. Being married has diverted me from the habit of studying men."

"It diverted me, too. I didn't even study the one I was married to."

Lixie strolled out to the tables and stood beside Langford Elsworth as he finished a story that brought a loud roar of approval from the cowboys gathered close to listen.

"You seem to be having a very good time."

"Yes, quite so. Having Edwin here brings all sorts of memories."

"And you have a captive audience." She pointed to the cowboys. "This outdoor supper was quite a good idea, wasn't it?"

"Mrs. Miller, are you rubbing it in?"

"Yes, I am, Langy-dear," she drawled.

All conversation ceased when a cowboy galloped up the darkened driveway and reined up near the tables. Most of the men reached for carbines and rifles that were leaning against the tables near them.

"A rider's comin' in!" the man shouted as he leaped from his lathered horse.

"Who is it?" Elsworth questioned.

The cowboy let the reins drop to the dirt, and the horse shied away from the crowd. "He said he was a friend of Mrs. Miller's."

Lixie pushed through the milling crowd of men. "Was it Jefferson Carter?" she asked.

"I don't rightly know, ma'am," the thin-faced man with buck teeth replied.

"What does he look like?" she pressed.

"It's dark, Mrs. Miller. I couldn't say what he looks like."

Elsworth stared into the darkness of the driveway. "Where is he?"

"He said his horse bruised his hoof. He wanted to take it slow."

"So that's why he hasn't shown up yet." Lixie scurried to the front door of the big house.

Harriet Fletcher blocked her way. "You look fine, Lixie."

"I just need to . . ."

Harriet put a hand on Lixie's shoulder. "Trust me. You look very nice."

"Then why am I so nervous?"

"You and I both know the reason for that."

"It's silly, isn't it? At my age."

"At your age? To enjoy male companionship is a lifelong pleasure. I believe we were created that way."

"I really look all right?"

"If you looked any better, I'd feel like a milkmaid."

"Now that's a lie. A glorious, wonderful lie, Lady Fletcher. And thank you for it."

Harriet pushed Lixie back to the yard. "Go visit with that strong-shouldered, square-jawed, straight-shooting man with the dancing eyes."

"Have you met Mr. Carter?"

"No," Harriet laughed.

"Then how . . ."

"What other kind of man would put such a bounce in a woman's step?"

"Do you think it's odd for Langford to invite me up, and then I visit with Jefferson?"

"Sweet Lixie, the one wonderful advantage of women our age is that we can visit with absolutely anyone we want to!"

"What about Bonita?"

"I will not leave her side."

"I really look all right?"

"I believe I see a man riding up by the barn."

"Okay . . . I've talked to the man two times and chased him off both times. I'll attempt to do better this time."

"Perhaps you should just smile and nod your head and never speak," Harriet laughed.

Lixie glanced down at the Indian girl who was licking her spoon. "Mrs. Fletcher will stay with you awhile, sweetie."

The girl pointed the spoon at Lixie. "*Bonita.*" She grinned.

"Yes, and this *bonita* lady," she pointed to Harriet, "will stay with you for a little while."

The girl pointed the spoon at herself. "*Bonita,*" she called out.

"Yes, we are all *muy bonita.* In fact, you could call us the *bonita* sisters! It's one of the delightful advantages of being the only women on the ranch."

When Lixie turned back toward the temporary tables, most of the cowboys surrounded the newcomer. They slowly parted as she approached.

"Here's your friend, Lixie!" Mean Mike blurted out.

The lantern light reflected on a round-faced man with a dirty white shirt and unfastened black tie.

"Mr. Noble! What are you doing here?" she blurted out.

"Why, I came to see you, of course," he blustered.

"But—but—but . . ."

"Paco told me you came to the CS."

I must remember to hogtie that child and drag him through a prickly pear patch. "But where is Jefferson Carter?" she quizzed.

"Who?"

"Mr. Carter. The attorney from Santa Fe," she demanded.

Noble smeared road dust into the sweat on his chin. "I did see him today."

The cowboys that surrounded her blocked most of the lantern light, and she could barely see Noble's face. "Where did you see him?"

"At a walnut tree near a road to someplace. I cut across a road near a tree, and that crazy livery stable horse began to buck. I rode him for quite some time, but I lost my grip and landed on my, eh, my backside. Anyway, when the Santa Fe lawyer rode up, I was sitting under the tree. He retrieved my mount. Quite a nice fellow."

"No wonder the horse bucked. You were sittin' under the massacre tree," Johnny White declared.

"Massacre?" Noble gulped.

"Never mind." White shrugged. "You made it without gettin' slaughtered."

Noble pulled off his hat and wiped his forehead on his shirt sleeve. "I didn't see one savage. Did you?"

"One is resting on the front porch," Lixie announced. "But I would hardly call her a savage."

"You must be joking!" Noble blurted out.

"No, she's an injured ten- or eleven-year-old girl. Where did Mr. Carter go after he retrieved your horse?"

"Said he was following an Indian trail to the northwest."

"Northwest? We found their tracks going southeast toward the Hachitas," Elsworth reported.

"I'm not a tracker. I'm just a famous author on the trail of an exciting new book. But right at the moment I'm hungry. It surely is nice to have such a meal prepared for me."

"You were not invited," Lixie blurted out.

"Now, Lixie-dear," Elsworth drawled, "on this ranch even a driftin' cowboy gets a meal and an overnight stay. Of course Mr. Noble is welcome."

"Thank you, Mr. Elsworth. You're a gentleman."

"You will stay in the barn," Lixie insisted.

"We have some extra room in the big house," Elsworth countered.

"Where do you put those drifting cowboys who spend the night at the CS?" she asked.

"In the barn," Johnny White offered.

"It's better than sleeping out under the Apache moon," Noble mumbled.

"Mr. Noble, I want you to know that I will still not give you an interview. And I sincerely do not want you to write a book about me," Lixie proclaimed.

"Are you goin' to write a book about Lixie?" Mean Mike called out.

"Yes, indeed," Noble declared as he sat down at a table and grabbed up an empty plate.

"Maybe you can put me in it," Johnny called out.

"Johnny White!" Lixie scolded.

"I ain't never been in a book before, Lixie. It might be my only chance."

"Neither have I!" another called out.

"You can put us all in it," Mean Mike called out.

"Well, boys, that just might be," Noble agreed. "Pass those chops. Why don't you all sit down and tell me what you know about Mrs. Miller? Is this sweet potato pie? There must be biscuits here. Yes, I believe there just might be a place for some of you in one of the chapters. Will one of you boys rustle me up some preserves or jam? You know, I just might do a book about the historic CS Ranch. Wouldn't that be—is that apple pie over there? My favorite. Do you suppose one of you could go warm it up in the kitchen? Yes, a book about the CS Ranch. Why, I could feature a different one of you in each chapter. I'll need hot coffee, boys, and I do mean hot."

Lixie stalked back to the big house as the men clustered around the one and only Charles Noble. Harriet sat in the willow chair, her hand holding Bonita's. The girl was stretched out on the pallet, her eyes closed. "I take it that's not your man," Harriet probed.

"That is the one man on the face of the earth I absolutely do not want to see. Why does the Lord allow this to happen to me? It's cruel. Very, very cruel. I could have stayed in Lordsburg, missed Jefferson Carter, and been hounded by Charles Noble. I didn't need to come here for this!"

"I thought you came here to help a friend in need and reach out to a cute little injured girl."

"Harriet Fletcher, don't you start being my conscience."

"I know, I shouldn't have said that. Forgive me."

"Oh, no."

"You won't forgive me?"

"Oh, I forgive you. And you should have said it. I know it's true. But I do not want to talk to that man. Let me stay with Bonita."

"You've hardly left her side."

"That's my reason for being here, you said."

"One of two reasons."

"You can help me by playing the hostess to Mr. Charles Noble. Why don't you have him write a book about you?" Lixie suggested.

"Yes, that would be an aid to sleeping all over the country." Harriet smiled. "Actually, I might talk to him. I do want to write a book myself."

"Oh?"

"About the Yavapai County War in Arizona."

"And Stuart Brannon?"

Harriet Fletcher vacated the chair. "And my Edwin and many others. I'm sure I can keep him busy awhile."

Lixie kissed the woman on the cheek. "You are a queen in my book."

Harriet squeezed her arm. "Queen? Oh, my, those in England even refuse me the title of Lady."

Three hours later the makeshift tables stood empty. The lanterns offered only a dim outline of the headquarters' shadows. Lixie stood at the railing of the veranda and surveyed the deserted yard. There were still lights in the cookhouse where she imagined the Mendozas scrubbing plates and pans. There were no lights in the barn. A bright one in the bunkhouse beamed where Mr. Charles Noble had been suckered into a game of whist with Mean Mike Mason and several others.

Harriet Fletcher had retired to the guest cottage, while Edwin and Langford chatted in the library in the big house sipping strong tea and poring over maps of Spanish land grants in New Mexico. Behind her on a pallet of quilts, Bonita slept on her back with pillows arranged so she could not turn her head left or right.

Somewhere out in the night, six men with carbines provided the first line of defense in case of a night attack. Leaning against the wall on the right side of the woven willow chair was a short-barreled shotgun that caused Lixie's shoulder to ache every time she glanced at it.

She studied the night sky. *The stars don't care what happens down here. They hang in the night sky and shine in the darkness. They don't worry about their purpose. They aren't concerned about their position. A star doesn't sulk if another one shines brighter. Stars are exactly where You put them, Lord. Their task is simple. Maybe not easy, but uncomplicated, simple. Just shine. Shine on full-moon nights. Shine on new-moon nights. Shine on cloudy nights. Shine on clear, cold nights. Shine when the whole world can see you. Shine when no one can see you. Shine when people on earth are laughing. Shine when they are crying. Shine when they die. Shine when they wish they were dead.*

Lord, I'm really getting tired of my melancholy. I have no idea in the world what to do about it.

Lixie ambled back in the shadows to the wicker chair and sat down next to the sleeping girl. She tugged a quilt over her lap and stuffed a cotton-ticked goose-down pillow behind her head.

They all think I'm strange for insisting upon sitting up with Bonita. They have no idea how much I need to be needed. How wonderful it would be to have one person who can't survive without me, one person whose world would collapse without me in it. We should have adopted children. By now I would have grandchildren.

She glanced down at the sleeping girl.

Maybe I could adopt Bonita. Of course, she has a family . . . somewhere. A family who is very worried, I'm sure. Besides, how would it be to adopt an Indian girl? What would people say?

Lixie began to laugh. "What would they say? Nothing that they don't say already!" *Why on earth do I worry about what people say, Lord? From now on I will only worry about what You say. What do You say about my treatment of Bonita?* "When I was hungry, you fed Me? When I was naked, you clothed Me? When I was hurting, you comforted Me? As you have done it to the least of these . . ."

Bonita is not the least.

Charles Noble is the least of these.

No, that's not true. Someone like . . . like Ramona Hawk. She is the least of these. When I was in prison, you visited Me. Lord, if You'll just see that she gets back into prison, I'll go visit her.

Bonita is far from the least.

She trusts me. At least for an evening, she needs me.

Perhaps it's been a good night after all.

Lixie dozed in and out of sleep. She checked on Bonita, then slept some more. She said goodnight to Lord Fletcher and slept again. She awoke when the cowboys changed guard at midnight. Then she slept some more. She thought she said something to Johnny White, but that could have been a dream.

Her eyes were shut, her head collapsed against the pillow when she thought she heard someone walking toward the big house. She blinked her eyes, but with everything so dark she could see nothing.

All lanterns were out.

The stars were bright.

There was no moonlight.

The desert air felt still, fresh.

The dust settled.

Only half awake, she could smell the rose perfume that Harriet had dabbed on Bonita.

Then she heard another sound—a muted crunch.

Her hand dropped to where the shotgun had been propped against the wall. It wasn't there.

She strained to focus on the yard, but her eyelids were so heavy she just wanted to close them and fall back asleep. Her shoulder ached. Her back ached. Her neck was stiff.

Maybe it's one of the boys making the rounds. I should greet him, but I'm too tired to talk. I'll just act like I'm asleep. Perhaps I am asleep.

But what if it's not one of the boys? What if it's . . . What if it's one of Bonita's relatives coming for her? She opened her eyes wide but could see nothing but the stars and the vague outline of the buildings in the yard. *They couldn't get past the guards.*

There was another crunch from the yard. Her eyes flipped open again. She sat up. The pillow dropped behind her back. *Of course they could! Where is that shotgun?* She groped and felt only the clapboard siding.

There was another step, then silence.

Why can't I see anything? The stars are lighting the yard, but I can't see! It's like . . . like a dream. A bad dream.

Something hard hit the wooden steps. Lixie bit her lip. *A shoe*

. . . a boot . . . It hit the step. Indians don't wear heavy boots . . . or do they? How would I know? I should scream and pull the blanket over my head! No, I need to find the shotgun. I put it right here next to my right hand, but it's gone! This has to be a dream.

Lixie spotted what looked like a shadowy figure on the porch. It took another step, then waited as if expecting something to happen.

"Who's there!" The voice was deep, and to Lixie's surprise, it wasn't hers.

She forced her lips apart but couldn't form a word. *Lord, I want to wake up. Wake me up now please!* "Get—get out of here. I'll shoot!" she blurted out. Then she pulled the blanket over her head.

"For pete's sake, don't shoot, Mrs. Miller," the voice implored.

She heard a match being lit and dropped the blanket just as the light faded. There was no one in sight.

"Where are you? I warned you I'd shoot."

"The shotgun is at your feet. If you're goin' to sit guard duty, at least hold it in your lap."

Lixie reached down to her feet and felt the cold, slick barrels of the gun. She plucked it up. "Where did you go?"

"Where it's safe," the voice from the yard replied. "What are you doing on the porch in the middle of the night?"

"What are you doing sneaking up on me?" Lixie dug the pillow out from behind her back.

"I wasn't sneaking. I was being quiet. I didn't want to wake anyone."

She put the pillow behind her head and leaned back. "You were sneaking. Who are you?" Lixie's eyes ached. She closed them and found relief.

"You know me."

"This is an annoying dream. I'm very tired. Who are you?" she demanded.

"Jefferson Carter."

She didn't open her eyes. "Don't toy with me, mister. Who are you? Light a match again. I want to see your face."

"I don't have any more matches."

"What are you doing here?"

"You invited me. Remember?"

"I'm very, very tired. Would you just whisk away and invade some other lady's dreams?"

"You want me to leave?"

"I want to sleep. I invited Mr. Jefferson Carter this afternoon, this evening—not in the middle of the night."

"I got detained."

"It's too late."

"Too late for what?"

"If this were not a dream, I'd tell you. How do I know you're Jefferson Carter?"

"How do you know I'm not? Can't you recognize my voice?"

"I can't even recognize my own voice. It's too distracted. I'm going to sleep. Go away." She pulled the blanket over her head.

"I found it!" he exclaimed.

"Good. Take it and leave," she insisted. "What did you find?"

"Look!"

When she opened her eyes, a flash of light reflected against the blanket. She dropped the blanket to her lap. The flame died, and she could see no one.

Why do we have dreams about people we can never see?

"Look, you can't hide under that blanket and pretend I don't exist."

"You don't exist, Mr. Carter."

"Reach out and take my hand."

"I most certainly will not. Go away."

"I thought you wanted me to stop and visit."

"I wanted you this afternoon. I wanted you to show up when Mr. Charles Noble crowded in. I wanted you here to watch the stars and hold my hand and tell me you needed me. That's what I wanted, Mr. Jefferson Carter."

"I don't understand."

"Of course you don't. Dreams never make sense. Does anyone on the face of this earth need you, Mr. Jefferson Carter?"

"What?"

"I was wondering today if anyone in the world really needed me. Does anyone need you?"

"I believe I have clients that need me for a while."

"Yes, well, that is better than nothing. But you are a shadow that keeps disappearing. You can't keep a match lit more than two seconds. You're slow to figure things out. Maybe it's a good thing we met like this because you are obviously not Mr. Jefferson Carter."

"Who do you think I am?"

"Well, if you were the real Jefferson Carter, you would be a ruggedly handsome man with strong shoulders, gray hair, and a compassionate heart. You would be one who would need Lixie Miller just to be Lixie Miller. One who, when he says he will stop by, always keeps his word. One who doesn't give a hoot what others think about Mrs. Miller. One who is willing to live a quiet life in blessed security. One who panics when he thinks of living without me, who is so true that there is never a hint of infidelity." Lixie's eyelids felt so heavy she allowed them to droop closed. "That's what I was hoping for, Mr. Handsome Dream Attorney from Santa Fe." Her voice faded to a whisper.

"Mrs. Miller, I hardly know you."

She kept her eyes closed. She couldn't tell if she were speaking aloud or just thinking a response. "And whose fault is that? You said you traveled all the way to Lordsburg just to see me."

"I traveled to give you a message and follow a lead on the whereabouts of little Charley McComas and to meet you."

"It doesn't matter."

"Why?"

"Because I'm sleepy, and you're a distraction."

"A distraction?"

"It's common knowledge that nightmares rob a person of sleep."

"I've never been called a nightmare before."

"You have now. Float on out of here. I'm tired. I just don't feel like dreaming anymore about you. It was a childish fantasy."

"What fantasy?"

"About you and me, of course. I'm way too old for such thoughts. If I'm lucky, I'll wake up later and not remember any of this."

"Who's that on the pallet beside you?"

She let her arm flop down to her side but couldn't find Bonita's hand. "My bonnie-girl."

"I didn't know you had children."

"There are many things you don't know about me."

"And many you don't know about me either."

"That's obvious. You don't have the nerve to face me."

"I told you, I don't have any more matches."

"That's all right. I have my eyes closed."

"I think I'll go sleep in the barn."

"Yes, indeed."

"Perhaps we can talk in the daylight sometime."

"I talked to you all afternoon. Didn't you hear me?"

"I wasn't with you."

"You were right there in my daydreams."

"I was?"

"Just like now. Good night, Mr. Carter."

"Good night, Mrs. Miller. I'm sorry you're so troubled in heart. May the Lord grant you His peace."

Peace? That's what I need. I need peace. I need to sleep through the night. Without nightmares. Without reliving the past. Without inventing the future. Lord, Mr. Carter is right. I need Your peace.

She dozed for a minute. Then her eyes blinked open, and she sat up straight. "Who is right? Was he really here?" There was a cold sweat on her forehead. She lowered the blanket from her head. Lixie couldn't see or hear anything, but she could feel the cold barrels of the shotgun lying across her lap.

Five

Lixie Miller woke up with a stiff neck, a side cramp, and a numb left foot.

A small brown hand tugged on her sleeve.

She rubbed her eyes and glanced out on the pastoral scene of a New Mexico dawn. What grass was left on the hills had been brown for months and blended with the color of the dirt. The sky was the color of a dull robin's egg. Only the willows along the creek and the limp hanging leaves of the cottonwoods were green. The chair felt rock-hard on her backside. The morning air tasted fresh.

Lixie studied the huge purple bruise on the girl's forehead. "Good morning, Miss Bonita. Your head looks much, much better." Lixie brushed the thick bangs out of the girl's eyes. "I certainly hope you slept better than I did. Dreams kept waking me up. Do you dream, darlin'? Of course you do—everyone dreams. But what does a little Apache girl dream of? Ponies? Playing? Pretty things . . . and boys? Strong, wiry, little brown-skinned Apache boys, I suppose."

Lixie stood up, and the girl did too.

"You feel like getting up today? That's good, but I don't want you to over-do it." Lixie staggered toward the veranda railing. "You need to eat some more, regain your strength. Then in a day or two, we'll see if . . ." *Lord, I've known this girl less than a day, and I can't bear to think of her leaving.* "Bonita, we'll take one day at a time. I have no idea if you understand a thing I say. Sort of like some men I know."

Holding the girl's hand, Lixie limped out into the yard. Her foot finally came out of the tingly stage. "I need to go wash and clean up and do some rather personal things, but I don't want to leave you alone. I can't barge over and bother Lady Fletcher. So what am I going to do with you?"

The girl peeked out from under the huge purple bruise on her forehead and pointed to Lixie. "*Bonita*," she announced. Then she pointed to herself. "*Bonita*," she repeated.

Lixie strolled over to the cookhouse and peered inside. A light burned in the kitchen.

"Anyone home?" she called out.

When she ambled into the empty dinning room, Bonita clutched her arm and huddled next to her. Lixie glanced into the kitchen and saw Emile Mendoza breaking eggs into a large bowl.

"Good morning, Mrs. Miller," he called out. "How is little Bonita?"

Lixie rested her free hand on the girl's narrow dress-covered shoulder. "Better, I believe. But the bruise is quite ugly."

Emile grabbed an egg in each hand, cracked them, emptied their contents into the bowl, and discarded the shells all in one motion. "Did you sleep at all?"

"Not too much," she admitted. "I'm not used to sleeping out-side in a chair. But I trust I'll catch up tonight."

"Tony offered to take a shift with the girl."

"If we can settle her into a routine, that might be a possibility."

Emile wiped his hands on his white canvas apron. "Did you want something to eat?"

"The smell of biscuits in the oven does make me hungry. But I thought I'd give Bonita a little something to nibble on while I go up to my room to clean up."

"How about some bread, butter, and jam?" he offered. "It will be another half an hour before I have much of anything else ready."

"That would be wonderful." She looked down at the girl. "I imagine you would like some jelly bread, wouldn't you?"

Lixie studied Bonita as the girl licked her lips. *Somehow she knows I'm talking about food. But what else would I talk about in a kitchen?*

"Did you see Johnny White yet this morning?" Emile called out.

"No, we just woke up."

Emile rummaged through a cupboard above the counter on the far wall and pulled out half a loaf of sourdough bread. "He has something to tell you. He told me to let him know when you woke up." Fat sizzled in a huge cast-iron frying pan on the woodstove.

"I'll go check with Johnny and then come get the bread and jam."

"How about a glass of fresh milk for her too?"

"I think that would be very good."

Lixie sauntered toward the barn. Bonita clutched her arm and tried to keep in step.

Mean Mike sprawled on the front step of the bunkhouse, pulling boots over sockless, skinny feet. "Good morning, you two," he called out. "Ain't it a chipper of a day?"

"You seem quite happy, Mean Mike. You must have slept well."

"Nope, but I'm happy all right. I hope you ain't mad at me."

Lixie studied his thin, unshaven face. "Why?"

Mason leaned back on his boot heels. "I reckon I took him to the cleaners."

"Who?"

"Your friend, Mr. Charles Noble."

"Did you beat him in whist?"

The lanky cowboy pulled out a handful of change. "I won me $2.37 cash."

"That was quite a game. Mean Mike, where's Johnny White? He wants to see me."

"He's out back in the round pen. He's giving Doctor a good workin' over."

"Doctor?"

"We got a pair of black stallions here at the headquarters. One is called the Professor. The other is the Doctor."

Behind the huge unpainted barn stood a rectangular corral. At the south end of it, a round corral was built in a fifty-foot circle of thick posts and planks. The fencing was almost solid. The gate was closed, and from the ground Lixie could barely peek inside. She climbed up on the rails and peered over. Bonita climbed up beside her, still grasping Lixie's arm.

Johnny White was on the far side of the pen, his back to them. A long-legged black horse was standing with his head down and a gunnysack tied over his eyes. Johnny cinched down the saddle, then stepped back and studied the animal. He wiped the palms of his hands on his denim jeans and swung up onto the saddle.

The horse danced backwards. Johnny gripped the reins tight, settled down in the saddle, and dug his boots into the stirrups. He took a deep breath and yanked the sack off the horse's eyes.

The horse dropped his head and began to buck. On the second jump, the horse almost tipped over backwards. Johnny's hat tumbled to the dirt. The horse spun to the left and kicked his rear hooves above Johnny's head.

White glanced up at Lixie and Bonita, and immediately the black horse came up off all four feet and twisted in midair. Johnny sailed over the horse's head and landed facedown in the loose dirt.

"Oh dear," Lixie moaned. "I do believe that was not the intended result."

Bonita giggled and climbed up on the top rail of the round pen. She circled Lixie's neck with her arms.

With head reared back, the black horse trotted in circles close to the fence. He came within two feet of Lixie and Bonita.

"Are you all right?" Lixie hollered.

Johnny struggled to his feet and brushed off his jeans and shirt. "Reckon there ain't nothin' busted but my pride. I wasn't countin' on an audience."

"Did we cause that accident?"

He retrieved his hat as the black horse circled the pen. "No, ma'am. Me and him play this same game every Saturday mornin'."

Lixie studied the flashing dark eyes of the circling stallion. "He only bucks on Saturday?"

"Yes, ma'am."

"How does he know which day of the week it is?" she asked.

"'Cause Saturday is the only day I ride him." Johnny dusted his hat off, jammed it back on his head, and strolled toward them. "How's your girl?"

"Better, I believe."

Bonita gripped Lixie tighter as Johnny White approached.

"She'll have that horse tattoo on her forehead awhile, I reckon. You get her to talk any more?"

"Our entire vocabulary seems to be the word *bonita*."

"*¿Dónde está su familia?*" Johnny asked the girl.

She bit her lip and laid her head on Lixie's shoulder.

"Do you think she understood?" Lixie asked.

"She knew I was askin' about her. Either she didn't understand, or she wants to ignore me. You goin' to turn her loose today?"

"She can run away anytime she chooses," Lixie said. "But we will have to look for her family at some point."

"She surely seems attached to you."

Johnny White had a wad of dirt stuck to his cheek. Lixie resisted the urge to reach down and brush it off.

"I don't know why I was the one adopted. I rather enjoy it, of course."

"Kids is that way," he added. "They can sense who their friends are. Which is more than I can say for some horses. The Doctor has no idea how near he is to becoming a gelding."

"We don't want to interrupt your work, but Emile said you were looking for me."

Johnny leaned his back against the fence and watched the circling horse. "I've got a message to give you from your friend."

"Oh?" The image of a round-faced, grinning Charles Noble flitted across her mind. *Why does he keep insisting that he's my friend? He's actively working against my best interest. That's the definition of an enemy, not a friend!*

"He left early, said he had a few things to go check out, but he was definitely coming back so that you two could have that talk."

"I hope you told him not to bother coming back. I've tried every way possible to dissuade him."

"Eh, no, ma'am, I didn't tell him nothin'. I thought you was lookin' for him yesterday."

Lixie sighed and tried to press the wrinkles out of her forehead. "Looking for him? I'm delighted he left. He really is a pest."

Bonita pulled her arms back from Lixie's neck and continued to scrutinize the circling black horse. She sat on the top rail and scooted away just a little. Lixie reached over and patted her knee.

Johnny White turned around to face Lixie. "Ma'am, I never claimed to know much about women, but maybe I know even less than I reckoned. I thought for sure you was lookin' for that Santa Fe lawyer to show up."

Lixie felt her shoulders slump. "Mr. Carter? Are you talking about Mr. Jefferson Carter?"

"Who did you think I was talkin' about?"

"Mr. Charles Noble, of course."

"Oh, no, Noble's sleepin' it off in the barn loft. It was Mr. Carter who left you a message."

Lixie's head pounded. "He was actually here?" she gasped.

"He came in late last night. I thought he meandered over there and talked to you."

Lixie shook her head. "No . . . no . . . that just couldn't have been him!"

Johnny rubbed his chin. "It wasn't?"

Lixie closed her eyes and let her head drop back. "I can't believe this, Johnny White. This isn't real. Every day gets worse. I feel like a complete, absolute idiot. I was asleep. I was babbling. This is insane! Why did he try to visit with me in the middle of the night on the front porch of a ranch house where I was doctoring a sick child?"

Johnny White's mouth dropped open. His eyes searched the corrals as if hoping to be rescued. "Eh . . . eh, I don't know, Mrs. Miller. I'm just a cowboy."

"Did you say he was coming back?"

"He told me to tell you he'll be back this afternoon."

"But we're going on a picnic."

"I told him that if we ain't here, we'd be at the river."

"What did he say?"

"Somethin' about picnics bein' rather frivolous. Does that mean fancy?"

"That's close enough." Lixie leaned forward and rested her forehead on her fingers. Then she closed her eyes and sighed. *Lord, when does it let up? When do I have that peace? That's what Mr. Jefferson Carter wished me. May I have Your peace. I want Your peace, and I want it right now!*

"Lixie, are you all right?" Johnny White asked.

She opened her eyes and smoothed the wrinkles at their corners. Bonita was standing on the inside of the next to the top rail. She towered above Lixie and Johnny White.

"Have you ever experienced the peace of God, Johnny White?"

"Are you preaching at me?"

"No, I'm preaching at myself. Sometimes things seem so out of control that I have to stop and go back to the basics. Sometimes my life bucks just like that black stallion, but I have to ride it every minute of every day."

"Is peace when you're riding a dead-broke horse? Or is it the confidence you have even when you're on the back of a bucker like this one?" Johnny asked.

"Now *you* are preaching at me," Lixie said.

"Really? No one has ever accused me of that before."

The horse circled the far side of the pen and started to lap back toward them. The Indian girl pointed at it and shouted, "*Bonita!*"

"You think the horse is pretty?" Lixie said. "Yes, you're right, darlin'."

When the trotting horse circled toward them, Johnny hugged the fence line next to Lixie. As the black nose of the horse pulled even with Lixie, Bonita leaped on its back and clutched its thick mane.

"No!" Lixie called out.

"*Bonita!*" the girl shouted.

"Stop her, Johnny!"

The cowboy leaned back against the round pen railing and watched the Indian girl gallop the horse round and round.

"Stop her?" he hollered. "I'd like to hire her! Look at her ride. Lixie, look at her ride!"

The girl straddled the horse in her jeans, her dress skirt shoved up around her waist. Her long black hair flagged out behind her. A wide, white-toothed smile greeted them as she circled the horse again.

"You got a mighty cute daughter, Mrs. Miller."

"You know she's not my daughter."

"Me and the boys figure you ought to just adopt her."

"That's impossible. She has a family."

"I'll tell you what's impossible—for some little belt-waist Apache girl to outride ever' cowboy on the CS."

"But she's doin' it, isn't she?"

"She's the only one who can ride the Doctor without getting bucked off first. She's not only ridin' him, but she's enjoyin' ever' minute of it."

The girl bounced and giggled on the back of the long-legged stallion. *Now that, Lord, is exactly what Your peace should look like.*

Elizabeth Miller had just gotten Bonita settled on the porch in front of a tall jar of milk and three thick pieces of bread smeared with butter and chokecherry jam when Lady Fletcher strolled out of the guest cottage and over toward the big house.

"Good morning, *bonita* sisters. I trust everyone slept well."

"You look chipper," Lixie called back as Lady Fletcher approached.

"And you didn't answer my question."

"I believe Bonita slept well."

Harriet stopped at the bottom of the stairs and examined the girl. "The swelling went down, but that bruise certainly looks horrible."

"It's best she doesn't look in a mirror for a few weeks."

"How about you, Mrs. Miller? I surmise you had a horrible night sitting up in the chair?"

"I would rather not talk about it."

"About what?"

"About Jefferson Carter showing up in the middle of the night, and I . . ."

"He didn't!"

"Yes, he did. And I babbled on and on, half-asleep until he decided to ride off."

"You didn't!"

"I did."

"He left already?" Harriet pressed.

"Yes."

"Wait a minute. The man appears in the middle of the night, expects you to be coherent, gets riled when you aren't, and rides off before sunrise? Good riddance, Lixie dear!"

"It does sound rather strange, doesn't it?"

"I should say so. He's not exactly Pat Garrett hoping for a mid-night rendezvous with Billy the Kid."

"He did make sense about one thing. He said he hoped I would find the Lord's peace in my life. I truly believe that's what's missing."

"You talked about God's peace with a man in flickering lantern light in the middle of the night?"

"It was pitch-black. No lantern."

"You didn't see his face?"

"I didn't see anything," Lixie reported.

"This does seem rather strange."

"The word *insane* came to my mind this morning. I've decided to give up on the situation."

"What situation."

"The one with Mr. Jefferson Carter."

"What do you mean, give up?"

"I think it would be best if I never see him again."

Harriet stepped over next to Bonita. "I, for one, would like to meet Jefferson Carter at least once, to see what kind of man turns Lixie Miller into chokecherry preserves."

"Speaking of sticky faces, you should see this young lady ride bareback."

"You two have been horseback riding already?"

"Bonita just rode the rankest horse in the remuda."

"Good for her!"

"Harriet, will you sit with Bonita while I go clean up?"

"Certainly." Harriet plopped down in the woven willow chair.

Lixie touched the girl's shoulder. "Honey, you stay here with Lady Fletcher. I'll be right back after I clean up." She started for the front door of the big house.

Bonita leapt to her feet and clutched Lixie's arm.

"Sweetie, you stay here with me," Harriet coaxed. "We'll eat some bread and visit." She reached out, but the girl hid behind Lixie.

"You really need to stay here," Lixie instructed.

Bonita held tightly to her arm.

"Oh dear, I believe you two are rather attached," Harriet said.

"What am I going to do? I have to clean up."

"She probably will be afraid to go into the house. Just march right in there and see what she does," Harriet suggested.

Lixie Miller sat on the edge of the unused bed in the guest room at the top of the stairs and unlaced her high-top shoes.

Bonita bounced on the feather mattress beside her.

Lord, I know I've been whining to You about wanting to be needed. But I don't think I have to be needed this much. I can't even change my clothes without two little, round brown eyes watching my every move. Perhaps I can amend my whine. I want to be needed moderately.

By the time they left the room, Lixie had reset her hair in combs, washed her face, neck, hands, and feet. She changed earrings and fastened a small silk rose to the sleeve of her left wrist.

Bonita still wore denim trousers under her blue calico dress. She exited the room with a red ribbon in her hair and a red silk flower on her wrist. She was still barefoot.

At eleven o'clock Captain Ethan and Mary Ruth Holden arrived with an escort of two outriders. Soon the Holdens, Fletchers, Langford Elsworth, Lixie Miller, and a silent, wide-eyed Bonita lounged on the veranda.

"Paco asked about you," Mary Ruth said.

"I've only been gone one day."

"He checks up on all his friends."

Lixie turned to Harriet Fletcher. "Paco is a precocious Mexican boy about Bonita's age. I seem to attract the younger set."

"This one has been permanently attached to you since we arrived," Mary Ruth continued. "That's a horrible bruise."

"It was much worse last night," Lixie said.

Elsworth waved across the yard. "It looks like your good friend, Mr. Noble, woke up."

"The boys kept him up until almost dawn playing whist," Lixie replied. "Langy-dear, you fed him and housed him. It's time for him to move on."

"We can't turn him out by himself with Apaches roaming the countryside," Elsworth cautioned.

"The marshal reported that a small band of bronco Apaches crossed the railroad tracks near Sopar last night and are headed toward the Hachitas and Mexico," Captain Holden reported.

"You see, there's no danger," Lixie announced. "Mr. Noble can ride back to Lordsburg."

"But Johnny White told us Mr. Carter is on the trail of another band going back to Arizona," Elsworth countered.

"Mr. Carter was here?" Mary Ruth quizzed. "Lixie, why didn't you—"

"I don't want to talk about it," Lixie snapped. The words scattered like buckshot from a short-barreled shotgun.

"Yes, well, so much for that conversation." Mary Ruth turned to the men on her right. "Mr. Elsworth, I understand we're going for a picnic along the Gila River?"

"That is what we planned."

"Are you sure it's safe?" Lady Fletcher probed.

"I'm taking a dozen armed men. The only problem will be hauling enough food to feed them all."

"Is that close to where Bonita had her accident? Perhaps someone will be looking for her there," Lixie said.

"What if they are? Will you have trouble giving her up?" Lady Fletcher challenged.

Lixie reached over and held the young girl's hand. "Of course I will. But there's no choice in the matter. Kidnapping is still a serious crime, I believe."

"We will take two carriages and one wagon to the picnic," Elsworth announced.

"That's good. We women get a carriage to ourselves!" Lixie called out.

Elsworth cleared his throat. "I say, I hadn't thought that . . ."

"Now I'm sure you men want to visit about different things than we do," Harriet remarked.

"Oh, yes, how nice. Just us three girls," Mary Ruth remarked.

"Four," Lixie corrected. She squeezed Bonita's sweaty fingers.

The caravan pulled out when the sun was straight overhead. Elsworth drove the carriage that included Lord Fletcher, Captain Holden, and Charles Noble. Lixie drove the second carriage. Bonita huddled next to her, and Harriet and Mary Ruth sat in the backseat. The wagon was driven by Tony Mendoza. His father, a book in hand, sat next to him. Johnny White and Mean Mike Mason rode twenty yards in front of the carriage. The other ten mounted men rode to the sides and behind the wagon, carrying carbines across their saddle horns, revolvers holstered to their sides.

Little Beaver Crossing consisted of three dozen cottonwood trees, willow brush, and a meadow not much bigger than the yard at the CS Ranch. After miles of dusty desert, it looked like an oasis.

Six of the men were posted on the perimeter of the meadow. The rest helped Emile and Tony Mendoza set up the picnic. The women retreated to the shadiest spot in the meadow.

Charles Noble trailed after them. "I believe I'll call this chapter 'Picnic Among the Apaches.'"

"The only Apache is a ten-year-old girl," Lixie said.

"The reader isn't concerned with details. They long for a grand panorama, the wide view—not a narrow literal telling of the story."

"You mean, you don't want to get too close to the details?" Harriet asked.

"Precisely!"

"Then I suggest you would be better off sitting over with the men," Mary Ruth proposed. "You don't want to get bogged down with women's chatter about details."

Lixie grasped her hands in front of her waist. "That's right. You need the wide view."

"That doesn't mean—"

"Of course it does," Lixie proclaimed.

"It—it—does?" he stammered. "What does it mean?"

"That sitting over by the wagon will give you a better impression, a clearer perspective of this day. You'll be a much better writer for it. I'm afraid you'll be quite bored when we start discussing how to sew buttons onto a serge coat sleeve," Lixie argued.

"Or why refined cane sugar makes better cookie batter," Mary Ruth added.

Lady Fletcher held her chin up and nodded her head. "Yes, or how to remove sweat stains from men's cotton shirts."

"Hmmmph," Noble mumbled. "I suppose you could be right. A wider perspective?"

He trudged back toward the wagon as Lixie unfolded a three-point wool blanket. "Now if any of us discusses mending, sewing, or cooking, the others may pull off her hat and toss it in the river!"

"Do men really think that's what we talk about when we're alone?" Harriet asked.

"Most have no clue at all," Lixie said.

Mary Ruth untied her hat. "They would be surprised to hear us talk about politics, social issues, and religion."

Lixie let out a laugh, and a wide-eyed Bonita began to giggle. "I'd be surprised if that's what we're going to talk about."

"We all know what the subject is today," Mary Ruth proclaimed.

"Certainly." Harriet nodded. "We'll discuss Lixie's mysterious Mr. Jefferson Carter."

Lixie put her hand over her mouth. "My what?"

"Now, now, Mrs. Miller, don't act so coy. You knew that would be discussed."

Lixie rubbed Bonita's back in a slow, circular motion. "I thought we discussed it enough on the way out."

"You jest. We came to absolutely no conclusion at all," Harriet declared.

Mary Ruth tugged off her gloves. "I think she should marry the man and adopt Bonita."

"I can't believe you said that," Lixie gasped.

"Does she protest too much?" Mary Ruth asked.

"Quite," Lady Fletcher concurred.

Lixie fanned herself with her black straw hat. "Let me remind you that I've offended him and chased him off every time he's shown up."

"But he keeps coming back. He's a determined man," Harriet pointed out.

"He's a complete stranger. I know nothing about him."

"He's an attorney with a good reputation in Santa Fe. His specialty seems to be land grant cases, which means job security for years to come. Ethan and I have already discussed it," Mary Ruth trumpeted.

"I don't even know his vices," Lixie said.

"Nor he yours," Harriet reminded her.

Lixie felt her face blush. "He's probably too young for me."

Mary Ruth tilted her head and batted her eyelids. "Too young for what, dear?"

Lixie waved her hands. "I don't know anything about his faith!"

Harriet traced her finger across the wool blanket. "He did mention he hoped you can find the Lord's peace. That's a spiritually mature thing to say."

Bonita lay down on her back and put her head in Lixie's lap. Lixie stroked the girl's cheeks. "I'm sure he thinks I'm an idiot."

Harriet sat straight up. "She does have a point there."

"Yes, I can see where that could be his interpretation of the situation," Mary Ruth acknowledged.

Harriet nodded her head. "Quite so. You are right, dear Lixie.

Mary Ruth, I'm afraid Mr. Jefferson Carter is out of the question. Hmmm, I wonder if Mr. Charles Noble is married."

"What? Wait . . . don't give up on Mr. Carter so easily!" Lixie protested.

"We were just listening to you, dear," Mary Ruth chided.

"If you two begin to talk about me and Charles Noble, I will personally pick you up, hats and all, and toss you into the Gila River. Do I make myself clear?"

Harriet untied the ribbon on her straw hat. "Quite so."

"I presume this means we should just talk about Jefferson Carter?" Mary Ruth plucked a blade of meadow grass and waved it like a wand.

"Yes, that would be preferable." Lixie studied the Indian girl. *Lord, here she is among foreigners, can't understand a word, is separated from family, has no idea in the world what the next day, the next hour will bring. And yet she's so trusting she can sleep in my lap. That's that I want. That's exactly what I want.*

"Which is precisely what I said when we first sat down," Harriet continued. "We simply must discuss Mr. Jefferson Carter."

"What is Lixie going to say and do when he returns today?" Mary Ruth pondered. "Should she be silent about the past, shall I say, less than satisfactory encounters with him? Should she claim she doesn't remember what she said during the night?"

"Or perhaps she should throw herself at his feet and beg forgiveness for being an idiot," Harriet suggested.

"Oh, you two are a real help. I'm not going to lie or be deceptive. Nor will I ever apologize for being groggy when awakened in the middle of the night," Lixie maintained.

"Yes. Of course. If he stops by the picnic, we will simply disperse in a timely and subtle manner," Harriet said, "and leave you two to visit."

"Three," Mary Ruth corrected. "Bonita won't leave her side."

"If Mr. Carter happens to come back, and if he happens to want to talk to me, could you both see if you can entertain Bonita?"

"Lixie, dear, we'll try, but you know how little success I had this morning," Harriet said.

Lixie studied the sleeping girl's face. "Do you know what would be quite humorous? If Bonita really could understand English and was listening to every word."

Mary Ruth clapped her hands. "What a book she could write!"

"If she could write," Harriet added.

Lixie softly touched the purple bruise on Bonita's forehead. The young girl's eyes blinked open. She sat straight up, looked around, and appeared to be listening to something.

"What is it, honey?" Lixie asked.

Bonita pointed to the rocks east of the river.

"Is something over there? What is it?" Lixie stood up. "I don't see anything."

The dark-skinned girl crouched behind Lixie.

"Langy-dear!" Lixie called out to the men near the wagon. "Bonita thinks there's something or someone up in those rocks."

Mr. Elsworth pulled off his hat and scratched his head as he stared to the east. "I can't see a thing," he called back.

"Johnny White rode up that way to scout for tracks," Tony Mendoza shouted.

"Oh, there you have it," Elsworth boomed. "The girl probably saw him ride up there."

"Here comes Johnny!" Mean Mike shouted. "He's ridin' mighty fast for just a scoutin' trip."

Harriet stood beside Lixie. "How did she know someone was up there?" she whispered.

"Indians have trained their ears to catch the smallest sounds. Their survival depends on it," Lixie replied and turned to the girl. "It's just Johnny White." She pointed at the approaching rider.

Bonita lifted her arm and pointed it to the rocks.

"Someone is still up there?" Lixie asked.

Mary Ruth Holden stood on the other side of Bonita. "She is a very handy young lady to have around."

The women hurried over to the food wagon as Johnny White dismounted in the circle of men.

"Did you see anything?" Elsworth questioned.

"Lixie's friend is up there!" Johnny White pulled off his hat as the women approached.

"My friend?"

Johnny's brown face flashed a dimpled grin. "Mr. Jefferson Carter."

"I told you he'd be back," Harriet whispered.

"Did we decide that she should throw herself at his feet?" Mary Ruth giggled.

Lixie shielded her mouth. "You decided to go off and leave me alone."

"We did? That was frightfully inconsiderate of us, knowing how poorly you've done on your own in the past," Harriet said.

Lixie turned to the dark-haired cowboy. "Johnny, why didn't Mr. Carter come down with you?"

"He wanted me to bring him a spare horse."

"Is his buckskin lame?" she asked.

"Oh, no, it's just that they'd have to ride double, and his pony's tired."

"They?" Lixie asked. "Who's with Mr. Carter?"

Johnny glanced around at the other CS cowboys. "I didn't catch her name."

The crowd in the meadow lined up next to the supply wagon to wait as Johnny White returned to the boulders leading a buckskin gelding.

"He must have found some poor woman who was stranded," Harriet murmured.

"Yes, they are traveling on only one horse," Mary Ruth concurred. "That was definitely not planned that way."

"Her horse could have lamed up," Harriet said.

"Or run off," Mary Ruth replied.

"How do two people ride in the same saddle?" Harriet questioned.

Mary Ruth shielded her mouth with her straw hat. "Very chummy, I presume."

Harriet's voice was barely above a whisper. "What would a woman be doing out here alone?"

"Perhaps there's been a tragedy," Mary Ruth suggested. "Maybe the Indians killed her husband, and Mr. Carter rescued her."

"Maybe the Indians killed her father and mother, and she's just a girl," Harriet said. "Johnny didn't say how old she is."

"Maybe she's fat and ugly," Mary Ruth offered. "That's why she needs a fresh horse."

Harriet placed her fingers over her mouth. "Perhaps she's an Indian woman."

Mary Ruth's eyes widened. "Alone?"

"Come to look for her daughter!" Harriet said.

Lixie clutched Bonita to her side and then felt her pull back.

"Here they come!" Tony Mendoza shouted.

Everyone except Charles Noble stared east. He sat on a crate scribbling in a notebook propped on his knee.

For several moments all anyone could see was a trail of dust and three running horses. Johnny White led the trio. Jefferson Carter's horse was last.

"Looks like three men!" Mean Mike called out.

"The second one has long hair," someone shouted.

"It's a gal, boys!" another hollered.

"She's wearin' pants!" Tony exclaimed.

"Men's trousers and straddlin' the horse. Don't that beat all?" Mean Mike blurted.

"A man's shirt too. Maybe she's an Indian girl. . . . I can't tell," Tony said.

The crowd of cowboys surged forward with most of the men talking at the same time.

"She ain't no little girl; she's fully growed. I can tell that much."

"I don't reckon I ever seen a woman wear trousers."

"Her hands are tied, boys! Look at that. Ol' Carter has her tied to the saddle."

"How come he tied up a lady? That ain't right."

Langford Elsworth led the procession toward the incoming riders. "My word, it's Ramona Hawk!"

"The one that killed Tommy Avila?" Mean Mike spewed out.

Lixie watched as several men dropped hands to their holstered revolvers.

"She's sort of purdy."

"For a woman that age."

"And a killer."

Johnny White jumped off his horse before the animal stopped running. He caught the bridle on the buckskin and brought the horse to a stop in the middle of the meadow. The crowd surrounded the rider as he untied the woman's feet from the stirrups.

Harriet leaned over to Lixie. "They had her tied in!"

"She does look older close up!" Mary Ruth added.

Lixie folded her arms across her chest and scooted closer as the woman dismounted.

The woman's brown eyes sparkled as she stared right at Lixie and the other women. The wrinkles at the corners of her eyes were deep. A slight smile, almost a sneer, broke across her lips. "You ladies can't imagine how relieved I am to see you among this group."

"Relieved?" Lixie repeated.

"When a woman is left alone out in the desert, and she gets hog-tied and hauled into a group of men, she naturally assumes the very worst."

Langford Elsworth stormed toward her. "Miss Hawk, this is CS Ranch property. Every man here was a friend of Tommy Avila's. You must know that you have not entered a friendly environment."

"All the more reason I'm thrilled to see some other ladies here."

"Carter, how did you get your face scratched?" Mean Mike called out.

Lixie could see three parallel, bloody scratches on his cheek. "Some gals don't exactly listen to reason, boys."

"How come you's wearin' men's clothin'?" Mean Mike questioned.

"How come you are?" she challenged.

"Are we goin' to shoot her or hang her?" a cowboy at the back blurted out.

"I'm takin' her in," Carter announced. "There's a trial to be finished in Santa Fe, with the added charge of escape."

Ramona Hawk's glance darted to Lixie. "You ladies don't happen to have a dress you could spare me? I don't enjoy this masquerade."

"Those look like the same clothes one of the deputies was wearing when the three of you disappeared," Elsworth pressed.

"I borrowed them."

"What's that old boy wearin'? Your dress?" Johnny White quizzed.

Ramona Hawk flashed a dimpled, white-toothed grin. "No."

"How come you're wearin' trousers?" Mean Mike asked again.

"I was making a run for the border. I figured everyone would be lookin' for a woman." Hawk sized up each man as she talked. "We split up to cross the tracks. We were to meet south of Hachita. My horse gave out, and before I could steal another, Mr. Attorney showed up with a carbine in hand." Hawk looked at the leather thongs tying her wrists.

Lixie sidled up to Jefferson Carter. "Do you believe her?" she whispered.

"Nope," he whispered back. "She's a tough gal who's been through it all. She's not going to divulge anything. I figure it's all a ploy to get us off the track."

"What track are we on?"

"That's what I'm trying to find out."

Lord Fletcher strolled over. "What are your plans now, Mr. Carter?"

"I was hopin' to barge in on some dinner and then ride straight to Lordsburg to catch a train to Deming, then up to Santa Fe. Any Apaches between here and there?"

"Maybe half a dozen crossed the tracks last night near Sopar and are now headed back to Mexico," Captain Holden reported. "No one can figure out why they crossed over in the first place."

"This might be your lucky day, Miss Hawk," one of the CS

cowhands called out. "To get hung by cowboys is better than being skinned alive by Apaches."

"Being tied hand and foot and denied even basic courtesies is not what I call a lucky day," she mocked.

"I'd like to feed the prisoner before we go, but don't take the hobbles off her hands or feet," Carter said.

"I can't eat like this," Hawk protested.

"You can if you're hungry enough," Carter replied. He glanced at Lixie. "Afternoon, Mrs. Miller." He tipped his brown felt hat.

"Mr. Carter, welcome," she replied. "Do you need any iodine for those scratches?"

"I reckon they'll heal at their own rate. Lixie, do you have a minute? I'd like to talk to you."

"Certainly."

"I trust that you ladies will see that Miss Hawk gets fed?" Carter said.

Mary Ruth stepped up. "Of course."

Harriet squeezed Lixie's elbow. Lixie turned to stroll toward the cottonwoods with Jefferson Carter. Neither spoke until they were well away from the others.

"Lixie . . . last night I . . ."

"That was quite bizarre, wasn't it?"

"I reckon."

"I'm sorry I blabbed in my sleep. I trust you won't hold me accountable for whatever I said."

A slight grin broke across his face. "No, ma'am. I won't expect you to remember any of it, but I surely did learn a lot about Lixie Miller. It's kind of funny."

"I found nothing humorous about it."

"What I mean is . . . I learned about you when you talked in your sleep. And just a few minutes ago, I learned a lot about Ramona Hawk by listening to her cuss me out."

"That must have been quite a scene. With her reputation I'm surprised she didn't shoot you on sight. How exactly did you capture her?"

They were walking closely enough that their arms bumped.

"I was on my way to meet you here at the river when—"

"You were coming to meet me?"

"All of you, I suppose. Johnny White said you were havin' a picnic. I really did want to talk to—"

"Bonita?" she pressed.

"Mrs. Miller, I wanted to talk to you also."

"And you found Ramona Hawk along the way?"

"Right back up in those boulders, about ten minutes before Johnny White rode up."

When they reached the cottonwoods, they turned west and skirted the willow saplings.

"You sneaked up on her?"

"I came up out of the draw and spotted someone spying on your caravan."

"She was watching us?"

"She was stretched out on her stomach on top of the boulders, with a man's hat pulled down to shade her eyes. I saw the long black hair, but from a distance thought she was an Apache. All I could see were the duckings and long-sleeved shirt, boots and hat."

"Why was she watching us?"

"She wouldn't say. To figure out how to steal a pony, I reckon. I waited a while to see if there were more Apaches anywhere. Then I left my pony and slipped up on her."

"Not many men ever sneak up on Ramona Hawk."

"If I had spotted her in a purdy dress like yours, I would have gone ridin' up to save her and probably been dead by now. I had a carbine six inches from her ear before she knew I was there."

"I presume you were surprised to find it was Ramona Hawk."

He pulled off his hat. His hair was very thick and very gray. "Shocked would be a better word. She tried to sweet-talk me until she rolled over and saw I was one of the Santa Fe attorneys. I've never heard even a bullwhacker who could cuss like that."

"How did you ever get her tied up?"

"You can see by the scratches it wasn't easy. I sacked her."

"You what?"

"I tied a gunnysack over her head and her hands behind her

back and let her cuss and flail around until she wore out. I was delighted when Johnny White rode up."

"The boys want to hang her," Lixie cautioned.

"I can't let that happen. Even the worst in our country deserves due process of the law."

"Well spoken, counselor. What was it you wanted to talk to me about?" *His hair has much more gray than I remembered. I wonder how old he really is?*

Carter plucked up a small, dry stick, broke it in half, and tossed it out in the river. "The boys at the CS said you took in a little Apache girl."

"Sort of."

He reached down for a pebble the size of a double eagle. "Would it be possible for me to talk to her?"

"She doesn't speak English."

He skipped the rock across the water. "Does she speak Spanish?"

"Perhaps a little. I'm not sure." Lixie picked up a pebble the size of a quarter.

"I want to know if she's seen little Charley McComas. There are rumors that he's in the Sierra Madres."

She tossed her rock in the water. It sank at first splash. "What about that group of Apaches that crossed the tracks near Sopar going south?"

"I don't know. I was hoping maybe the girl can tell me."

Lixie spun around. "Bonita!"

He stepped up alongside her. "What's the matter?"

"She's been at my side since we found her." Lixie reached out and clutched Jefferson Carter's arm. "Where is she?"

"She wasn't with you when I rode up. I figured you left her back at the ranch."

"No, we didn't! She was right there at my side." Lixie held her skirt up to her ankles and jogged. Her right hand slipped down into his hand as they scurried across the meadow.

Harriet Fletcher and Mary Ruth Holden sat on the nearest blanket. Both stood as the couple approached.

"Where's Bonita?" Lixie called out.

Harriet glanced at their hands. "I take it you had a good visit."

Jefferson Carter dropped Lixie's hand.

"Where is Bonita?" Lixie repeated.

"We assumed she was with you. If we had known you two were alone, we could have provided a chaperon," Harriet replied.

"Lady Fletcher, I'm extremely worried right at the moment. Where's Bonita? You said you'd watch her," Lixie demanded.

"But she wasn't here," Mary Ruth repeated.

Edwin Fletcher, smoking a clay pipe, strolled over. "Is something the matter?"

"I can't find Bonita," Lixie blurted out.

"I say, what did happen to that girl?" He turned toward the men who clustered near the wagon where Ramona Hawk was guarded. "Langford, have you seen the little Indian girl?"

Elsworth, Ethan Holden, and Mean Mike Mason ambled over to Lixie and the women.

"She done ran off, Mrs. Miller," Mean Mike reported.

Lixie surveyed the meadow. "What do you mean?"

"When Johnny and them rode up, Bonita ran off toward the river."

"But—but—she was right at my side."

"You was distracted, I reckon," Mean Mike replied.

"But why didn't you tell me?"

"I figured you knew about it. You was standin' right there. I wasn't goin' to interrupt your stroll with Mr. Carter."

Lixie rubbed the perspiration off her forehead. "We've got to find her. We've got to find her right now."

"Perhaps she recognized where she was and went after her family," Edwin Fletcher offered.

Lixie wrung her hands. "But they are nowhere around here."

"Maybe she's just down there playin' in the river. You know how kids are," Mean Mike suggested.

"She wouldn't just leave me like that!" Lixie insisted.

"But you did plan on her leaving sometime, didn't you?" Mary Ruth queried.

"Not like this. I must find her."

"We'll all go look," Harriet said.

Lord Edwin Fletcher lowered his voice. "I say, I do believe Lady Fletcher and I should stay near the wagon. I perceive some of these men would lynch the Hawk woman if there were no witnesses."

"I'm afraid he's right," Ethan Holden said. "We'll stay too."

"Mean Mike, will you come help me look for her?" Lixie asked.

"Yes, ma'am. I'll get Johnny. He's the best tracker we got on the CS."

"I'll go with you," Jefferson Carter offered.

"And leave your prisoner?" she asked.

"Lord Fletcher is right. If the presence of two ladies doesn't temper these cowboys, nothing I could do will stop them."

With Johnny White and Mean Mike Mason out in front, Lixie Miller and Jefferson Carter hiked back across the meadow to the meandering row of cottonwoods that lined the river.

"Mr. Carter, please forgive me for grabbing your hand like that. I was very upset. I should not have been so familiar."

His eyes searched the cottonwoods, his voice barely audible. "We all have times when we need a hand to hold."

Six

Johnny White was already halfway into the six-inch-deep stream when he called back to Lixie Miller. "You and Mr. Carter take this side of the river. Me and Mean Mike will wade across and search the other."

Still summer air hung in the willow thickets as Lixie plowed her way through. "I just don't know why she ran off."

Jefferson Carter, his hat in hand, hiked a step behind her. "Seems to me, either a person runs off or is chased off by fear. If she just ran away, I reckon you have to let her go and trust her into the hands of the Almighty."

She paused as he held back the brush that blocked her way. "My mind agrees with you, but my heart has a real struggle with that." Lixie surveyed the mud along the river's edge for footprints. "Bonita!" she called out. The word died quickly.

This time Jefferson Carter led the way. "If something spooked her, then she'll try to figure out a way back. She won't go very far— just to a place she feels safe."

Lixie's thin cotton stockings rubbed inside her lace-up shoes. "I wanted her to feel safe at my side." She searched through the thick brush. "Bonita!" Then she continued to hike. "What could have frightened her?"

Carter squatted and peered behind a thicket too dense to penetrate. "Perhaps it was three horses riding up fast and furious."

"No, she loves riding fast horses. You should have seen her on that black stallion at the ranch." Lixie brushed leaves off the sleeves of her dress. "Bonita!" she called out.

Jefferson Carter looked back through the cottonwoods at the distant meadow and the wagon surrounded by CS cowboys. "Perhaps she was afraid of one of the three people who rode up."

"Do you need to get back to your prisoner, Mr. Carter?"

"No, everything's fine, I trust."

"Bonita!" They hiked across a break in the brush. Dried leaves and sticks crunched underfoot. "She isn't afraid of Johnny White. He's been around her for two days."

"Which leaves me and Ramona Hawk."

Lixie glanced back to catch him looking straight at her. She felt like throwing her shoulders back and sucking in her stomach. *Keep steady, Elizabeth Miller. You are looking for a little girl, not auditioning.* "I can't imagine how either of you could touch her off. Bonita heard something up in the rocks before Johnny White even came back."

From across the river she heard Johnny White holler, "Bonita!"

Carter hiked up alongside her. "What do you mean?"

"She started pointing at the boulders before we knew you were there." Lixie tugged a linen handkerchief from her sleeve and dabbed the back of her neck. "She became very agitated."

"Hard to figure, isn't it? Ramona Hawk is a dangerous woman, but at first glance she looks, well . . ."

"Attractive?"

"No woman looks very attractive wearing a man's shirt and trousers." Carter glanced over his shoulder at the people in the meadow. "But she doesn't look scary. Besides that, she was tied up."

Lixie reached back and clutched the sleeve of his white cotton shirt. "Jefferson, maybe that's it!"

"A tied-up woman made the little girl run?"

"Yes, think about it. With her long black hair and dark complexion, Ramona Hawk could be mistaken for an Indian. You said so yourself."

"And I came thundering in with a woman all tied up, so Bonita got scared and perhaps thought I was coming for her?"

"And that you will bind her and take her away—especially if she's seen white men come and capture others in her band that way."

"Or maybe she's been treated that way herself."

"No wonder the poor thing is frightened. Where can she be?" Lixie pulled back green-leafed willows between her and the river's edge. "Bonita! Honey, it's all right. Come on out!"

Jefferson pushed his hat to the back of his head. "She's hiding, and here I am beating the brush with you. She probably thinks I'm trying to find her to cart her off."

"Oh dear, it might not be good for her to see us together."

Carter stared across the river at White and Mason. "I'd go back to the others, but I hate to leave you alone here. It doesn't seem right."

"Perhaps you could drop back a few yards."

"She'd know I'm here."

She grabbed his arm and led him toward the cottonwoods. "Then go back, and I'll continue to look on this side of the river by myself."

He stopped walking. "I can't do that. I can't leave you out here alone."

She brushed the hair back off her eyes. "I'm not alone. Johnny and Mean Mike are right over there."

His voice sounded like the summation of a court case. "No, it's just not right. Something could happen."

"What could happen?" She studied his narrow eyes. He seemed to look straight past her. "Jefferson, you said one band of Indians was headed to Arizona. Ethan said the others were in the Hachitas by now. There seems to be little chance of Indians being around here."

"People have been wrong, dead wrong, about predicting Indian movement before. Besides, there are more enemies than Indians."

"What do you mean?"

"If Ramona was telling the truth, and her two accomplices rode on ahead of her, there's a chance they'll come back and look for her."

"Thanks for your concern, Mr. Carter, but I really think you should go back. There are worse things than facing an enemy. Losing a child, for instance."

"I'll just lag back of those cottonwoods a bit."

"You'll do nothing of the kind. You go protect your prisoner," Lixie insisted, but she didn't let go of his shirt sleeve. *Lord, I'm really not all that strong a woman. What I like more than anything is to have a strong arm to hold onto. All the time.*

"But what will I tell the Fletchers and Holdens? That I deserted you?"

She patted his hand. "Tell them I'm with Johnny and Mean Mike and that we thought your riding into the meadow might have been what frightened Bonita. Now go on, Mr. Jefferson Carter."

He pulled his .45 Colt revolver from its holster. "Here, you tote this."

She folded her arms across her chest. "I most certainly will not."

He shoved the revolver back in his holster, and the smile dropped from his face. "Then I'm not leaving."

"Why?"

"I don't have it in me to desert an unarmed woman in this situation," he announced.

"Are you playing chivalrous with me, Mr. Jefferson Carter?"

His eyes softened, and when they did, the creases at the corners became more prominent. "I'm not playing, Lixie. This is me. I can't be any other way."

She reached her hand out. "Then give me your pistol."

He pulled the revolver from his holster and handed it to her, grip first. "You know how to use it?"

Lixie flipped open the loading port, pulled the hammer back to the first stop, and spun the chambers to see five bullets. "Why do men assume an army wife knows nothing about firearms? Those two men across the river asked me the same thing about a shotgun yesterday morning, right before you rode up, if I remember right."

"Was that when you were wrestlin' one of them in the back of the wagon?"

She slowly let the hammer back down on the empty chamber. "Mr. Carter, I was not 'wrestling' anyone and am insulted that you said that."

He blushed. "Then let me apologize. I was teasing you, and it didn't come across right. Lixie, if the truth were known, I was just jealous."

"Jealous?"

"I suppose you've seen that all along. A man's imagination can run away with him."

Lixie watched him chew on his tongue. *Just what were you imagining, Mr. Jefferson Carter?*

"I'm leaving," he blurted out. "But don't go too far downriver. If you don't find your girl by the time you reach the edge of the cottonwoods, come back, and we'll use the horses to search."

"Thank you, Mr. Carter."

"Do you reckon the two of us will ever have a peaceful discussion, Lixie Miller?"

"I'd like to keep trying. After I find Bonita, of course."

"So would I." He turned. "At the first sign of trouble, fire a shot. You'll have a band of cowboys at your side in minutes."

Lixie walked with him toward the cottonwood trees. The gun in her right hand hung at her side. "And one attorney?"

"Yes, ma'am. I'll be the first one here. I carried a badge and a gun for a long time before I ever decided to become a lawyer."

He strolled on out toward the meadow as she stood holding the revolver. "What made you decide to do that?"

"Prison." He turned his back and hiked away.

Lixie ambled toward the river. *Prison? What do you mean, prison? You were a prison guard? Or you had friends unjustly incarcerated, so you wanted to become an attorney? Or you spent time in prison? No, no, no. I'm a better judge of men than that.*

Lixie scoured the willows that lined the river.

A good judge of men? The only man you ever chose, Lixie Miller, turned out to be a lifelong scalawag that had you in the dark for years. You're a lousy judge of men, Elizabeth Cartouche Miller. Admit it.

A hawk screeched overhead, above the canopy of cottonwood leaves. The river made a muted lapping sound on the muddy banks as it meandered along. Lixie's shoes were silent except for the occasional breaking of twigs. The only movement she saw was in sporadic glimpses of Mean Mike and Johnny White on the other side of the river.

Prison? Why did he say that, then turn around, and leave? I can't believe he would do that. Was he teasing me again? Or tormenting. What kind of man would do that? What was he in prison for? I mean, if indeed he was in prison, which I'm sure he wasn't. What if he murdered someone? What if he shot his wife? I know he isn't married now, but a man that age must have been married at one time. Why did I say that? I can't believe how little I know about the man. I must ask Langy-dear. He was at the Hawk trial for a while. Maybe he heard something about this man. I could write to Gracie and Colt. They know Mr. Jefferson Carter.

We simply must sit down and talk for a few hours. I want to know his past. His present. His future. Where was he a lawman? What about prison? Did he ever serve in the army? Is he now, or was he ever married? How much does he know about the general's notorious widow? How old is he? Does he have to have biscuits and gravy for breakfast every morning at 5:30 A.M.?

This is insane. Do you see what I'm doing, Lord? I'm babbling to myself. I'm playing a game with reality. My mind creates stories as fictional as those of Charles Noble. I should be a writer.

That's it. I should write a book! It would be about a strong-willed, independent woman who goes west to seek a place of accomplishment and . . . and starts an orphanage for . . . Indian children . . . but faces opposition from . . . a sinister army officer . . . whom she exposes with great peril to her own safety. The evil officer, who is trying secretly to steal Indian land because he discovered gold on it, sneaks up to the orphanage. It just happens to be the night she is sleeping on the veranda with a toddler who is dying of . . . something horrible . . . smallpox . . . eh, dysentery. Anything that kills a child is horrible . . . and the officer is creeping up to . . . eh, to start a fire! Yes, he is going to burn the orphanage down and . . .

And the woman falls asleep. The villain comes closer and closer in the coal-black night. Now he's on the stairs. She senses something. Fighting to wake up, she pulls back the hammer of the revolver she clutches in her right hand. The little sick girl hears the footsteps on the porch too, and slowly slips her hand up into the lady's and squeezes . . .

A small, sweaty hand slipped into Lixie's hand and clutched it tightly.

"Oh!" Lixie gasped. "I'll stop him!" She pulled the trigger with the Colt peacemaker still pointed into the muddy dirt.

The explosion caused them both to leap back.

Bonita cried out and threw her arms around Lixie's waist.

Miller dropped the gun.

Wild splashing sounds came from the river as Mean Mike and Johnny White, guns drawn, sprinted through the water.

Lixie was hugging the girl and crying when seven riders thundered up, Jefferson Carter leading the pack. "What happened?" he shouted to Johnny White who broke through the brush.

"We just got here."

Carter leaped from the saddle and trotted up to Lixie. "Is anyone hurt?"

"What were you shooting at?" Mean Mike said.

Lixie hugged the girl and rocked her back and forth. "Oh, honey, you had me so worried. I didn't know where you went. It's okay, baby. . . . It's okay. Mama didn't mean to fire the gun."

Did I just say, "Mama?" One day with her, and now you're a mama? You're having a collapse, Lixie Miller. Lord, You know how many years I sobbed my heart out wanting children. I've got to come out of this. I have to regain some composure. What's happening to me? Sometimes I believe I'm truly going mad.

Jefferson Carter put his hand on her shoulder. "Lixie, are you all right?"

She nodded. "I'm sorry, boys. Bonita sneaked up behind me and grabbed my hand. It so startled me, I fired off a shot by accident. That scared us both."

"Where was she?" Johnny White asked.

"In the willows. I never saw her until she sneaked up on me." *And I have no intention, Mr. Jefferson Carter, of ever letting you know what I was daydreaming about.*

Carter retrieved his revolver from the ground beside her. "Bonita's found, and no one's hurt. Those are the important things."

Bonita clung to Lixie's arm again. "Thank you all for coming so soon. It's a great comfort to know how quickly you got here," she added. "You'll never know how secure that makes a woman feel."

"You two want to ride my horse back? I can walk," Carter offered.

Lixie's arm circled the girl's thin shoulder. "No, thank you, I'd like to walk. Perhaps I can coax out of her why she ran off."

"I'll walk with you," Jefferson Carter offered, "unless you think that will disturb her. I'd like to try to talk to her also." He turned to the cowboys with dripping wet duckings and boots. "Why don't you two ride my pony back?"

Carter led Lixie and Bonita away from the river in sight of the distant picnic ground. He strolled near the trees, his hands at his sides. Lixie walked beside him, Bonita clasped to her right arm.

"Do you think Bonita's scared of me?" he asked.

Bonita dropped Lixie's arm and scooted over by Carter. She took Lixie's left hand and shoved it into his arm and then returned to her position, clutching Lixie's other arm.

"How did she know I was talking about her?" he asked.

Lixie looked down at the girl with dried tears on her dirty face. "She must have spied us running back to the picnickers hand-in-hand. I don't think she's scared of you, Jefferson Carter."

"Are you, Mrs. Miller?"

Lixie took a couple of long strides to keep up with him. "Should I be?" She slowed down to let Bonita catch up.

"I'm kind of curious, Lixie. What do you know about me?"

"Very little. But then what do you know about me?"

"You are Elizabeth Kathleen Cartouche Miller, born in 1833 in Richmond, Virginia, the only daughter of a doctor. You married 2nd Lieutenant Rockford Miller when you were eighteen. You promptly moved to St. Louis, Missouri, and then spent the prewar years in Kansas, Nebraska, Colorado, Dakota, and even a stint in California during the war. Through raw ambition and personal friendships, your husband rose to the rank of general. Your two younger brothers served in the Army of Virginia under Lee, and both lost their lives heroically. Your father was penniless after the war. He moved your mother to the British territories somewhere west of Manitoba. A few years later you received a letter saying that they had both died of consumption. You and the general, for reasons unknown, never had any children. Four years ago you traveled for a surprise visit to see your husband and . . ."

Lixie stopped walking and pulled her hand off his arm. "Where did you get all of that? How did you? Were you spying?" *I feel like a plucked turkey hanging at a meat market. Who is this man, and how did he find out all this?*

He took her hand, but she pulled it away. "I need to know how you know all this."

"I read it," he said.

"Where?"

"In the notes of Mr. Charles Noble while you were down here looking for little darlin'. Is it all true?"

She put her arm back into his. "I suppose so. At least, that much is correct. Why were you reading his notes?"

"They were lying there on the crate, and I, well, shoot, Lixie, I wanted to know more about you."

Lixie waited for Bonita to pull a thorn out of her bare foot.

"Why?"

They began to hike again.

"Because I have a hunch that we're both looking for the same thing."

"And what's that?"

"You know," he murmured.

"And what do you think we're looking for?"

"Seems to me we're both hoping to come to peace with our past and find purpose in our future. Isn't that true?"

"Was that in Mr. Noble's notes as well?"

"No, it was in your eyes and the tone of your voice."

"Explain yourself, Mr. Carter."

"Your eyes dance. All the men see that. But they miss the fact that you are always on the verge of tears. Your voice is always confident, teasing, even strident . . . except in the middle of the night when you aren't pretending. Then it's searching . . . vulnerable."

She pulled her arm away again.

"Did you do that because I was wrong or right?" he asked.

She reached out for Bonita's hand. She could feel her heart race, her breath shorten. "I did it because I realize that I know far too little about you to be talking this way or walking this way."

"Does that mean you're uncomfortable and want to change the subject?"

Lixie thought she saw a sly smile creep across his face. The lack of a breeze made the air stifling. Perspiration beaded on her forehead and upper lip. "Yes, it does."

"Let me tell you a secret. When I was a young man, I used to be quiet, patient, and subtle in my conversations with ladies."

"I expect you were good at it."

"I might have been the best there ever was. I was so subtle no lady ever figured I was interested at all. But let's change the subject before I say something that I'll regret, and I have to relive this conversation in a thousand sleepless nights."

"Now that, Jefferson Carter, I can relate to." She looked down at the girl. "I really would like to know why Bonita was so frightened she ran off."

He pointed at the cluster of people around the wagon. "If it wasn't me, perhaps she was scared of Ramona Hawk."

Lixie looked at the girl's round brown eyes. She seemed to be staring at the wagon. "Bonita doesn't even know Ramona Hawk."

Carter squatted beside the girl. "How do we know that?" He looked right at Bonita. "Honey, do you know Ramona Hawk?"

The young girl looked up at Lixie and then back at Jefferson Carter. She took his hand and pulled him back around to Lixie's side.

"I don't think the name phased her," Lixie said. "Besides, what would a little Apache girl know about a Confederate spy, bank robber, and . . ."

"Gun runner?" Carter added. "If Ramona Hawk was selling guns in Mexico, as many believe, she might have been in the Sierra Madres where Bonita was."

Lixie combed Bonita's stiff, thick hair with her fingers. "If

Hawk sold guns to the bronco Apaches, wouldn't Bonita see her as a friend?"

Bonita hid behind Lixie's skirt as they approached the group at the picnic. Harriet Fletcher waltzed toward them. This time Lixie bent over, eye level with the girl. "Darling, are you afraid of the woman in men's clothes?"

Bonita looked at her with big, anxious eyes.

Jefferson Carter leaned over and pointed toward Lixie. "*Bonita?*" he questioned.

The girl nodded.

He pushed the girl's finger to herself. "*Bonita?*" he said again.

She smiled and nodded.

"How about Lady Fletcher?" He pointed a finger at the approaching woman.

"*Bonita,*" the girl murmured.

"And Mrs. Holden?" Carter pointed at Mary Ruth.

Bonita nodded.

"And how about the woman in the wagon?" He pointed past the cluster of men at Ramona Hawk. "Is she *bonita?*"

The girl violently shook her head from one side to the other. "*Malo!*" she rasped. "*Malo!*" She buried her face in Lixie's dress.

"Bad? She's a bad lady?" Carter questioned.

Bonita kept her head hidden behind Lixie.

"Mr. Carter, it looks like you're right. Maybe it was Ramona Hawk who frightened her. What did she do to this child?"

Carter stood up. "I have a feeling Ramona Hawk isn't about to tell us."

"She hasn't had to face an irate Lixie Miller!"

Jefferson Carter put his hand on her shoulder. "If you could force some confession, these cowboys would lynch Ramona Hawk for sure."

Lixie clenched her teeth. "How do we know she doesn't deserve to be lynched?"

"That's for the legal authorities to decide, not a bunch of cowhands."

"I know. I know. It's just that her presence brings pain and bad memories to Bonita, and I can't do anything about it. It's a helpless feeling." *Do not pat my shoulder and sound condescending, Mr. Carter!*

He folded his arms across his chest. "That's exactly why I became a lawyer."

"A lady, especially one my age, has no chance of ever becoming an attorney."

"Somehow, Lixie Miller, I find it hard to imagine anything you couldn't do."

Harriet Fletcher met them as they approached the others. "How's the crowd doing with Hawk?" Jefferson Carter asked her.

"They're not real happy. They say they let the law take care of her once, and she escaped," Harriet reported.

Carter glanced over at the cowboys. "I'll take the prisoner and leave."

"You're liable to have volunteer assistants," Lady Fletcher observed.

"There's safety in numbers," he murmured, "except when it's a lynch party."

"You can't go out alone," Lixie cautioned.

"It seems like the lesser of two evils."

"But just as fatal," Lixie said. "You said yourself that her partners might come back for her."

"Edwin and I will go with you," Harriet announced.

Carter pulled off his hat and wiped his forehead on his shirt sleeve. "That's not necessary. You have other plans."

"Oh, no. We simply must see Lordsburg!" Lady Fletcher offered.

"Why? It's just a railroad town," Carter said. "No one wants to go there."

"There has to be some unique feature that draws those from outside," Harriet pressed.

Lixie stroked Bonita's hair. "Like the Saturday night cockfights?"

"I absolutely refuse to watch that."

Mary Ruth Holden ambled over to where they huddled.

"Other than that, we have the normal shops, saloons, a railroad station, and a bell foundry . . . that's all."

"A what? A foundry?" Harriet questioned.

"They make bells," Lixie explained.

"For churches?"

"Churches, governmental buildings, bunkhouses . . . for anything."

Harriet tugged at her silver earring. "Are they any good?"

"Paco says they are the best in the Southwest and perhaps in the world," Lixie said.

"That's it. Lord Fletcher and I must go check them out for a chapel bell at our Arizona ranch."

"You have an Arizona ranch?" Lixie asked.

"Stuart Brannon keeps trying to get us to buy one next to his, and we just might someday, so we need to inspect the bells," she explained.

"Are you goin' to go this afternoon?" Jefferson Carter inquired.

"Yes, we must."

"We will go back too," Mary Ruth said. "We insist that you stay at our house. We have plenty of room since our other houseguest has moved out."

"Don't rent my room permanent, Mama. I'll be back," Lixie laughed. "I'm going with all of you, because if Lord and Lady Fletcher aren't at the CS Ranch, there's no reason for me to be there."

"What about Bonita?" Carter asked.

"She'll go with me, of course," Lixie said as she hugged the girl. "We'll look for traces of her family on the way back. Do you think Lord Fletcher will go along with that scheme?"

Harriet held her folded hands under her chin, tilted her head, and batted her eyes. "How can he refuse?"

Except for the two cowboys who went back to the CS headquarters to inform Mr. Whetlock of the proceedings, the entire picnic crew packed up and headed toward Lordsburg.

Johnny White and Mean Mike scouted the road, followed by

the farm wagon, driven by Tony Mendoza. His father sat alongside him. Perched on blankets and tied to the tailgate was Ramona Hawk, guarded by Jefferson Carter, armed with a carbine and seated on a wooden crate. Several CS cowboys rode behind the carriages. A mild easterly wind kept most of the road dirt from fogging back on the caravan.

"Sorry you couldn't ride with the ladies," Elsworth said to Lixie as he drove the second carriage.

"This is best. The Holdens and Fletchers can keep watch on the prisoner." She patted the girl's hand. "And little Bonita is too scared to get any closer than this to Ramona Hawk."

"I shudder to think what scares her so," Elsworth said.

"I know. I don't think I could remain calm if I knew. Perhaps it's the Lord's grace that keeps us in darkness."

Even when he was driving a carriage, Langford Elsworth's posture was perfect, and he towered above Lixie. "Miss Hawk presents an interesting case in jurisprudence, doesn't she?"

Lixie watched the back of the Holdens' black leather carriage. "You mean, trying to keep her alive so we can hang her?"

"Quite," Elsworth said. "That does seem to be the case. We strive very hard for legalities. Justice sometimes takes a backseat. For instance, there is no doubt that she murdered Tommy Avila and Joe Addington."

"Gracie and Colt told me all about it. Her guilt is beyond debate. So the question becomes, what is a fair punishment? And who should inflict that punishment?"

"And a deeper question—," Elsworth pondered, "will she ever be brought to trial at all?"

"Your hired men don't want that."

Elsworth tugged his tie loose and unfastened the top button on his white shirt. "Lixie, all of us are susceptible to wanting revenge, I'm sure. But right at the moment, I think there is a case to be made for justice. There are few in New Mexico who would think a free Ramona Hawk will never murder again. At what point does society circumvent an inadequate system to see that justice triumphs?"

She folded her hands in her lap. "Some would say never, I suppose."

"But if your founding fathers had adopted such a philosophy, this land would still be an English colony."

"Not this land, Mr. Elsworth," she corrected. "This would be a Mexican colony, or perhaps Spanish."

"Quite so, but the point remains valid."

"We are a nation of laws. For the most part, voluntary compliance of the law. It's dangerous to circumvent that. There's no room for selective compliance. There are times to trust a higher court."

"Well spoken, barrister!"

"That's the second time in an hour I've been called an attorney."

"You have a commanding presence, Mrs. Miller."

"Some say I look on the verge of tears at all times."

"Nonsense. Who says that? Obviously someone with poor eyesight. Quite the opposite is true. If ever there was a self-confident, assured, independent woman, it's Elizabeth Miller."

The road contoured along the base of the Burro Mountains where the dirt and scattered clumps of grass were the same buckskin color. At the top of the draw, huge boulders narrowed the roadway before it dropped down on the desert floor.

The wagon and carriage ahead of them pulled to a stop. The men on saddle horses milled about. Jefferson Carter jumped out of the wagon and hiked back to their carriage. "The Fletchers said this pass was where Bonita had her accident."

Lixie saw his eyes take in her whole appearance. "What do you think we should do?" *Lord, I must confess that I like it when he looks me over. It's a feeling I haven't had in a long, long time.*

"I'm wondering if we need to split up? Some can go on to make Lordsburg by dark and get Ramona Hawk in jail. Others can lag back and look around for traces of Bonita's family."

"I say, do you think it's safe to divide up?" Elsworth probed.

"I believe so," Carter responded. "From here to Lordsburg is fairly open. There should be little trouble. We can divide the men into two groups and still have half a dozen guns with each party."

"I suppose that does make sense," Elsworth admitted.

Lixie reached up and held onto the Indian girl's hands that circled her neck. "Naturally Bonita and I will stay. Perhaps she'll recognize something."

"And we need to send the carriage with the Fletchers and Holdens along with Ramona Hawk."

"I can stay with Mrs. Miller," Elsworth offered.

"I'd like you to drive that wagon with Hawk, if you don't mind. The threat is from your men, and I judge that if they listen to anyone, they'll listen to you, Mr. Elsworth."

Elsworth pulled off his felt hat and wiped his forehead with a white linen handkerchief drawn from his vest pocket. "Yes, but have you considered what would happen if I choose not to constrain them?"

Carter glared up at Elsworth. "Now that never entered my mind, Mr. Elsworth. I figured you for doing the right thing, no matter what. That's the British way, isn't it?"

"I'm afraid your appeal to patriotism sounds a little hollow in the wilds of New Mexico Territory. However, given the circumstances—"

"And the fact that Lord and Lady Fletcher are watching," Lixie reminded him.

"Yes, quite so. I will verbally try to dissuade them, of course. But I doubt if I could shoot my own men."

"That's understood, Mr. Elsworth."

"But doesn't that leave Mrs. Miller somewhat understaffed?" Elsworth protested.

"I plan on staying with Mrs. Miller and the others," Carter announced.

"Don't you think your prisoner will need your protection?"

"I'm convinced having righteous women as witnesses is a greater deterrent to crime than all the lawyers in Santa Fe."

"I believe you could be right about that," Elsworth admitted. "I say, you will want to drive this carriage then." Elsworth looped the lead lines around the hand brake and climbed off the carriage.

"Mr. Elsworth, I hear Johnny White is your best tracker. Could he and Mean Mike be two of the men who stay back?" Lixie requested.

"Any others you would like to select?" Elsworth asked.

Jefferson Carter studied the men. "Give us the ones most likely to shoot Ramona Hawk."

The sun was three-quarters of the way across a pale blue, cloudless New Mexico sky when the others pulled away from the boulders and rolled down the slope on the Lordsburg road. The hoofbeats faded quickly, leaving a taste of dust in the air. Not until the wagon was out of sight did Bonita loosen her arms from Lixie's sweaty neck.

"That's right, sweetheart. The *malo* lady is gone now."

Carter offered a hand to help Lixie down and then lifted Bonita off the carriage. He started to set her down, but she clung to his neck.

"Oh, my. You have been officially accepted." Lixie grinned.

Carter set the girl to the ground, and Bonita grabbed Lixie's hand.

Johnny White meandered up to them. "Lixie, where do you want me and the boys to look?"

Lixie pointed south. "All I know is that Harriet said Bonita ran out from behind those two big rocks on the left and never made it across the road. I suppose we should head out in all four directions."

"What are we lookin' for?" a tall, thin cowboy with a long-barreled revolver questioned.

"Indian movement, boys," Jefferson Carter explained. "Little Bonita could have been with the group going to Arizona or with the ones going back to Mexico. See if you can find a campfire circle or tracks or anything that sets a trail."

"Apaches don't leave a trail," Mean Mike said.

"They don't leave a trail when they think they're being followed, but someone was traveling with children. They weren't expecting a battle. Maybe the kids wandered out behind a yucca and left tracks. We've got to look."

"Don't reckon to break my back for some Indian girl," the tall man complained.

"You mean if she were white and separated from her family, you'd be looking?" Lixie challenged.

"Yes, ma'am, I would."

"Do you see how this little girl hangs on to me?" Lixie pointed out. "Why do you think she does that?"

"'Cause you show her love, I reckon."

"Yes, she doesn't know she's supposed to hate all white people. You have to learn bigotry. When did you learn it?"

The man stiffened. "I had lots of friends get killed by Indians."

"So have I. Lizzie Custer was a close personal friend. But this little girl hasn't killed anyone. I can't understand anyone who'd refuse to help a child. However, we don't need your help. You can sit at the carriage and wait."

"I didn't say I wasn't helpin'," he grumbled.

"Thank you, and I apologize for sounding judgmental. I get very emotional when it comes to children."

Jefferson Carter pulled off his hat and surveyed the side of the mountain. "You two boys hike along the road to the south, and you other two take the road to the north. Anyone passing from Mexico to Arizona has to cross this road somewhere. Johnny, you and Mean Mike ride out west and cut a wide arc to see if there are any tracks. If it was that bunch on their way to Arizona, they had to go west. Lixie and I will take Bonita and hike back up into the boulders and see if there are any traces up there. That's where she darted out."

Johnny White swung back up into the saddle. "What if we find something?"

"Come back and get us. And if there's any trouble, fire a shot."

The hillside behind the boulders was steep. Lixie pushed against her knees to help her climb each step. Jefferson Carter, carbine in hand, led the way. Bonita dropped several steps behind Lixie.

"She doesn't act as if she has been here before," Lixie said as she caught her breath.

Carter reached his hand down to her. "Perhaps we're not in the right place. The Fletchers could have been mistaken."

Lixie grabbed his hand, and he pulled her up the hill. "Or maybe she was running so fast she didn't pay any attention to where she was. She certainly didn't hear the carriage."

Carter hiked up a little farther and then studied the descent.

With hands on her knees, Lixie climbed toward him. "Why would she be running that hard?" she puffed.

"Either she was chasing something, or something was chasing her," Carter offered.

Lixie stood huffing, resting her hand on her hips. "Mr. Carter, I really don't think I can climb up much farther. And we aren't having any luck finding tracks on this granite."

They both waited for Bonita to catch up with them. "You might be right. I was hoping to climb a little farther just to get an overview, but it's so steep a person would get totally out of control trying to run down from here."

"What do you mean, out of control?"

"Did you ever run down a hill so steep you couldn't stop yourself if you wanted to?"

"No, I never have."

"This is that kind of place."

"What happens?"

"You either run into something or find a level place and begin to slow down, but you have absolutely no control over your body."

He glanced at Lixie.

She peered back at the girl who now squatted down and drew in the decomposed granite with her finger. "Which is precisely what might have happened. Bonita could have lost control and couldn't stop, no matter what was happening."

"She might not have been chased at all. It might have been just a game or something, and she couldn't stop," he admitted. "But it doesn't explain why she was alone."

"Or why no one has come to look for her. She's such a precious thing. I can't believe no one cared."

Carter climbed on top of a boulder and gazed on up the hill. "If she merely got to running too fast, probably there's nothing up here that will help us."

"Are you saying we're wasting our time climbing this mountain?" she puffed.

"Perhaps. Why?"

"Because, Mr. Jefferson Carter, I do not intend to push my tired bones up this steep hill for nothing."

"Shall we go back and see what the others found?"

"As long as it's downhill."

When Lixie turned around, Bonita stood and blocked her path. "We're going back to the carriage, honey."

Bonita pointed up to the small granite mesa on top of the mountain.

"No, honey." Lixie pointed the girl's arm back the other way. "We're going back down."

The little girl stood still and pointed her arm back up the hill. "*Malo*," she announced.

The hair on the back of Lixie's neck stiffened at the word. "¿*Malo*? Bad person? Bad lady? Someone's up there? Someone *was* up there?"

Bonita reached over and shoved Lixie's hip up the hill.

"I believe she wants us to keep going." Lixie shrugged.

"Are you up to it?" Carter asked.

"I'll try," Lixie offered. "You might have to carry me."

"I can do that."

"I was joking, Mr. Carter."

"I wasn't. You want me to prove it?"

"No." *You liar, Lixie Miller. You'd love for him to carry you!* "When I collapse, you certainly have permission to carry me."

"And you me." He grinned as he hiked on up ahead.

"Now that would be a sight." She felt Bonita's small hands continue to push her on. "Imagine me hiking off this mountain with a handsome forty-five-year-old man over my shoulder!" Lixie managed to shout.

"Fifty-two, and it's been a long, long time since I've been called handsome . . . if ever."

"I don't believe it!" Lixie stopped and put her hand on the small of her back and tried to stand straight.

"Which don't you believe?" he queried.

"Both. Are you really fifty-two years old?"

"Yes. I thought you knew that."

"No. I didn't know that."

"You didn't ask me, so I figured you knew already or didn't care."

"I couldn't figure out how to ask without sounding personal." Lixie took three more steps and then clutched his sleeve. "Can we wait here? I really need to catch my breath."

"How much farther?" he asked Bonita.

She pointed on up the mountain.

"I was afraid of that," Lixie groaned. "Do you know how much I will ache tomorrow?"

"Do you want to go back?"

"No. She wants to show us something."

"Do you have any guesses what?"

"I suppose it might be where she camped for the night or something," Lixie suggested.

"Which could show us footprints of her family." He stepped around behind her and put his palms on the small of her back.

"What are you doing?"

"I'm going to push you up the hill."

"Oh, you don't have to . . . oh, my, that does help." The firm pressure on her back kept her headed uphill.

"Are you sure you want us to find her family?" he said.

"I want what's best for her. I'd cry for weeks, but that would not be all that abnormal."

"Don't worry about crying when she's gone. Crying is all right."

"You complained about me looking as if I'm on the verge of tears all the time."

"It wasn't a complaint, Lixie. I merely said you were at the edge all the time. I reckon a real long cry would do you good."

"Why do you say that?"

"It seems to me crying is a form of release. Sometimes we have things that need to be released."

"Released to whom?"

"The Lord, I reckon."

"Are you saying I have things that I need to release?"

"I reckon we all do."

"Even successful attorneys?" she pressed.

"Successful? How do you think an attorney measures success?"

"In won verdicts?" she asked. "Or in annual income? I don't know."

"Like for anyone else, success is measured when I've done something that will last beyond my life. I have no wife. No children. No business. No ranch. No place in history. I'm afraid success is still in the future for me, and I'm not a young man."

"That all surprises me."

"Why?"

"You have a confident presence, like a man of many accomplishments."

"I too am on the verge, Lixie Miller."

"Of crying?" she asked.

"Perhaps not tears. But on the verge of . . . well . . . that's another story." He stood up and straightened his back slowly. He hiked on up to the top and then reached back for her hand. His strong arm pulled her up the mountain.

"What story?"

He turned to help the girl to the summit. "Bonita, darlin', we made it to the top. Now what?"

The girl pointed south.

"It's quite a view up here. You can see in every direction. We can almost see back to Lordsburg. Silver City must be over there." He nodded east.

The collar of Lixie's dress was sweat-drenched. A slight breeze felt cool to her face. "I'm sure it's a great place for Indian scouts to watch for miles in every direction." She plopped down on a chair-sized boulder. "Or just collapse and die of exhaustion."

Bonita meandered over and sat on Lixie's knee. "Darlin', you're right. It's a *bonita* view, but Mama is tired!" Lixie glanced at the grinning Jefferson Carter. "Okay, you can laugh all you want, but for a day or two, I've been a mama."

"I'm not laughing, Lixie. I understand."

"We are a rather forlorn pair, Mr. Carter."

"I don't intend to be melancholy with this beautiful view." He surveyed the small crest. "I don't think anyone would camp up here. It's too exposed to the elements."

She pushed herself to her feet, walked over, and stood next to him. "Do you think that dust column is from the Holdens and Fletchers and all?"

"I would guess so."

She put her hand on the girl's shoulder. "I wonder if this precipice has a name?"

"How about Bonita Peak?" he suggested.

"Oh, yes!" When she clapped her hands, Bonita immediately clapped her hands and giggled. "No matter what its name, I will always call it that!"

"You have a disarming smile, Mrs. Miller."

"Thank you, Mr. Carter. Now are you going to tell me what you are on the verge of?"

"No."

"Are you going to tell me about that vague reference to prison?"

"I was in prison, that's all. It's nothing I'm proud of."

"Were you wrongfully accused?" she pressed.

His voice was very soft as he continued to stare across the desert floor below. "No, I admitted my guilt."

"Am I going to regret asking you why you were in jail?"

"I reckon you will."

"Oh dear, that does make it awkward, doesn't it?"

Bonita tugged on Lixie's arm.

"Darlin', let me stand here a minute and catch my breath. I'm an old lady."

The girl kept tugging.

Jefferson Carter pulled off his hat and scratched his head.

"What do you suppose she wants to show us? There's nothing up here."

"Bonita, why don't you just point to it. I'll look from right here."

The girl tugged again on her arm.

"Trying to reason with a girl who doesn't understand what you say is rather futile."

Bonita walked over to the south edge of the granite ledge.

"Careful, darlin'," Carter called out. "It drops straight off there."

Bonita scooted to the edge and looked down.

"I don't think she minds me, Mama."

"What am I going to do with my girl?" she laughed. "Children are the same in any race. The reason I never had any children is not a mystery, Mr. Carter. In the Bible it's called a barren womb. And, yes, I've shed many a tear over that but none in the last ten years. Now I've told you more than I was planning to. It's your turn."

"What do you want to know?"

"Let's see . . . how about what you are on the edge of, why you were in prison, why you never married. I am right in thinking you've never married, aren't I?"

"I've been expecting these questions ever since we first met at the Sonoran Hotel restaurant in Lordsburg."

"I thought that if it became an important topic, you would tell me," she countered.

"Are these important topics to you, Lixie Miller?"

"Are they important topics to you, Jefferson Carter?"

"Not really. Let's just drop the matter."

"Certainly," she responded.

They both stepped up to the precipice next to the girl with the waist-length black hair.

Lixie gazed at the distant Pyramid Mountains beyond Lordsburg.

"Tell me about those things, or I will personally throw you off this cliff," she mumbled between clenched teeth.

"It's quite a steep drop," he said. "So I believe I should tell you I've been married six times and have over twenty children. So many I lose count."

She stepped back from the edge of the cliff. "That's preposterous!"

"How do you know for sure, Elizabeth Miller?"

"I don't believe that story for a minute!" she snapped.

"Okay, would you believe I have never been married and never had any of my own children?"

"Yes, I believe that. What do you mean, none of your own children?"

"I raised my brother's two boys. He died in the war."

Lixie stepped back beside him. "And his wife?"

"When she heard of Washington's death, she went out into the hog barn and shot herself."

"Oh, my." For the first time she looked straight down the side of the cliff. "Perhaps we should move back. This is a rather frightening drop." Bonita pointed down at the rocks. "Yes, it's a pretty view, honey, but move back." She glanced up at Carter. "How old were your nephews at the time?"

"Madison was thirteen, and Monroe was eleven. But they never called me Daddy. I was always Uncle Jeff."

"Is everyone in your family named after a president, Mr. Carter?"

"Yep. Even my little sis."

"And her name?"

"Fillmore."

Lixie turned and slugged him in the arm. "Now you're teasing me!"

He feigned a flinch. "Her name is Tyler. Isn't that a dynamite name for a woman?"

"Yes, it is. I like that. Where does she live?"

"San Antonio. Her husband is a horse doctor." He slipped his hand around hers. "It's quite majestic up here, isn't it?"

She took a deep breath and let it out slowly. "It's peaceful, Mr. Carter. You were right last night. That is what is most missing in my life."

He tugged on Bonita's hand. "Come on, darlin'. Let's head back."

She yanked her hand back. "No!" she blurted out.

"Oh? You *do* know an English word," Lixie said.

"I imagine it's sort of universal," Carter remarked.

"But I've never heard her say it before."

"You've given her everything she wanted. She's had nothing to protest."

Bonita pointed down the cliff.

"What do you see, honey? Is there an animal down there? What is that, Mr. Carter?"

"Where?"

"On the ledge over by that stunted pine. Is there something on the ledge?"

"Oh, my word," Carter murmured.

"Oh . . . no!" Lixie gasped. "It looks like . . . a . . . body!"

Her knees buckled.

The distant desert seemed to bubble up in front of her eyes.

As if she were a marionette, her joints went limp.

She tumbled forward into blackness.

Seven

Lixie's eyes blinked open at the sound of a single gunshot.

She reached out to brace herself for the fall.

She wasn't falling.

But she was on hard granite. Cold, rough stone pressed against her back. She caught her breath, but there was no pain.

No pain at all.

Her head rested on something soft. Two wide brown eyes stared down at her. Bonita stroked her hair and rocked her head back and forth. Lixie closed her eyes. *A cliff. A man's body. A man's mangled body. I fainted and fell . . . forward!*

Her eyes shot open. She noticed tears on the little girl's face.

"Hi, baby," Lixie murmured.

Bonita grinned and blurted out an Apache sentence so fast that Lixie couldn't tell when one word ended and the next began.

"My sweet Bonita, that's more talking than I've ever heard from you." She reached up and stroked the girl's smooth, brown, tear-streaked cheeks.

A shadow fell across her face. A broad-shouldered man towered over her. His chin was chiseled, but his eyes were soft, framed with well-tanned wrinkles. "Are you doing better, Mrs. Miller?"

"Yes, Mr. Carter. I feel quite foolish. I fainted, didn't I?"

"Yes. But I don't reckon a person has any control over when they faint."

"I would hope I could choose a better place. I thought for sure I was going to fall off that cliff."

He squatted on his haunches next to her and pushed his hat back. "You did."

"And I didn't get hurt?"

He stared off to the south. His voice softened. "I sort of grabbed you . . . before you went all the way over."

A wave of tingles rolled across her upper body. "Sort of grabbed me?"

"I did grab you," he confessed. "Sorry about the dress."

She looked down at her dress, which looked all in place with a tint of road dust. "What did you do to my dress?"

He stood straight up and looked ten feet tall. "It got ripped a little in the back," he mumbled. "It's a small tear. I'll be happy to buy you a new dress. It was strictly an accident. I was scared to death you were goin' over the edge."

That explains the cold rock on my back. "Mr. Carter, if you ever have to choose between saving my life or tearing my dress, please tear the dress."

"Yes, ma'am, I'll remember that," he smiled. "Does this sort of thing happen to you often?"

"I believe it's the first time in my life I ever fainted." Lixie slowly sat up and then hugged Bonita. "Darlin', you did a good job of takin' care of Mama!"

"The first time you ever saw a dead body?" he asked.

"No, as a matter of fact, I've seen many a soldier die, even a few that had been mutilated after the battle. But it was the first I've seen where the buzzards had gotten to him. I believe I was tired from the climb and totally caught by surprise. After a battle I was prepared for what we found." She reached up her hand, and he pulled her to her feet.

"Oh my, this dress is a little drafty."

Carter pulled off his leather vest. "I think you should wear this."

"Thank you, Jefferson. I believe you're right." She pulled on the dark brown vest that smelled of leather, sweat, and man. Lixie let it hang loose and didn't button it in the front. "What do we do now?"

"I'm goin' to get the other men up here with ropes. We'll try to go down and identify that poor old boy. Maybe one of them knows who he was."

"Are you going to bring him up?"

"I don't think there's enough left of him. We'll cover him with rocks. That's the best we can do."

Lixie brushed the girl's long black hair back over her shoulder. "I wonder what he had to do with Bonita. She knew the body was there. She hiked right over and pointed to it. It was what she wanted to show us."

"And she didn't seem to have any other connection with it. She wasn't happy or sad. It was just an event to be reported." Jefferson Carter surveyed the mountaintop. "Perhaps you and Bonita should hike back down and wait at the carriage."

"For her sake as well as mine. There's no reason to view that sight again," Lixie said.

"We'll keep one or two of the boys down there with you as guards. We don't want to take a chance in case there's trouble."

"You think those who did this are still around?"

"All I know is that this seems to be a place where bad things happen."

Mean Mike Mason stretched out in the lengthening shade of the boulders, his hat pulled down, a carbine in his lap. With Bonita in hand, Lixie strolled south on the road.

"Bonita, do you know what happened to that man up there?" Lixie asked.

The girl swung their clasped hands back and forth. She chewed on her tongue.

"Did you have to watch something ugly? Did someone shove that man off the cliff? What happened to his clothing? Who is he? Is he the one who was chasing you?"

The girl glanced up and blurted out a long sentence in Apache.

Lixie gave the girl a hug. "This is progress. Yesterday I couldn't get a peep out of you, and today you are blabbing your head off. Of course, neither of us understands the other . . . but that's probably true in many families."

They walked along the road looking at the dirt, but the only footprints Lixie saw were those made earlier by the CS cowboys. "Baby, if you see anything that looks like your family's tracks, you'll tell me, won't you?" *I'm not sure what I'm really looking for. Do I want a message in the dirt: "Apache girl . . . go this way." Maybe if she got excited and pointed and wanted to take a certain route across the desert . . .*

Lixie laced her fingers in Bonita's and continued to tramp along the road. "Young lady, just what do you think of Mr. Jefferson Carter? He seems very sincere, but there is a mystery about the prison thing. I'm afraid to press him on it. Maybe I'm scared to find out the truth. What do you think I should do?"

The girl promptly pointed at the olive green succulent leaves of yucca and blurted out another Apache proclamation.

"Yes," Lixie replied, "that's exactly what I was thinking. If the relationship is to go any deeper, I will certainly have to know more about him."

The girl reached up and lightly stroked her bruised forehead.

"Oh, baby, is that still hurting bad?"

The girl tugged on Lixie's leather vest until she bent over. Then she put both palms on Lixie's cheeks and looked her in the eye. "*Bonita,*" she announced.

Lixie hugged the girl. "Darling, you'll never know how wonderful it feels to have you call me pretty." The girl clutched Lixie's neck. "Perhaps you do know, darling. Perhaps you do."

Hand in hand, they continued their stroll. The only sound was the crunch of Lixie's shoes and an occasional shout that rolled down from the men on the granite summit of Bonita Peak. To the west the barren playa ran to where the Arizona border waited for the setting sun. At the point of the road's steep descent, Lixie paused and inspected the uninhibited land in front of them.

"You know what, sweet girl? Some people think this is an arid, unproductive desert. Do you know what I see? Peace. It is so peaceful. So quiet. So undisturbed. It makes me want to whisper and walk softly. I wish my heart and soul and mind could be this quiet. I know all of this doesn't make any sense to you, but don't worry. It doesn't make sense to anyone else either."

Bonita broke into a rapid, detailed description. She pointed south toward the Mexican border. Then her voice lowered to almost anger as she pointed west and continued her diatribe. When she finished her explanation, she spat in the dirt toward the west and stomped on it with her bare foot.

"Oh my, I take it the San Carlos reservation in Arizona is not your favorite place. That's interesting. I do hope you were sayin' nice words and not being vulgar or blasphemous. You might not like what is over there, but it will provide us with a beautiful sunset tonight, won't it?"

They crossed the road and hiked back to the horses and carriage and the napping Mike Mason. Bonita tugged her dress up to the waist of her trousers, scratched her side, and then dropped the dress back down.

Lixie brushed the dress down in the back. *Okay, we might have to work a little at being ladylike. Fortunately, she was wearing trousers, and there were no boys around.*

Bonita lifted her foot and picked a small stone out from between her toes. She threw the pebble across the road and hit a small stick lying on top of a boulder.

I believe You're doing this to me on purpose, Lord. A friendly little reminder of vastly different cultures and social habits. I know she's not mine to keep. But this might be the only day that I have a child this close to me. The memories might have to last the rest of my life.

When I read a good book, it pulls me in, and for a moment I'm living in that fictional world. Just for a day or so, I'm enjoying this fictional world. Let me play like she is mine. Please, Lord, let me pretend awhile. It's the first time in years that I've felt relaxed . . . and important to someone.

"Bonita," Lixie called out, "let's skip. Do you know how to skip?" She began with first her right foot and then the left.

The girl giggled and broke into a barefoot skip alongside her. They kept it up hand in hand for twenty yards.

"Baby," Lixie puffed, "this is more exercise than I've had in years! Oh, whoa . . . maybe we should stop. Mama's getting tired."

When they stopped, Bonita pulled her hand free, trotted a couple of steps away, jammed her hands into the powdery dirt of the roadway, and turned a perfect cartwheel.

Lixie clapped. "Oh, yes! That was very good!"

Bonita pointed to her and blurted out another long Apache sentence.

"Me? You want me to turn a cartwheel? You have to be joking, baby. I'd fall and break every bone in my body. Mama's too old for that." She grabbed the girl's hand and continued to walk. *I'm too old to be your mama. I'm old enough to be your grandmother. That's a depressing thought.*

Lixie stopped as they got close to where the boulders pinched the road to its narrowest.

"Honey, does any of this look familiar? Is this where you got hurt?"

Bonita took Lixie's finger and pointed it at her bruise.

"Yes. Is this where you hurt your head?"

The girl walked out into the middle of the road, bent over at the waist, and tapped the dusty road with the palm of her hand.

I will ignore that incredible dexterity. "Exactly at that spot? That is rather interesting. Then you would have been up there where the men are and come running down to burst out in front of the Fletcher carriage. You just couldn't stop, could you, baby?"

Bonita waved her hands, showing the path she had run and the collision with the horses. There was an excited Apache explanation for each hand motion.

"Darling, how I wish I knew what you're saying. Surely someone in Lordsburg understands Apache. If not, I'll ask Colonel Banks to send an army interpreter over. Wouldn't that be delightful, Bonita? What if we could actually talk to each other?" *What would she actually say to me? Would she call me Mama? Or Grandma? Would she say I wear too much powder on my face? Would she say I hover and cling too much? Would she say, "I want to go home!" Maybe I don't want to know.*

Mean Mike Mason stood up as they approached. "Little sis's dress looks mighty fine on her, don't it?"

"You have a very good eye for clothes."

"My mama taught me that."

"Will you be going to see your mother at the same time you see your little sister?"

"Yes, ma'am. The whole family lives in Missouri, except for me."

"I imagine you have a great time when you go home."

"Yep. I reckon there ain't nothin' better than family. Where's your family at, Lixie?"

She glanced down at Bonita's bruised forehead. "The war eliminated my family."

"I'm sorry to hear that, ma'am."

"Today I have a family. Miss Bonita here is my temporary adopted family."

"Yes, ma'am, you two looked like you was havin' fun, skippin' and playin'."

"Bonita was showing me the exact spot where she had the accident with the horses." She gave the girl a hug. "Weren't you, honey?" Lixie motioned with her hands Bonita's run down the mountain and the collision.

The girl then pointed to Mean Mike's carbine and cocked her elbows as if holding a gun. Bonita tracked an imaginary target and repeatedly pulled her trigger finger.

"Someone was shooting?" Lixie asked.

"What were they shootin' at? Were they shootin' at the carriage?" Mean Mike pressed.

Bonita broke into a rapid string of Apache words. Then she grabbed the barrel of Mean Mike's '73 Winchester carbine and pointed it at herself.

"Oh, my word!" Lixie blurted out. "Someone was shooting at you, sweetheart?"

"I reckon that's what she's sayin'," Mike said. "Can't figure out why anyone would shoot at a little girl."

Lixie hugged the girl. "Oh, baby, who would shoot at you? Who was it?"

Bonita pointed back up the mountain. "Someone was up there shooting? Was it that man who fell off the cliff?" Lixie tried through motions to depict the man on the rocks beside the cliff. "Was he the man who shot at you?"

Bonita shook her head. She spoke slowly and softly, her chin tucked against her chest. Lixie watched the girl's eyes. As she concluded the Apache monologue, the word *malo* spilled out with the others.

Lixie bit her lip.

"I suppose she figures we understand all that," Mean Mike said.

"I hope we can get her to tell us the same thing when there's an interpreter around. Mean Mike, would you excuse us for a minute? We need to have a girl talk."

"Girl talk? Shoot, you two don't even speak the same language."

"There are some female things, Michael Mason, that are universal and go beyond language," Lixie declared.

"Yes, ma'am." He tugged his hat down in front and ambled over to the carriage.

Lixie lifted the girl's chin until their eyes were only inches apart. She held up her hands as if aiming a gun and then pointed back up the hill. "Baby, was it the *malo* lady who shot at you?" Lixie acted as if she were pointing a gun.

Bonita slowly looked up and down the road as if someone were watching them. Then she nodded her head.

Ramona Hawk shot at my girl? Why? Why would she do that? Why was she up on that cliff? And why was a little Apache girl a threat? And why, oh why, did I try to stop the CS cowboys from hanging her?

The sun had slipped behind the western mountains when Jefferson Carter, Johnny White, and the others climbed down off the mountain. Lixie stood by the carriage. Bonita and Mean Mike threw rocks across the road at a stick of wood propped up as a target.

"It's about time they come back down," Mean Mike said as he

meandered over to Lixie. "She beats me at throwin' purtneer ever' time."

The girl returned to her side, and Lixie put her arm around her. "Perhaps you should teach her to play whist," Lixie said.

"Not her. She'd probably beat me there too. Don't let that bruise and those big brown eyes fool you. She has a quick mind, and she likes to win."

Lixie looked down at the girl. "You impressed Mean Mike, darlin'."

Bonita responded with a full stream of Apache words.

"What do you reckon she said?" Mason quizzed.

"I'm sure she said how much she was impressed with you too."

He rubbed his thin chin. "You think so?"

"Since we have no idea what she said, let's just pretend that's what it meant."

"I like that!" He gazed up at the men hiking down the hill. "You know, it might be nice to have a gal you can't understand. Then you could jist pretend her words were compliments and be happy."

"We'd better get on the road," Jefferson Carter called as he and the others approached. "We'll be drivin' in the dark as it is."

"What happened up there?" Mean Mike called out.

The tall, thin cowboy pointed at Bonita. "Some of her kin did it."

Lixie held the girl close.

"That's not true," Carter cautioned.

"A white man stripped of his clothes and body mutilated. Sounds like Apaches to me."

Carter stepped right up to the tall cowboy. "Those are lies, and you know it. The buzzards had pecked at the body, not Indian knives. And I've never heard of any Indian who killed a man, took his clothes, and left his boots."

"He had his boots?" Lixie asked.

"Yep."

"Mr. Carter is right," Johnny White called out as he mounted up. "No Indian would leave boots."

"I say it was her kind. We all know how them Apache women carve up a body," the tall man insisted.

Jefferson Carter leaned toward the taller man. "Mister, you are talkin' about things you know nothin' about."

"Are you callin' me a liar?" the man shouted. His hand rested on the holstered revolver.

"I'll call you stupid if you draw that gun," Johnny White yelled. "Mount up, Harold, before you do something real foolish."

"I ain't scared of no Santa Fe lawyer," Harold blustered.

"You ought to be scared of a tough former U.S. marshal from the Indian Nation," Johnny White retorted.

Harold backed away from Carter. "Is that you?"

"Yep."

"Why did you quit marshalin'?"

"I kept shootin' people."

The tall man turned toward his horse. "I didn't mean it was this little girl who done it. I just meant it looked like Indians. I could be wrong," he murmured.

The road was straight. The stars provided just enough light to see silhouettes. Johnny White and Mean Mike led the way. The other cowboys dropped back behind the carriage. From time to time Lixie could hear them talking but never could distinguish the words. Bonita fell asleep with her head in Lixie's lap and her legs sprawled across Jefferson Carter's.

When the outriders dropped back far enough, she leaned toward Carter. "What really happened up on top of the mountain? I have a feeling you didn't want to tell everything to these cowboys."

Carter kept his eyes focused straight ahead. "I'm trying to piece it together. It's not a pretty story."

She sat up straight. "And it involves Ramona Hawk?"

He spun around. "How did you know that?"

"Bonita told me."

"What do you mean?"

"She showed me where she ran in front of the carriage and then motioned that someone was shooting at her."

"Ramona?"

"I asked her if it was the *malo* lady—that's what she calls Hawk—and she nodded yes."

He glanced down at the girl sprawled across their laps. "I reckon that confirms it. I had surmised the same thing. First of all, the old boy up there looks an awful lot like one of the Santa Fe guards that disappeared with Hawk, but I can't be sure."

"Was he a hostage or a participant?"

"I can't figure it out. I had assumed that both the guards helped her escape. Here's what I do know—he and Ramona Hawk were up there on top of Bonita Peak."

"Why do you think they were there?" she interrupted. "It's not a good hideout."

The carriage hit a bump, and she cradled Bonita's head.

"It's a good place to sit and watch someone drive up from Lordsburg if you wanted to spy on someone."

"You think they planned an ambush?" Lixie tugged at her silver and black onyx earring. *I wish I had a comb, a mirror, a washcloth . . . or that it would hurry up and get dark.*

"That's a theory. There are no stagecoaches on this road. Nor mine payrolls. No one of major importance around here. But it gets more complicated. Hawk is now wearing the man's clothes."

"But not his boots. Were the boots still on the man's feet?" Lixie asked.

"No, they were tossed over the cliff with the dress," Carter reported.

Lixie rocked slowly back and forth, stroking Bonita's soft, warm cheek. "A dress? Ramona Hawk's dress?"

"It looked like the one she wore during the trial. It had sort of a scooped Santa Fe neckline."

Lixie's tongue moistened her lips. *And just why, Mr. Carter, did you remember Hawk's neckline?*

"It was torn in front," he reported.

"As if someone grabbed the front of her dress and ripped it?"

He slapped the lead lines and picked up the speed of the carriage. "That's what it looked like to me. But there's more."

She stared down at the sleeping girl's face. *Sleep, baby, maybe you shouldn't hear this.*

"I believe the man died of a gunshot. He was shot in the chest at close range. There are powder burns on what's left of his long handles. I don't see how he could have lived through that."

"He was shot while standing on top of the mountain in his long-handle underwear and then tossed over the cliff?"

"That's my best guess," Carter said.

"And then someone tossed a dress and his boots over as well?"

"Apparently. He could have been her hostage all along. I don't suppose we'll get an answer from Hawk. She's good at throwing off the authorities. There are other reasons for gettin' a dress torn."

Lixie tugged the leather vest together at her neck. "I do appreciate your letting me wear your vest." She reached down and held the little girl's hand. "Why did she shoot at Bonita?"

Carter patted the girl's ducking-covered knee. "Maybe little darlin' saw Hawk murder the man."

"But why would Hawk care?" Lixie inquired. "She's wanted for murder already. She's running for the Mexican border. What difference does it make that an Apache girl saw her? Tell me, Mr. Attorney, is any court in New Mexico Territory going to use an Apache girl who can't speak English to testify against a white woman?"

"Probably not."

"How much do the CS cowboys know?" Lixie asked.

"Not much. I knew if I mentioned that I thought Hawk might have killed that old boy, they'd ride out of here and try to stop the others before Lordsburg."

"If justice is getting what you deserve, at what point do we stop being overly concerned about keeping this woman alive?"

Jefferson Carter slapped the lead lines on the horses' rumps. The carriage bounced and swayed across the desert road. "I have to follow every legal step. I've seen firsthand what happens when you don't."

"I know you're right. I guess I've never known a woman closer to the heart of evil."

"And the Evil One," he added.

"Precisely." It was dark enough that Lixie could not see the dust stirred up by the horse's hooves, but she tasted it with every breath. "Will you be the one who takes her back to Santa Fe?" she asked him.

"I expect the sheriff or U.S. marshal will escort her back. There's a possibility I'll travel with them."

"I'd rather you wouldn't. She's a scary woman to be around. Every time men get around her, someone dies. I don't want it to be you. I worry about you, Jefferson Carter. You have to look out for yourself."

"I appreciate your concern for me." He was quiet for a moment. "In fact," he sighed, "you will never know how much I appreciate it. Lixie, this will sound very presumptuous, but it feels good to have someone worry about me, even if we've barely known each other three days. Some people think that because I've never married that I'm a loner. Oh, I've been surrounded by friends all my life, but very few have ever worried about me. Do you know what I mean?"

She traced her fingers lightly across Bonita's soft brown nose. "I know that being independent is overrated."

"I reckon I wouldn't talk like this in daylight."

"Why not?"

"Because I would have to look at the rejection in your eyes."

"My eyes aren't rejecting you, Mr. Carter."

"But I would have worried about it more in daylight. There are some things that can only be shared in the dark of night. Maybe that's what's so difficult about being alone. There is never anyone there in the dark of night to talk to."

Lixie breathed deep breaths as his words stirred up the pain in her own heart. She couldn't stop the tears.

"Are you crying?"

"How could you tell?"

"I don't know—it just seemed like you were. I didn't mean to be so melancholy that I made you cry over me."

"I have no idea if I'm crying over you or crying over me."

"You?"

"Jefferson Carter, you have just described my condition exactly. I've been trying to define my feelings ever since I arrived in New Mexico. And in a couple of sentences you summed it up. There is no one to talk to in the dark of night."

"I reckon we're a pair."

"I reckon we are," she drawled.

He put his arm around her shoulder and gave her a quick hug. Then he dropped his arm back to his side. "I know this sounds crazy, but it's like we are longtime friends. Lixie, someday we need to sit in the shade, sip lemonade, and get caught up on the last fifty years."

"I believe you're right. When do you think we could do that?"

He scratched the back of his neck. "We have to play out this scene with Ramona Hawk first."

"I need to find Bonita's family," she added.

"And I have a law practice that needs me back in Santa Fe by the middle of the month. Plus, I did promise the Ware family in Ft. Scott, Kansas, an update on news about little Charley."

"So you did come to Lordsburg to learn about the McComas boy?"

"Yes and no."

"How's that?"

"I promised Eugene Fitch Ware that I would check the latest news along the border about his nephew next time I was down this way. But I told him I didn't know when I would have time. When Ramona Hawk escaped, my calendar was suddenly empty. I had counted on being tied up for ten days."

"So you said, 'I'll go look for little Charley McComas?'"

"Now here's another dark-of-night confession that you probably wouldn't get from me in daylight. I said, 'This is my chance to go to Lordsburg and meet Lixie Miller.'"

"Counselor, you're going to need to produce some evidence to support that allegation. As I remember, we were total strangers until three days ago."

His voice rumbled just a little louder than the clop of the

hooves and the rattle of the carriage. "Unfortunately, my evidence went to Iowa."

"Gracie?"

"The Parnells and I hit it off, and since we were staying in the same hotel in Santa Fe—"

"You live in a hotel?"

"Yes. That's rather sad in itself, isn't it? A man my age without a home. Without real roots."

"No, no, I didn't imply there's anything wrong with it. Please go on."

"After the first meal with the Parnells, Gracie began saying that I just had to come to Lordsburg and meet her very good friend Lixie Miller. From then on, every meal we had together, it was 'Lixie says this' and 'Lixie says that.' She was very persuasive," Carter said.

"I must speak to her about that."

"Will you thank her or condemn her?"

"That remains to be seen."

"Anyway, I concocted a plan to come visit the Parnells, on the pretext of checking on Charley McComas, and to meet the—"

"The general's notorious widow?"

"To meet the notorious general's widow, Lixie Miller. But Ramona ran off, and the Parnells went to Iowa. So I decided to barge in without introductions. I have to admit I didn't do too well at that first meeting. I have a feeling it would have been different if Gracie had been there to introduce us."

"Mr. Jefferson Carter, I am extremely flattered. I don't believe I've ever had someone travel two hundred miles to meet me before."

His voice was hardly audible. "I find that hard to believe."

"I married young, Mr. Carter. A general's wife has a very insulated position. But I don't want that to sound like a complaint. I chose to be an army wife and for most of my life had no real regrets. It's a supportive community, but by design the general's wife has few peers."

Johnny White rode back by the carriage. "Looks like a campfire up the road a few miles."

"I don't remember any houses along this stretch of the road," Carter called out.

"Nope. Could be some pilgrims spending the night," Johnny replied.

"A strange location for a camp—no protection, and a fire like that would be a beacon for miles," Lixie said.

"Maybe that's what they want," Carter mumbled.

"You think it could be a trap or ambush?" Johnny called back.

"We can't take a chance," Carter cautioned.

Lixie cradled Bonita's head as they continued to roll and bounce down the desert road. "What should we do?"

"I'll go warn the others," Johnny proposed. "Then we'll bunch up close, cock our carbines, and approach slowly. Lixie, your favorite shotgun should be under that seat."

"If I have to shoot it again, I won't be able to lift my right arm for a month," she called back.

"It could be nothin' at all, Lixie, but I'm kind of skitterish after seein' that ol' boy dead up on the granite mountain."

Soon there were two cowboys riding behind the carriage, one on each side, and two in front. All carried Winchester '73 carbines across their saddles.

Lixie stroked the girl's forehead. "Baby, it's time to wake up."

A little hand reached up and clutched her fingers in the dark. "Time to sit up, Bonita. . . . Look, there is someone camping up there."

The Indian girl sat up and scooted in between Carter and Miller.

The distant campfire made silhouettes out of Johnny and Mean Mike riding ahead of them.

"Do you really think it's trouble?" Lixie asked.

"I think it's someone who wanted us to find them."

Lixie felt Bonita's arm slip into hers. "The Fletchers and the others?"

"There's a sinking feeling in my stomach," Carter replied.

"Do you think they hung her already?"

"There isn't a tree for thirty miles. They could have shot her, but I doubt if she was hung."

"Look!" Lixie pointed into the night. "That's definitely Harriet Fletcher. I can recognize that stately profile anywhere." Lixie hugged Bonita's shoulder. "Oh my, what has happened? I'm afraid to find out." She glanced down at Bonita and in the darkness could barely make out the young girl's white-toothed smile. "Ramona Hawk isn't here," Lixie blurted out.

"How do you know that?" Carter asked.

"Every time Bonita is around Ramona Hawk, she gets agitated and frightened. And right now she has a big smile."

"Are you saying Bonita has supernatural powers?" he questioned.

"No, I'm just saying that the Lord's given her the ability to sense a threatening situation. Some animals seem to be able to do this. Maybe it's an acute sense of smell or hearing."

"What if Ramona Hawk is dead? Do you think our girl will pick that up too?"

"Our girl?" Lixie shot back.

"She did volunteer to sit in the middle."

Bonita chattered in Apache as they approached the fire.

Ethan Holden offered his hand to help Lixie and Bonita climb down. "She escaped," he announced.

"Oh, no!" Lixie moaned. "How did that happen?"

"It was my fault," Harriet Fletcher said. "The wagon axle started locking up unless we drove slowly. Right after dark Hawk made a play for a rest stop."

Mary Ruth Holden came over to the others. "She said she had to take care of some woman business."

"And you untied her?" Carter questioned.

"She was wearing men's clothes, remember? Claimed she needed to be untied," Ethan Holden reported. "We untied her feet but left her hands hobbled."

"So," Edwin Fletcher continued, "Harriet and Mary Ruth offered to step out in the brush with her. A couple of the boys circled deep just to block any attempted escape."

"I even carried a shotgun," Lady Fletcher reported.

"When we were a few yards from the men, we . . . well," Mary Ruth admitted, "we turned our heads, of course."

"And she ran off?" Lixie asked.

"She shoved Mary Ruth into me and grabbed for my gun. I yanked back and she let go. I tumbled to the dirt," Harriet explained.

"I stumbled on top of Harriet," said Mary Ruth.

"By the time we got up, she was running into the night." Harriet looked down at her empty hands. "I could have shot her in the back. It would have killed her, no doubt. But I just couldn't do it. I just couldn't."

Lord Fletcher stepped to her side. "Of course, you couldn't. My word, who can shoot a woman in the back?"

"The CS cowboys mounted up and went after her," Mary Ruth said.

"And they haven't found her?" Carter questioned.

"Not yet," Lord Fletcher replied.

"They will shoot her if they find her, won't they?" Lixie said.

"I suppose they will," Ethan Holden conceded. "She will certainly shoot them if she gets a chance."

As Johnny White and Mean Mike walked their horses over to the carriage, the other cowboys galloped off into the dark.

"I suppose they're goin' out after Hawk?" Jefferson Carter queried.

"Yep." Johnny White said.

"How about you two?" Lixie inquired.

"Someone has to stay and protect the women and children," Johnny explained. "Besides, it'll be crazy out there in the dark. They're liable to shoot each other."

"You built this fire for us to see?" Carter asked.

"And we built it for a trap. We reasoned that Hawk was out on the desert without a weapon or water. If she saw everyone ride off except the women, she might sneak back and try to steal what she needed," Lord Fletcher replied.

"The men hid in the shadows, and we sat by the fire," Harriet explained.

"We were the bait," Mary Ruth added.

Ethan Holden shrugged. "Of course, it didn't work."

"It worked in *Stuart Brannon and the Border Rustlers*," Harriet mused.

"Speaking of books, where is the formidable Mr. Charles Noble?" Lixie questioned.

"He and Langford rode off with the wagon," Mary Ruth said.

"We did snipe one bag of food out of the back," Ethan offered.

"Mr. Noble said this was turning out to be a better story than *The General's Notorious Widow*." Harriet chuckled.

"For that, I am truly grateful. I never thought I'd say this, but I do hope he's careful. Out in a pitch-black desert with a murderous woman and a dozen trigger-happy cowboys, it does sound ominous," Lixie said.

They all strolled over toward the fire where Bonita sat in the dirt and ate a plain biscuit. Jefferson Carter stood behind her, and she leaned back against his leg. "Are we supposed to wait for them?" he asked.

"I told them we would wait for you to catch up and then decide. They expected to have her apprehended by now. Mr. Carter, what would you suggest we do?" Lord Fletcher inquired.

"I agree with Johnny." Carter's voice was strong, almost loud. "There are enough cowboys with guns out there in the dark. I suggest we head on into Lordsburg, notify the authorities, and form a search party for the break of day."

"I'll telegraph up and down the line," Ethan Holden offered. "She'll have to cross the tracks somewhere."

"We could notify the border also," Lord Fletcher suggested. "She'll want to get into Mexico as soon as possible."

"I'm not so sure," Lixie blurted out.

"Why is that?" Fletcher asked.

Bonita handed a half-eaten biscuit up to Lixie. "Because she could have been in Mexico by now if she had tried." She bit off a piece and handed the biscuit back to the girl.

"Are you saying Hawk doesn't want to go to Mexico?" Harriet Fletcher probed.

Lixie swallowed the very dry biscuit. "I'm saying she doesn't want to go to Mexico broke."

"So she has stealin' to do?" Mean Mike suggested.

"She'll need money and a new dress," Harriet surmised.

"First, she'll need to live through the night," Johnny White muttered.

"And where is the nearest place to steal money and clothing?" Carter asked.

"My word, Lordsburg, of course!" Ethan Holden gasped.

"What are the odds of her hiking out of the desert without being apprehended or shot?" Lord Fletcher questioned.

"Probably much better than the odds that the CS cowboys won't shoot each other," Carter said.

"Let's ride," Mean Mike said. "An evenin' at the Matador is a lot more appealin' than stumblin' across the desert in the dark."

Within minutes the fire was out. The two carriages, led by Johnny White and Mean Mike Mason on horseback, rolled south toward Lordsburg.

Bonita settled in with a cold biscuit in one hand and a chunk of ham in the other.

Lixie fixed a biscuit sandwich and handed it to Carter. She rolled a piece of ham and chewed off a bite. When she finished the ham, she began humming a hymn to the sound of the creak of the wheels and the clop of hoofbeats on the dusty road. A blanket of stars hovered above them, and the only breeze she felt was that created by the movement of the carriage. *This has been one of the most bizarre days of my life, Lord. And yet . . . there was something so divinely peaceful about it. I don't know if You are teasing me or rewarding me. But for a few wonderful moments I'm just Lixie Miller, a New Mexico woman, riding in a wagon with a broad-shouldered man and a darling girl. I know, Lord—he isn't my man, and she isn't my girl. But for a moment—a few peaceful moments—let me pretend they're mine.* She took a deep breath, let her shoulders relax, and stopped humming.

"You're quiet, Mr. Carter. Do you regret lagging back with me instead of staying with your prisoner?"

"No."

Bonita reached down for the canvas food sack. "Help yourself, baby." Lixie held the bag up for the girl to dig through. "I'm not sure what's in there, but you're welcome to any of it."

There was a crisp, juicy crunch.

"I assume she found an apple." As they came up over a rise, she saw lights on the southern horizon. "Do you suppose that's Lordsburg?"

"Yep," he replied.

"It's not getting closer very rapidly. It must be a long way off."

"I reckon."

The crunching stopped. "Bonita, hand me that core. I'll discard it for you."

Lixie reached over and took the girl's hands. One was sticky, the other crumb-covered.

"Oh dear, I do believe she ate the core, seeds and all." Lixie continued to hold the small hands as the carriage rattled into the night. *Lord, I know so very little about this girl. It's obvious You brought her into my life to teach me some things. I hope I can teach her as well. I trust I'll teach her more than how to eat an apple.*

After a minute or two, Bonita tugged her hands free and explored the food sack again.

"Mr. Carter, is everything all right?"

"Yep."

"I don't want to be a pest, but what are you thinking about?"

"You."

"Me?"

"Yep."

"Is that it? Is that all you're goin' to say?"

"I was ponderin' on why it is I'm not all that upset about Ramona Hawk's escape. I want her locked behind bars as much as anyone. Hung too, if that's what a jury decides. But I was thinking it through and figured had I been there with Hawk, the exact same thing would have happened. I surely would let a woman have a stop, and I couldn't shoot anyone in the back.

"And besides, had I been there, we wouldn't have had our little chat, and I don't reckon I'd trade that for all the outlaws in New Mexico. I know I should be anxious, but I have such a peaceful feeling. It's a beautiful night: You and little darlin' ridin' along beside me. The steady rhythm of the carriage. You hummin' 'Guide Me, O Thou Great Jehovah.' Maybe it's just the Lord telling me to be still and watch Him work. I don't know. In the midst of an out-of-control day, it's a peaceful respite. Does any of this make sense?"

Lixie held her breath. *I can't believe he's saying these things!* "Yes. Actually, my thoughts were frightfully similar."

"When I was a marshal in the Territory, I'd have nights like this. I'd be camped out on some little stream. Somewhere down the road or around the river bend a gang of violent men waited for me. Yet I knew I was in the right place, doin' the right thing . . . and there was a calm that seemed to flood all around. I realized that I didn't know what the morning would bring, but it didn't matter. The Lord was in charge, and I could accept that. Lixie, have you ever felt that way?"

"Occasionally."

"Now you're the one being quiet."

"It's strange, but even with all this turmoil, I'm enjoying the ride too," she admitted.

"There are some scenes that feel just right."

"And some relationships that set a mind at ease."

"What do you suppose the Lord is telling us by this?" he asked.

"To enjoy the ride because every trip has a destination."

"And what's our destination?"

There was a long pause as the carriage dipped down into a dry arroyo and up the other side.

Lixie's voice was soft. "Lordsburg."

"I believe you're right. There's no reason to worry about tomorrow. For another hour or so, it will be you, me, and the baby, Mama."

"She's growin' up, Daddy."

There was a lightness, a tease in his voice. "I know. It seems like yesterday she was sprawled across my lap."

"I like the way you play the game, Jefferson Carter. There's sorrow in your eyes but kindness in your voice."

His words came like a dead weight falling from a balcony. "I killed an innocent man, Lixie."

Her hand flew to her chest. She pressed hard as if to slow her anxious breathing. "Is . . . is that why you went to jail?"

"Yep."

"Was it in the Indian Nation?"

"Yep."

"Were you a marshal at the time?"

"Me and my partner, Norman Jaques, had come up on the Harmon place about sunset. We figured that Drywood Tillson and Hack Moore would be showin' up, looking for fresh horses to steal. They were ahead of us. We didn't know that Mr. Harmon was up in the hills cutting logs for a barn, leaving Mrs. Harmon and the twin girls by themselves.

"So like dummies we rode up to the front of the house and almost got ourselves shot. We could hear the women screaming inside. Me and Norman decided the first priority was rescuing the ladies, even if that meant losin' the two outlaws.

"Norman snuck around to the back door. I camped out at the front door where the Harmon horses were grazing. We had decided that they might try to use the women as shields as they made a run for the horses. We said that if a woman came out, we wouldn't shoot, but we wouldn't let them take the women with them.

"Anyway, there was a commotion. I knew they were going to make a break. They fired a couple of wild shots in my direction and then came bursting out on the porch in the evening shadows."

She leaned forward to hear better. "The first one through the door was a man. I shot him."

"Who was it?" Lixie gasped.

"Norman. They captured him at the back door, but they didn't know how many marshals were out there. So they made a break out the front 'cause it was closer to the horses. They gagged Norman and shoved him ahead of them."

"But it was just an accident."

"The courts called it manslaughter."

"And the jury convicted you?"

"No jury. I pleaded guilty."

"How many years did you get?"

"Three. But the judge pardoned me."

"So you didn't go to prison?"

"I went. I turned down the pardon."

"Why?"

"Because of LoriAnn and the baby."

"Who is she?"

"Norman's wife. I just couldn't look her in the eye."

"How long ago did this happen?"

"Sixteen years, ten months, and fourteen days." His voice faded out, and the only sound left was that of carriage wheels and horse hooves. Then the stillness was broken by a long string of Apache words and something soft shoved into Lixie's hand.

"Did little darlin' give you a biscuit?" she asked.

"Yep," Carter replied.

"I wonder what she just told us?"

His reply came muffled in biscuit crumbs. "That the conversation was getting too serious."

"I appreciate your telling me all that, Jefferson. We all live with mistakes and regrets."

"But not all of them have cost a good man his life."

Lixie reached across Bonita and tugged on his sleeve until he reached his hand out. She laced her fingers in his. They felt warm, strong.

She felt a sticky little hand grab the top of hers.

"It's our pretend family, Mr. Carter."

"I reckon you're right," he concurred. "One day at a time."

"One hour at a time," she said.

They rumbled behind the Holden and Fletcher carriage until the lights of Lordsburg blazed brightly ahead of them. As they approached town, the fog of dust they followed was more apparent. Carter slowed the team to avoid the Fletcher carriage's dust. They had just dropped down into a gully when Bonita threw her arms around Lixie's neck.

"She's not cold, but she's shaking!" Lixie held the girl tight. "What's the matter, baby?"

Bonita lifted her nose, took a deep breath, and pointed out into the darkness of the desert.

"*Malo*," the girl whimpered.

Eight

Even though the knock at the door was light, Bonita hid behind Lixie's skirt. She studied the girl's brown face. *Apprehension, but not terror. There is no malo lady behind this door.* "Now, sweetheart, there's nothing to be afraid of. We are home in Lordsburg. It's not our home." Lixie scurried over to the front door. "But it's our home for now."

She swung open the front door and peered out on the dark porch. "Paco!"

"Did you know they can't find Ramona Hawk, and some people say she's going to come to Lordsburg to rob the bank and might try to get even with those who captured her at the depot?" The boy pushed shaggy black hair out of his eyes.

"Perhaps it's not a good time to be out on the streets," Lixie replied. "Would you like to come in, Paco?"

"Not until that girl quits glaring at me."

"Oh dear. Bonita, this is my good friend Paco. And Mr. Paco, this is my . . . my . . ."

"Your good friend?" he offered.

"Yes, my good friend Bonita." Lixie stepped aside so they would face each other, but the girl ducked behind her again.

Paco peered around Lixie. "*¿Cuantos años tiene usted?*"

Bonita let loose a long string of Apache words and then buried her head in the back of Lixie's dress.

Lixie waited for Paco to enter the front room and then closed the door behind him. "You don't happen to speak any Apache, do you?" she asked him.

"Nope," he said. He surveyed the entire front room from floor to ceiling. "Tío Burto . . . Mr. Hernandez knows some Apache words."

When Lixie hugged the girl close, Bonita put her arms around her waist. "He does? That's wonderful! Would your Mr. Hernandez mind if Bonita and I visit? I'll get him to translate, and we can finally talk."

Paco wandered over to a side table and plucked up a small brass duck. "No, he wouldn't mind. He likes to have visitors." He turned around. "This duck won't float, you know."

"I'm sure you're right," Lixie said. "Let me turn off a few lamps, and we'll go visit Mr. Hernandez."

"Why have a duck that doesn't float?" He set the brass object back down on the table and cocked his head sideways. "You want to see my Tío Burto right now?"

Lixie took her black straw hat off a peg by the door. "Yes. Is it a bad time?"

"Sort of." He wandered over to the divan and flopped down. "They say if you shoot enough buckshot into a duck, it'll sink."

"Yes, I imagine it would." Bonita made sure Lixie stayed between her and Paco. "Why is this a bad time to see Mr. Hernandez?"

"'Cause he's not home. None of them are." Paco hopped off the divan and bolted to the table in front of the window. He stared at the swinging pendulum of the clock. "Did you ever make a clock, Mrs. Miller?"

"No, I never have. When will they be back, Paco?"

"Monday. They went to Las Cruces. Some cousin died, and they went to the funeral. I made me a clock once out of wire and tin cans."

Lixie put her hat back on the peg. "You made a clock? I'm very impressed."

"Yep, and it was a good one. The only problem was, it didn't work."

"That can be a difficulty."

"But I sold it to a kid for thirty-one cents."

"I trust you told him the clock didn't work."

"Yep. He said it didn't matter 'cause he couldn't tell time anyway."

Bonita inched her way to Lixie's side but kept her chin on her chest, her eyes focused on her own bare toes.

"With your Aunt Julianna in El Paso and now the Hernandezes in Las Cruces, where does that put you?"

"It's all right. They left me a key to the foundry. I am to feed the mules."

"But where are you going to stay?"

"With you, of course." He grinned.

"With me?"

"I could stay by myself, but I knew you would not want to be in Gracie and Colt's house all alone."

"That was thoughtful of you."

"That's the way I am. Of course, I did not know you would have her." He frowned at the girl.

"Her name is Bonita."

"Did you know the Hernandez brothers have a bell named Bonita?"

"That's nice. What does it sound like?"

"Like the 'town' in 'O Little Town of Bethlehem.'"

"Oh?"

"I think it's a G, but what do I know?"

Lixie started for the kitchen. Both children followed her. *They could be brother and sister—same height, similar black hair, big brown eyes, brown skin . . . and bare feet.* "Well, darling," she said, "it looks like we're going to have company."

"It's all right as long as she doesn't bother me," Paco replied.

Lixie fought back a grin. "Actually, I was talking to Bonita."

"Why?" Paco quizzed. "She doesn't understand what you say."

"How do I know for sure? Anyway, I like to pretend just the same. I believe you two are about the same age."

Paco rubbed the back of his hand across his round, brown nose and then wiped it on his shirt. "Yes, but one of us is much more mature than the other," he bragged. "Did you notice how crowded Lordsburg is tonight?"

"Yes. I heard that many on surrounding ranches came to town because of rumors of Apaches. I didn't know there were that many people living out on the desert. I suppose it's a boost in business for the hotels and restaurants." She put her hand on the boy's shoulder. "Have you had supper yet, Paco?"

He marched over and sat down at one end of the table. "Sort of."

"What does that mean?" Lixie questioned.

"I did eat at Mrs. Sinclair's boarding house after I took Buddy home, but that was a long time ago. My stomach is complaining."

"We were just making some jelly sandwiches. Would you like one?"

Paco stood up and peered at the kitchen cupboards. "I hope it is not grape jelly."

Lixie, with Bonita close behind, walked over to the wooden counter. "It's strawberry preserves."

"Is the bread fresh?" Paco sat down and rested his folded hands on the table. "I don't like stale bread. Did you make it tonight?"

"No, we stopped by the bakery. But it's fresh."

"All right. I suppose I could help you out."

"How kind of you," Lixie said. "Now go out to the back porch and wash your hands."

"I washed them today already." He inspected his fingers. "Anyway, I think I did."

"No food unless you wash up."

"Doesn't she have to wash too?" He pointed to the girl.

"No."

"Is it because you like girls better than boys?"

"Heavens no! It's because Bonita and I both washed up right before you came in."

Soon Paco was sitting at one end of the table. In front of him two thick pieces of sourdough bread and strawberry preserves perched on the heavy pottery plate. At the opposite end of the table, Bonita faced an identical feast.

"Would you like some apple juice, Mr. Paco?" Lixie asked.

"Yes, ma'am!"

As soon as she strolled across the room, Bonita jumped out of her chair and followed her.

"How come she's always got to be with you?" Paco asked between bites.

"Bonita is lost from her family. She gets afraid quite easily. It must be frustrating to hear us talking and not know what we're saying."

Paco looked up with red jam smeared on his chin. "I think she knows what we're saying."

"Why do you say that?" Lixie questioned.

"I can see it in her eyes," he announced. "You don't suppose she is shy because of my incredible good looks, do you? I've been told that my smile is quite fetching."

Lixie couldn't keep from grinning. "Yes, I can see that."

Paco tried to lick the jam off his chin with his tongue fully extended. "Why don't you ask her if my smile is too unsettling?"

Lixie pulled up a chair beside Bonita at the table. She pointed to the young Mexican boy. "His name is Paco."

Bonita looked at her with wide eyes.

Lixie pointed to the girl. "You are Bonita." Then she pointed to the boy. "He is Paco. Can you say Paco?"

"She is probably just too shy to say anything," he called out.

"Perhaps you're right."

The girl took a small bite of bread and preserves and chewed for a moment. Then she pointed to herself. "Bonita!"

Lixie nodded her head. "That's right. Now how about the boy? What is his name?" Lixie pointed at Paco.

"She don't know," he mumbled with cheeks stuffed with bread.

Bonita broke into a long Apache monologue. The tone was like a lecture. At the end she pointed at the boy and called out, "Paco!" She stuck out her tongue and then ripped off a big bite of bread.

"Oh dear, Bonita, that didn't sound very nice," Lixie scolded.

"It's okay, Mrs. Miller. She likes me," Paco declared as he bit into his bread.

"How can you tell?"

"Whenever a girl likes me, she sticks out her tongue at me."

"I didn't know this has happened to you before."

"Oh, yeah. Lots of girls stick out their tongues at me. Sometimes when I'm down at the depot, a train will pull in, and the girl never even gets off. She just looks through the window and sticks out her tongue at me. They can't help themselves, I suppose."

"You might like to wipe the jam off your chin, Mr. Handsome," Lixie suggested.

He wiped his chin with his fingers and then licked them.

"Yes, I do believe you two have much in common." Lixie raised her eyebrows. "You might want to use your napkin."

When he wiped his chin with the white cotton napkin, it stuck to his chin and dangled like a goatee.

Bonita started to giggle.

"She does have a fairly handsome smile, for a girl," Paco said. He jerked the napkin down.

A knock at the door brought Lixie to her feet and Bonita beside her. They scurried to the door and opened it slowly. In the shadows she spied a broad-shouldered man, hat in hand.

"Mr. Carter!" Lixie exclaimed.

"I thought maybe you would like a report."

"Yes, I would. Please come in."

"Hello, Miss Bonita."

"The children were having a snack."

"Children? You've expanded your family?"

Lixie pointed to the boy standing in the doorway with jam on his face. "Have you met Paco?"

Jefferson Carter stood a full head above Lixie. "I believe I've seen him around town. Evenin', son."

"Hi, Mr. Carter. I was supposed to find you the other night and tell you that Mrs. Miller wanted to see you real bad, but I told the wrong man," he blurted out.

"Paco!" Lixie scolded.

"Never mind," Paco mumbled. "Eh, did you shoot Ramona Hawk yet?"

"Nope. I sure didn't."

"Did you ever shoot anyone?"

"Yes, I did."

"I thought so. Some men tote a gun, but they never use it. That's strange, isn't it?"

"I suppose it is," Carter replied.

Lixie eased down on the divan. Bonita crowded in next to her. Jefferson Carter paced the room. "Have Langford and the CS Ranch cowboys come in yet?"

"Yes, they have. They found no sign of Ramona Hawk. Only the hobbles."

"The ones that had been around her wrists?"

"Yes."

"How in the world did she get those off?" Lixie asked.

"Looks like they were sliced with a knife."

"How did she get a knife?"

"Maybe she had one in her boot," Paco called out. "Joe Addington used to carry one in his. I saw it one time. 'Course it didn't do him much good when Ramona Hawk shot him."

"Did all the CS cowboys make it in safe?" Lixie queried.

"Yep, but there was one injury," Carter reported. "Charles Noble fell out of the wagon when it hit a barranca."

"How badly was he injured?"

"Broke his leg. The doc set it, sewed him up, and splinted it. Now we just need to find him a room."

Paco reappeared in the kitchen doorway with a piece of jelly bread in his hand. "I hear the hotels are full," he mumbled.

"We found one room at the Sonoran, but it was on the second floor. There's no way to get him up the stairs."

"How about boardinghouses?" Lixie asked. "Like Mrs. Sinclair's?"

"She's got those tall front steps and no first-floor rooms, unless she boots out the Berry sisters. She offered her parlor, but Noble said he wasn't about to share a room with a pig."

"Buddy's no ordinary pig," Paco called out.

Bonita leaned close, tracing her finger up and down Lixie's arm.

"What is he going to do?"

"Langford and Ethan are checking around. I'm sure they'll find him something."

"In the meantime, what's the plan for finding Ramona Hawk? And, please, you may sit down, Jefferson."

"I'm kind of dirty." He continued to pace. "The marshal swore in some of the CS cowboys for deputies. They'll patrol around town tonight."

"Do you think she's coming here?"

"If she wants to get to Mexico, she'll need a horse and supplies."

"I heard she might have friends in Hachita," Lixie offered.

"I heard that too, but is Hachita close enough to go on foot in the middle of the night?"

"No one on earth would try to cross that strip at night on foot, knowing that Apaches are south of the tracks."

"I suppose the marshal will want to watch the liveries, grocery stores, and the like," Lixie pondered.

"That's the plan. But with a town so crowded with strangers, it will be difficult to find one woman slipping in. At daylight they will try to find her tracks. Ethan Holden has telegraphed the army, the custom station house, and the other towns up and down the line."

"If she finds a horse and supplies soon enough, she'll be way south of here by daylight. I suppose that stealing what she needs will be easy for someone like Ramona Hawk."

Carter stopped pacing right in front of her. "If all she wanted to do was reach Mexico, she would have been there by now. I still say she wants something else. She wants to get to Mexico rich. Ramona Hawk does not go into anonymous hiding. I think she's a driven woman."

"Driven by what?"

"Evil. Pure, unadulterated evil."

"Is that a judicial or a theological verdict?"

"It's difficult at times to separate the two."

"If she wants money, perhaps she'll rob a bank or freight office."

"I don't think even the notorious Ramona Hawk can break a bank safe all by herself at night. She works best when she can intimidate people. Holden put four guards at the telegraph and express office. None of them have the combination to the safe. The banks have done the same."

"How about you, Mr. Carter? Are you going to patrol the streets also?"

"I told the marshal I'd ride out at daybreak and help him pick up the trail. I had plenty of tracking experience in Indian Territory. I reckon I'd better get a little sleep first."

"I trust you found a place to stay."

"Not yet. I wanted to give you a report first."

"I would offer you the divan, but it might not be all that comfortable."

"I wouldn't want to impugn your honor, Mrs. Miller."

Lixie burst out laughing and then covered her mouth with her hand. Bonita sat up and giggled. "You are speaking to the general's notorious widow. Nothing I could do would surprise anyone, I'm afraid. I've grown used to people pointing and whispering when I walk into a room. But thank you for thinking of me. In reality I will have Bonita around my neck at all times and Mr. Paco here to protect me."

"I can bite real hard," Paco said. He turned to Lixie. "Can I have her bread?"

"May I," she corrected.

"May I have her bread?"

"Whose bread?"

"You know . . . hers."

"Who?"

Paco sighed. "May I have Bonita's jelly bread since she isn't eating it?"

"No."

"No? After all that work?"

"I'll come fix you another in a minute. We have company now." She turned back to Carter. "The offer of the divan still stands."

"If I can't find anything else, I may have to take you up on it."

"Where are you going now?"

"Back to the depot. I want Ethan to send a private telegram up to Santa Fe and tell them we found one of the guards."

Lixie stood, with Bonita instantly at her side. "Please be careful, Jefferson Carter. Remember, one day we have promised to have a very long conversation. And I, for one, am really looking forward to that."

He headed for the front door. "You should keep your door locked."

"Why? We have neither horses, supplies, nor money."

"She saw you with the girl at the river and in the carriage. If she recognized little darlin' in her trousers and dress, she might assume you know something about what happened up on that mountain."

"What can a little Apache girl do to put Hawk in danger that all of the woman's other crimes haven't? That just sounds crazy to me."

"Ramona Hawk is smart but not completely sane. That's what makes her unpredictable and dangerous."

"What are you suggesting?"

"Keep a gun by the door. Don't open the door tonight unless you can identify who is out on the porch. That's all."

"Mr. Carter, I don't intend to live my life in fear."

"For my peace of mind, would you do that? Remember, it was Gracie and Colt who captured Ramona Hawk. You're in their house, and she doesn't know they went to Iowa."

"Since you put it that way, yes, I'll keep the door locked. I trust you'll keep me informed of any other developments."

"Yes, but I don't want to come wakin' up mama bear and her cubs." He winked at Bonita, who darted back behind Lixie.

"I'm not really her son," Paco said as he strolled over and stood beside Lixie. "We are very good friends."

"I'm glad you told me that."

Bonita shoved Paco away with her hand.

"Hey!" Paco yelped.

"Now, children," Lixie scolded.

Paco pointed at Bonita. "And she ain't my sister!"

"Good luck, Mama," Jefferson said with a broad smile. "You look good with children . . . really good."

"How come I have to sleep in the baby's room?" Paco complained.

"The Parnells have a two-bedroom house. Bonita and I will take the big room because there are two of us. That leaves you with the smaller room."

"But it's a baby's room," he whined.

"Ruthie is a toddler, that's true. But the bed is big enough for you. And very soft. I believe the feather mattress is thicker than the one in our room."

"I could sleep on the divan in the front room."

Lixie fluffed up the pillow on the small bed. "We might need to save it. With the town so crowded, it's possible we'll have to offer hospitality."

"I'm not sharin' my bed."

"That's fair enough." She folded down the white cotton sheets. "Do you have a nightshirt to wear?"

"I never use one. Do you?" he asked.

"I do have several cotton gowns, but I think I'll sleep tonight in my dress. I'm expecting to hear about the progress in finding Ramona Hawk, and I will need to be dressed if I go to the door."

"Can I read before I turn out the lamp?"

"By all means. I noticed Gracie has volumes of Shakespeare and Milton. Did you find one you would like to read?"

"Yep. It's *Stuart Brannon and the Señorita from Sonora*."

"Oh dear, I hope the material is suitable."

"Don't worry. I read the story two times before."

"Good night, Mr. Paco."

"Aren't you goin' to pray for me? When I stay with Gracie and Colt, Gracie always prays for me."

After prayers were said, doors locked, and lamps turned down, Lixie folded the comforter down from the top of the bed and lay down on her back, still wearing her dress. Bonita crawled up on the bed and lay beside her in her dress, pants, and washed feet.

"Baby, I do hope you will sleep better than last night. It has been a very, very long day. Your little forehead looks sore."

Lixie left the lantern by the bed burning on low and closed her eyes.

Bonita began to hum a tune. It was soft and syncopated, like none Lixie had ever heard. Yet it soothed and relaxed her.

Lord, the past forty-eight hours have been staggering. I started the weekend thinking I'd be entertaining Lord and Lady Fletcher. Now I'm in someone else's home with someone else's children. There's a wild woman on the loose. Maybe Apache Indians in the vicinity. A lawyer from Santa Fe watches over me. I have no idea what will happen next. No clue what is to become of Bonita. No guess as to what Ramona Hawk will try. And no hint about the future of the general's notorious widow.

In that way, things aren't any different than they were a week ago.

Yet for a few days I've felt alive on the inside—not dead or useless. And I like that. But I'm scared to death that in a few more days all this will be over, and I'll be even more depressed to return to my routine. Let me enjoy each day . . . each hour . . . each minute. Maybe long life has been overrated. Give me long days. Long, exciting, fulfilling days.

Small fingers poked into Lixie's side. When she opened her eyes, the room was dark. There was a faint aroma of coal oil, but the lamp was out. She reached out and took the small hand at her side. "What's the matter, darling?"

Bonita whispered soft Apache words.

She heard a distant knock at the door.

"Oh, someone is here?" She swung her feet to the floor and fumbled for a sulfur match. "It must be Mr. Carter. Perhaps he needs a place to stay after all," she whispered.

Lixie was surprised when the light flickered to see Bonita already up and standing in front of her. Lixie lit the lamp and carried it with her. The collar of her dress was sweat-drenched, and yet her bare feet felt cold on the wooden floor.

When she reached the front door, she hesitated.

I didn't even look at my hair. And my face powder, my rouge. What am I thinking? I can't . . .

Another soft knock.

But I must.

"Yes, who is it?"

"Sorry to disturb you, Lixie. It's Langford Elsworth. May I speak with you?"

"Certainly, but I do look a fright."

"I cannot imagine you looking anything but splendid," he replied.

"Thank you, Langy-dear." Lixie unlocked the door, and Elsworth hurried in.

"Oh . . . my," he mumbled.

"Would you like to take back that 'splendid' comment?"

"No, no. I didn't know you had a full house." He pointed to the couch.

She turned to see Paco sound asleep on the divan, one arm flopped to the floor where a shotgun lay within inches of his hand.

"I presume Paco didn't like staying in Ruthie's room. Did you need a place to stay?"

"I've got half my boys on patrol and the others camped out at the livery. I'll stay with them, and we'll go out about daybreak with the sheriff. But I'm looking for a place for Mr. Noble."

Lixie's shoulders sagged, and she let out a deep breath. *Lord, I can't believe You're doing this to me.*

"You heard he had a leg broken?" Elsworth said.

"Yes, I did."

"We had him tucked in down at the depot for the night because town is so crowded. But the midnight train pulled in, and they parked it."

"Why?"

"There are telegraph reports coming in from the west that the Apaches have torn up the tracks near Big Springs Arroyo. The Southern Pacific doesn't want to send the train until they have a daylight inspection. That means the depot is now a resting place for fifty passengers."

"Oh dear. And now you have to find a place for Mr. Noble?"

"Exactly. You know I wouldn't ask if I could think of any other solution."

"Yes," Lixie sighed. "I'll wake up Paco and send him back to Ruthie's room."

"Thank you, dear Lixie. You're a trooper!"

Elsworth gave her a quick hug around the shoulders and headed for the door.

"Go get Mr. Noble. We'll prepare things for his arrival."

"Actually, he's out in the wagon."

Lixie brushed the hair back out of her eyes. "Do you need help with him?"

"Johnny White's with me," Elsworth announced. "We should be able to handle him."

Lixie lit two more lamps, woke up Paco, and cleared the path to the divan before Elsworth and White assisted Charles Noble to enter the front room. Bonita stood behind her, a sleepy Paco stood at the door to Ruthie's room.

"Evenin', Lixie." Johnny White nodded. "Looks like you was sleepin'."

"I must look a fright."

"Yes, ma'am, you do. But some women look better in a fright than others gussied up."

Why doesn't a cowboy's blunt honesty upset me? "Mr. Noble, I'm sorry to hear of your injury."

"Few people realize the rigors of good research," he puffed.

"Set him on the divan. I'll check to see if Gracie has any more pillows or blankets."

"Good grief," Noble protested. "I can't sleep on that sofa."

"Why not?" Elsworth asked.

"It's much too narrow. If I roll over, I'll fall off and re-injure myself."

"Don't roll over," Johnny White suggested.

"Surely there's an extra bed," the writer mumbled.

"Mr. Noble, there's one regular bed and one child-sized bed in this house. As you must know, this is not my house, but it belongs to friends."

"That will work," he said. "Just help me get there."

"Where?"

"To the one bed. That's all I need."

"I'm afraid that's where Bonita and I sleep."

"I'm only talking about one night. I'm sure town will open back up after daylight," he insisted.

"Mr. Noble," Elsworth boomed, "Mrs. Miller was gracious to allow you to come into her home in the first place. I believe you'll have to make do with the divan."

"I will not. I have important books to write, notes to review. I'll need a lamp, a writing table, and an adequate bed."

"Lixie, do you want us to just dump him out in the street?" Johnny White offered.

"What! I'll sue!" Noble threatened.

"Mr. Noble, I've never in my life met a man who is so opposite of his name," Elsworth fumed. "You'll stay on the divan, or we will abandon you in the middle of Railroad Avenue. Is that clear?"

Elsworth and Johnny White deposited the heavy-set man on the couch.

"This can't be," Noble grumbled.

"Do you want us to tie and gag him for you?" Johnny White asked.

"We'll get along fine, thank you. I understand how an injury can make a person grumpy," Lixie said.

"I'm not grumpy," Noble snapped.

"Mr. Elsworth, Johnny—you go on and get some rest yourselves. We'll survive. On more than one occasion in the army, there was only the company doctor and myself to deal with the wounded."

"Thank you, Lixie." Elsworth gave her another quick hug and headed for the door.

Johnny White lagged behind. "I've never known any woman who reaches out and helps folks like you do, Lixie."

"Am I too frightful for you to hug me too?"

Johnny White shoved back his black felt hat and grinned. "No, ma'am. You ain't that frightful." He hugged her as if clutching a sack of oats and then turned loose and scurried out the door.

"I trust you aren't going to make me hug you," Noble complained.

"You can rest assured that will never happen. Now let me find you some blankets and a pillow," she offered.

"I'll need several pillows," he insisted.

"I'm not sure how many pillows Gracie has. I only know of three."

"I can get by with three for now."

"And just what are the children and I supposed to use?"

"You know how kids are. They can sleep on the floor without a pillow. Especially those two."

"What did you mean by that?" she snapped.

"Indians and Mexicans are used to sleeping out on the ground."

Lixie folded her arms and glared at the man. "If you are insulting my children, you will have to leave, Mr. Noble."

"I can't walk."

"Then you can crawl out the door."

"But they aren't your children!" he protested.

"Mr. Noble, as far as you're concerned, they are indeed my children. And I won't tolerate you treating them any other way. Is that clear?"

"No reason to get in a tiff."

"I expect you to apologize for that derogatory remark about my children."

"What remark?"

Lixie closed her eyes and shook her head.

"I'm sorry if my comments cast aspersions on their character."

"Thank you, Mr. Noble. I'll see if I can find you one pillow and one blanket."

"I need to keep my leg propped up."

"I'll see what I can do."

"Do you have anything to eat?"

"We might have some bread and preserves left."

"Is the bread fresh?"

Lixie glanced over at Paco.

"I'm going to sleep in Ruthie's room," he reported.

Bonita followed Lixie to the kitchen cupboard. She had just retrieved a loaf of bread and was starting to slice it when there was a thump and a shout from the front room. She and Bonita raced into the room at the same time Paco did.

"My word, don't just stand there," Noble insisted from the floor. "Help me up. I fell off the divan."

Lixie didn't bother looking at the clock. She knew it was some time after 1:00 A.M. when she closed the door of the Parnells' bedroom with Charles Noble in their bed. Paco was in Ruthie's bed. Bonita was asleep on the divan. Lixie surveyed the options in the front room.

Last night I slept in a chair on the veranda of the headquarters house at the CS Ranch. I am tired. Very tired.

She eyed the big oak rocking chair.

I am too old for this every night. My bones ache. It's like they hurt from the inside out. If I don't get some sleep, I will be of no use to anyone.

She dragged the rocking chair over by the divan and lined it with a wool blanket. *This is like a dream that won't end. I can't tell if it's a happy dream or a nightmare, but it just won't end.*

She flopped down in the chair and leaned her head against the hard wooden slats. *Even prison would be more comfortable than this. Maybe not those tiny brick cells in the brig at Ft. Laramie, but an ordinary prison would provide a cot or hammock or something.*

Lixie rocked forward to reach over and turn off the lamp. A light knock sounded from the direction of the kitchen.

Go away. I'm too tired to move. Who can it be at the back door? She glanced at the shotgun near the front door. *Perhaps I should just leave both doors open so I can get some sleep.*

She pulled herself to her bare feet, picked up the gun, and scurried through the kitchen to the back door. "Yes?" she called out.

"Lixie, it's me—Mary Ruth Holden."

"Oh dear." She propped the shotgun in the corner of the

kitchen and opened the door. Three people huddled in the darkness.

"Harriet! Lord Fletcher!"

"Yes, this is quite something, isn't it?" he replied.

"Please come in. What happened?"

"Didn't Mr. Carter tell you?" Harriet said.

"Tell me what? I haven't seen him in hours. At least, I think it was hours. Everything is quite confusing."

"Oh dear," Harriet Fletcher added, "I do hope he's come to no harm."

Lixie's eyes widened, and her heart raced. "What's going on?"

The three moved into the lantern-lit kitchen.

"One of the families camping in the streets came to the marshal about an hour ago to report a burglary," Lord Fletcher explained. "They were sleeping in their farm wagon when a woman dressed in men's clothing approached them with a knife."

"Ramona Hawk!"

"Apparently," Harriet said.

Lord Fletcher continued, "She took a Winchester, a sack of food, and—"

"A dress from the lady," Mary Ruth put in.

Lixie locked the door behind the guests. "Did anyone get hurt?"

"No," Harriet reported. "But that isn't the end of the story."

"What else?" Lixie turned the lamp up and set it on the kitchen table. Shadows danced on the walls around them.

"When the sheriff investigated, he found the men's clothes that Hawk was wearing down in an alley near where the wagon was parked."

"So she's changed clothes? That was expected." Lixie folded her arms across her chest. *I've spent my life fixing myself up to look presentable in public, and tonight I've greeted the whole town looking . . . my age.*

Lord Fletcher wrung his hands as if playing Lady Macbeth. "But the alarming thing was what was found in the pocket of the shirt she wore."

Lixie tried to brush her hair back over her ears. "What was it?"

"A clipping from the Santa Fe newspaper on the expected arrival of Lord and Lady Fletcher," Mary Ruth blurted out.

"Why did she have that?" Lixie asked.

"That's exactly what I would like to ask her," Lord Fletcher boomed.

Mary Ruth wiped the corners of her eyes. "Mr. Carter thinks she might have been planning to kidnap the Fletchers."

Lixie pressed her palms together and held her fingers to her lips. "Oh no! For ransom, I presume?"

"Yes." Mary Ruth nodded.

"I'm afraid she has an inflated idea of our importance," Harriet added.

"I don't really think she could have carried it off, but I have no other explanation for that being in her pocket," Lord Fletcher remarked.

"Or why she was up in the rocks spying on us when Jefferson Carter came upon her," Lixie said.

"It's rather far-fetched, but, nonetheless, Mr. Carter advised us not to take chances."

Lixie slipped her arm into Harriet Fletcher's. "I agree. What can I do for you?"

"Since we were in the same carriage, she knows that the Fletchers are with us. If she's after them, Ethan's sure she'll come to our house," Mary Ruth reported. "He's posted guards but wants us out. He and Rob will stay at the depot."

"We'll take the next train west, but that won't be until daylight, so we just need a place to camp," Lord Fletcher said.

"Yes, of course. We have a full house. Mr. Noble is in the bedroom. Paco's in Ruthie's room, and . . ." Lixie felt a small hand slip into hers. "Oh, here's my girl! I would be happy to offer our divan. Mary Ruth, there's a pillow and a blanket in the rocking chair. I'm afraid it isn't much."

"But where will you and Bonita sleep?" Harriet asked.

"We'll make do. Please, I insist. We slept last night on the front porch at the ranch, remember? Army wives and Indians—they don't come any tougher than us." Lixie brushed Bonita's bangs back off her bruised forehead.

"My word, Mrs. Miller, I'm much too tired to argue. You're a real sport," Lord Fletcher said.

That's me. The general's notorious sport!

When everyone got settled in, Lixie rolled up tea towels. She sat in one kitchen chair with her arms folded, her head resting on the makeshift pillow, while Bonita did the same in the chair next to her.

"Little darlin', I would imagine by now you are wishin' you were outside sleeping on the dirt in the Sierra Madres. Anywhere but here. It might be my only night to have a daughter, and I don't even get to tuck her in."

Lord, everything is so out of control now. I want to be faithful. I want to do the tasks You've given me. But I don't even have time to figure out what You're asking. And I'm much too weary to be of any value to anyone.

It could have been two minutes or twenty minutes or two hours, but Lixie sat straight up when someone knocked at the door again.

When she stood, she was surprised that her bones didn't ache. Her back didn't hurt. Her head felt clear. She went to the back door, shotgun in hand. "Yes?"

There was no answer.

"Yes, who is there?" she called again.

Still no answer.

Perhaps it's Ramona Hawk. She's trying to lure me into opening the door.

Again a knock.

That's the front door, not the back door!

She scurried through the darkened kitchen. *Whoever it is, I simply can't put up one more person!*

"Who is it?" she whispered at the door.

"Jefferson Carter."

Perhaps we have room for just one more. She opened the door and stepped out onto the porch barefoot.

His voice was a deep, deep whisper that tickled her throat. "Lixie, did the Fletchers make it over?"

It was so dark she could barely make out a silhouette, but she had no difficulty sensing his presence and smelling the spice tonic on his face. "They're asleep on the couch."

"They told you about the news clipping?"

"Yes, and they said you were supposed to come over first. I've been worried about you."

"Can we go inside and talk?"

"I'm afraid someone is sleeping in every room."

"Then we'll just sit out on the porch," he decided.

"Should I bring my shotgun?"

Even in the darkness she could see his white-toothed smile. "I promise to be good. You won't need the gun."

"Do you think I'll fall for that old line, Mr. Carter?"

"I can hope."

"Okay, Mr. Carter. I'll see if what you say is true." Lixie left the shotgun at the door and stepped out into the warm, star-filled night.

They sat on the wooden steps, shoulder to shoulder. "On the way over to see you, one of the deputies found me. He said someone tried to steal a carriage from Ramerez's livery but was chased off."

"A carriage? But a horse is easier to steal, and it would get her to Mexico more quickly."

"But you need a carriage for kidnap victims."

"You really think she's after them?"

"Can you imagine the international scene it would be to have a notorious Confederate spy capture an English lord and lady and hide out in Mexico? She could demand a reward from all three governments. No one knows those mountains except the Apaches, and they aren't in the mood to give anyone a tour."

Lixie felt his shoulder press against hers. "So what is the plan now?" She leaned back into him.

"Guard the Fletchers till the train pulls out in the morning."

"You think she'll follow them?"

"No, I think she knows she has to get to Mexico soon. This was on the way. Once they're gone, she'll try for quick money and race for the border."

"Are you going to surround this house with guards?"

"Just the opposite. We surrounded the Holdens' house with guards. To someone riding by, that would be the place housing something or someone valuable. No one will look here."

"And we don't need any guards?"

"Just one ought to do it."

"And you're it?"

"I volunteered."

"When are you going to sleep, Mr. Jefferson Carter?"

"When are you, Elizabeth Miller?"

"Next week."

"Oh?"

"Mr. Carter, I've been in Lordsburg for two months and spent most of my time lounging on the patio reading books. Soon enough all of this will calm down, and I'll be back in that same routine."

"You don't sound too satisfied with it."

"I enjoyed the first couple of weeks. It was time to think, relax, unwind from years of tension. But when it dawned on me that I might never do anything else, it became quite depressing. Have you ever been depressed like that?"

"Yep. For three years."

"In prison?"

"It's quite depressing."

"That's what my life was beginning to feel like. Prison. However, I'm sure these conditions are better than in prison."

"Oh? I never had to sleep out on the steps."

She slipped her arm in his. "It was hectic and comical inside. Your friend, Mr. Charles Noble, is quite overbearing."

"My friend? I thought he was *your* friend!" Carter laughed. "And where's your girl, Mama?"

"I believe she's asleep in the kitchen with her head on the table."

"Will she wake up scared?"

"She'll find me. She always seems to know where I am." Lixie patted his hand. "Now tell me how you overcame the depression of prison."

"It began when I got serious with the Lord."

"What did you do?"

"I started life all over again."

"Explain yourself, Mr. Carter."

"I wiped the slate clean in my mind about what I had been trying to achieve in life. I said, in effect, 'Lord, here I am, with all my strengths and weaknesses. What do you want me to accomplish with the rest of my life?'"

"And what did He say?"

"I kept hearing the verse about doing justice, loving mercy, and walking humbly with God."

"So that made you want to become a lawyer?"

"A U.S. marshal is concerned with the law, but the law can be cold and uncaring. As an attorney, I can express more of a passion for justice. You know what I'd really like to be?"

"A judge! You'd make an excellent judge!"

"How did you know what I was going to say?"

"It's just apparent you would be a good judge."

"Yes, but who's going to elect a man who went to prison for murder?"

"Manslaughter. And I'm sure there are many people out here in the West who would not let that stop them. You have to settle in a place, get to know the people, build up a reputation as a knowledgeable attorney, civic leader, and . . ."

"Family man?" The words tumbled out.

"I suppose that wouldn't hurt."

"That's a tall order for a man my age. By the time I accomplish all that, I'd be ready to retire."

"But it's not just having a worthy goal, is it? It's having a worthy life day by day as you reach that goal."

"You're a very encouraging lady."

"I'm a very sleepy lady."

"Do you want to go in now?" he asked.

"No. Do you want me to go in now?"

"No," he whispered. "Then tell me, if you could have a fresh start, Lixie Miller, what would you like to accomplish with the rest of your life?"

Lixie grew silent.

Finally Jefferson Carter cleared his voice. "Eh, you don't have to answer if you don't want to."

"I want to. I just had to think it through. If I were honest with myself, which is very difficult because I've spent so much of my life trying to pretend everything is all right, I suppose I really want to prove to myself that I can do it right."

"Do what right?"

"Marriage. Raising a family. Taking care of my loved ones. Taking care of my husband. Mr. Carter, this is not the kind of conversation that a woman should have with a man."

"Why not?"

"Some things are better not said."

"Say 'em, Lixie."

"If you must know, I feel like a failure as a wife and mother. As a mother, because I was never able to have children, and I dearly wanted them."

"You could have adopted some."

"My husband refused to raise 'some other man's baby.'"

"Why do you think you were a failure as a wife?"

"I think my husband's lifetime of infidelity explains that."

"It explains him but not you."

"That's quite easily said, Mr. Carter, but to believe it takes much more. Do you realize that the only thing I ever accomplished in my life was to get married, and I failed at that?"

"I think you're being tough on yourself."

"You asked. I was honest."

"Let me give you some advice, Mrs. Miller. You hold on to that vision. You just find yourself a man who will let you take care of him in every way and agree to adopt a family."

Her voice was soft, timid. "Have you got someone in mind?"

"How about Mr. Charles Noble?"

"What?" she choked. Lixie clenched her fist and slammed it toward his shoulder.

The blow glanced off the palm of his hand, and using her forward momentum, he hugged her close.

"What do you think you're doing?" she protested.

"Trying to keep from getting hurt. If I turn you loose, you might clobber me. Isn't that right?"

"Yes, it is. Your only chance for not getting hurt is to hold me tight."

"I reckon for self-preservation I'd better not let go."

"You're a very smart man," she whispered.

"How long do you figure I will need to hold you?"

"Until daylight at least," she said.

"The sun will break in less than two hours."

"We've wasted most of the night." Lixie laid her head on his shoulder and closed her eyes.

A distant gunshot caused Lixie to blink open blurry eyes. Her head was still on his shoulder. The night sky had turned light gray. Bonita stretched across the porch, her head in Lixie's lap.

At the second and third reports, Jefferson Carter leaped to his feet, pulled his revolver, and sprinted out into the yard.

Nine

Edwin Fletcher's wool vest was unfastened, his tie hung off to one side, and the top two buttons on his white shirt were not buttoned. "Where's the shooting?"

"It sounds like it's over near the Holden house," Carter called out from the yard. He shoved his revolver back into his holster.

"Oh, no!" Mary Ruth clutched her hands beneath her chin. "I need to get home."

"You most certainly don't," Lixie cautioned. "Ethan and Rob are at the depot. The marshal and his deputies are at your house. I'm sure they can handle it."

"Perhaps we should head to the train station right now," Harriet Fletcher suggested.

Bonita held on to Lixie's hand.

"You could be right. Get your belongings. I'll try and find a carriage," Jefferson Carter said.

Paco raced out to him. "The Hernandez brothers have a wagon at the foundry. They are gone, but I have a key. I'm feedin' their mules for them."

"Come with me, partner," Carter called out. "The rest of you stay inside. This might not have anything to do with Ramona Hawk, but we can't take a chance."

They all scooted back into the front room.

"My word, I can't believe a simple social call on a friend in New Mexico could cause this big a ruckus," Lord Fletcher huffed.

Lixie stood with her arms folded, peering out the front room window. "You're just at the wrong place at the wrong time," she said. "I have a feeling Ramona Hawk would have settled for any prominent person she could nab before going to Mexico. We'll just get you on the train and safely back to Arizona."

"I never thought any place would be wilder than Arizona," Lady Fletcher remarked.

"Keep it quiet out there. An injured man needs his rest," Charles Noble hollered from the back room.

Lixie kept her place at the window but yelled back, "Mr. Noble, we have an emergency out here!"

"Can't you have a quiet emergency?" he bellowed. "And tell them to stop those confounded gunshots."

"Would you like for us to take Mr. Noble with us and push him off a high trestle?" Harriet suggested.

"Ignore him. Shall I make us some coffee?" Lixie offered. "I can't send you off without anything. I've been a neglectful hostess."

"There's no time," Harriet said. "Your hospitality was generous as it was. Where in the world did you sleep?"

"Actually, we were out on the front porch, weren't we, Bonita?" The young girl stood in front of Lixie, also staring out the window. Lixie's arms were around her shoulders.

"The front porch? How simply horrid!" Lord Fletcher replied. "I wasn't thinking. A woman and child on the front porch alone? If Stuart Brannon finds out about this, he'll have my hide. It's inexcusable!"

"Actually, it was quite nice," Lixie admitted. "We weren't alone."

"Mr. Carter was there all night?" Mary Ruth asked.

"I suppose the night was mostly gone. He stopped by right after you all went to sleep," Lixie explained.

"Just how close did you sit all night, Elizabeth Miller?" Mary Ruth grinned.

"Very, very close, but the general's notorious widow need answer to no one but the Lord above. Of course, Bonita did sleep in my lap."

"Good for her." Harriet Fletcher stepped to the door. "Here

comes Mr. Carter and the little Mexican boy. He's quite a hand-some young man. And I didn't even know you had two children."

"I would take them both in a flash." Lixie hugged the girl and then released her. "Let's get you loaded up."

"Mr. Carter is waving at us. I wonder if he wants us to wait," Harriet cautioned.

Lixie glanced out the window to see Jefferson Carter sprint toward the door. Paco remained at the wagon, holding the lead lines. They were all huddled in the middle of the room when he burst in.

"What's happening out there?" Lixie asked.

Carter yanked off his black felt hat and ran his fingers through his mostly gray hair. "That's what we're trying to figure out."

Lixie studied Carter's narrow eyes. "Did anyone get hurt at Mary Ruth's?" she questioned. *He looks tired. Permanently tired.*

"Nope." Carter jammed his hat back on. "Marshal Yager said someone fired a couple rifle shots from two blocks away. The deputies and CS cowboys guarding the place got all excited and fired back. Fortunately, at this time of the morning no one was on the street."

"Why would anyone do that?" Lixie asked. *I believe he does look younger with his hat on. Don't we all?*

"Marshal surmises it was just a diversion."

"What kind of diversion?" Mary Ruth Holden asked.

"To force Lord and Lady Fletcher to make a run for the railroad station."

"You think Hawk is trying to flush us out?" Lord Fletcher asked.

"That's what we're wonderin'. She wouldn't know which house you are at and may have figured you aren't at the Holdens'. Ethan Holden said they checked the line to the west, and there are no tracks torn up or trestles burned."

Lixie felt Bonita's arm around her waist, and she ran her fingers over the girl's head. "But what about the telegram about the Apache trouble?"

"Ethan said it looked like someone tapped into the wire just west of town. It was all a hoax."

"This town filled up with people because of a hoax?" Mary Ruth asked.

"Apparently. Folks are going home now," Carter said.

"Why would anyone send such a telegram?" Harriet Fletcher quizzed.

"To stall the train and make sure any prominent guest would be boarding it during daylight hours," Carter offered.

"Are you saying Ramona Hawk sent a phony telegraph signal?" Lord Fletcher asked.

"Ethan said she knows Morse code and could read Grace Parnell's message as it came in last spring."

"You think she knows we're going to be on that train?" Harriet Fletcher asked.

"She knows you're going to *try* to get on that train. That's my guess," Carter said.

"What shall we do?" Edwin Fletcher asked.

"We'll test the waters. Lixie, I want you to wear Lady Fletcher's hat and cape. I'll take your hat and topcoat, Lord Fletcher. We'll ride down to the station just to see what happens."

"I most certainly will not put other lives in danger on our account," Lord Fletcher protested.

"There's no danger of losing our lives," Carter said. "She's not trying to kill you. If something does happen, as soon as she recognizes we're not the Fletchers, she'll sense a trap and pull back."

Lixie glanced around the room. "Is there a chance she spied us out in the yard and will come over here looking for the Fletchers?"

"That's what I was thinking," Carter continued. "So this is what we do. Five minutes or so after Lixie and I leave to go down to the station, I want the Fletchers, wearing our coats and hats, to hustle over to the bell foundry with Paco. It's closed and will be safe. As soon as we figure the game out, we'll come pick you up."

"So we're the bait?" Lixie asked.

"We're the diversion. Just like the random gunshots were a diversion at the Holdens'."

"Good heavens," Lord Fletcher observed, "it's like a chess game."

"That's exactly right," Carter agreed. "We're trying to antici-
pate her next move before we plot our own."

Bonita watched each one speak with a troubled look on her
face. "What about my girl?" Lixie asked.

"She can stay with me," Mary Ruth offered. "I'll go back to my
house and see if any cacti were shot down in their prime."

The girl clutched Lixie's waist. "Bonita won't leave my side,"
she reminded them.

"Actually, I want you to bring her with us," Carter announced.
"Why shouldn't Lord and Lady Fletcher be escorting the Indian girl
they discovered back to Arizona?"

"I said, keep it quiet out there. I'm trying to sleep," Charles
Noble hollered from the back room.

"And what about Mr. Noble?" Lixie inquired.

"Leave him here. Perhaps Ramona Hawk will decide to kidnap
him instead."

Mary Ruth Holden slipped out the back door and hurried
home.

Lixie and Carter, dressed in the Fletchers' coats and hats,
climbed into the carriage. Lixie stretched her hand to the backseat
and held Bonita's sticky hand.

"Let me review this, Jefferson. . . . You believe Hawk stopped
the train to force the Fletchers out of safety to the depot this morning and that she will try to capture them single-handedly before
they board?"

He slapped the lead lines. The bell wagon lurched out into the
dirt street. "That's one guess," he mumbled.

Lixie clutched her hat with one hand as a dust devil spun
across the street in front of them. "Why did Ramona Hawk leave
that clipping where it was bound to be found? She must have
known it would tip us off to her plan."

Carter surveyed every building they passed. "I'm sure she just
forgot it."

"I'm not. Something's out of place."

"She was trying to escape. You don't have time to think of
everything."

"No, by the time she demanded the lady's clothes, she had already escaped."

"What are you suggesting, Lixie?"

"Ramona Hawk was a spy for the Confederates for almost three years, avoiding capture time after time. She was tried and convicted of treason and sentenced to be hung, but she escaped a Missouri verdict and ended up in Mexico. She was apprehended for killing Tommy Avila and Joe Addington but escaped from the Santa Fe jail. You captured her yesterday afternoon, but she was loose within twelve hours. Ramona Hawk is no dummy who leaves important clues in shirt pockets unless she wants to."

"You think she tore that out of a Santa Fe newspaper and carried it around just to deceive whoever might chase her?"

"That doesn't sound reasonable, does it?"

"Nope," Carter replied. "But some of it does. She very well might know we wouldn't fall for the trail ploy. She would have another plan. Maybe she wants us to think we have her plan figured out."

"You mean the shots fired at the Holden home?" Lixie reached out for Jefferson Carter's arm.

"I mean, the stopped train. What if that too is a diversion?"

"Then she won't be around the depot," Lixie surmised. "But all the deputies and CS cowboys would be!"

Carter rubbed his chin. "Maybe she had the house spied out last night, but it was crammed with people. Maybe what she wants is to grab the Fletchers and head straight for the Mexican border."

"While all of us are at the depot!"

Jefferson Carter pulled the carriage over to the side of the street. "This is too complicated even for a lawyer. What do you think, Lixie? Are we just confusing ourselves?"

"What does your heart tell you?" she asked.

"It tells me not to let the Fletchers out of our sight." He turned the carriage around and raced back up the street.

"You're going back to the house?" Lixie asked.

"It's closer than the foundry. Let's check there first."

They took the Fourth Street corner so fast that two of the wheels raised off the ground.

Bonita began to laugh and shouted a string of Apache words.

"If I could speak Apache, I'd tell her how serious this is!" Lixie shouted.

"Let her have fun, Mama. Things will turn serious soon enough."

"Pull up. I'll run in and check while you turn the rig around," Lixie suggested.

When Carter stopped the carriage, Lixie climbed down and offered a hand to Bonita. Instead, the Indian girl climbed up into the front seat next to Jefferson Carter.

"Sorry, Mama," he shouted as he drove out to the center of the street, "she wants to stay with Daddy!"

Lixie scurried into the house. *Lord, she has been glued to me for only two days, and I thought it would last forever. She didn't need me nearly as much as I need her.* "Is anyone here?"

"Would you stop the screaming out there!" Noble wheezed.

She dashed to the bedroom door. "Did the Fletchers just leave?"

"How many times are people going to interrupt my sleep? As I told the marshal, they went to the foundry about the time you left for the depot."

"Marshal Yager was here?" Lixie probed.

"I don't know his name."

"What did he say?"

"He asked where the Fletchers are. Could you please post a note on the door that no one is to bother me. I'm trying to recuperate."

"Are you sure it was the marshal?"

"He was wearing an oval star badge. I know a lawman if I see one. Of course I'm sure. Now go away."

Lixie scampered back to the carriage now pointed the other direction. Bonita stood between Carter's knees, holding the lead lines.

"They must be at the foundry," Lixie reported as she climbed back up in the carriage.

"That's good. They'll be safe there," Carter replied.

"Come on, darlin'," Lixie coaxed, "we have to let Mr. Carter drive."

"I think we have a new driver," he said.

"Don't you teach her to drive fast," Lixie scolded.

"Mama don't want us to have any fun, darlin'."

Bonita looked at Lixie and rattled off something in Apache.

"Did she look over at you when I said Mama?"

"Sooner or later she'll learn what some words mean," Lixie said. "We don't need to race to the bell foundry."

"If the Fletchers are safe, then there's no reason to stir up dust and attract attention getting there."

"Mr. Noble said that the marshal stopped by and asked about the Fletchers. So Marshal Yager will be there with them," Lixie informed him.

"But the marshal was at the depot," Carter reported. "Didn't you see his horse?"

"I saw his horse, but I didn't see him. Maybe he hiked over."

"Why would he do that?"

"So Ramona Hawk would think he was at the depot."

"You might be right." Carter nodded. "Or maybe it was one of his deputies that stopped by."

"All I know is that Noble said a man with an oval star badge barged in and was looking for the Fletchers."

"Oval?" he quizzed. "The marshal and his deputies have round badges."

"Round, oval—what difference does it make?"

"The court bailiffs in Santa Fe had oval badges! Hawk's trial was attracting such a crowd that they hired extra bailiffs and gave them oval badges."

"The two guards that took off with Ramona Hawk would have had badges?"

"Yes. And one of them is around somewhere, and the other is

dead on Bonita Peak. There was no badge in his clothing left in the alley."

"She rifled the clothes for a badge and didn't find the clipping?" Lixie said.

"She did leave it for us! We've been playing her game all night!"

"And now she and probably the other guard are at the foundry because Noble told him that's where the Fletchers went!"

The huge unmarked building covered with corrugated metal that housed Hernandez Brothers' Bell Foundry was originally built , but never used, to manufacture railroad engine parts. Its wide front doors were closed and locked with chains and padlocks. One single tall wooden door to the side was propped open with a big bell clapper as if someone was afraid it would swing shut and lock behind him.

Carter handed Lixie the carriage lead lines and jumped down. "If you hear gunshots or any commotion, race down to the depot and get the marshal."

Lixie scooted over, Bonita next to her.

"This whole scheme was my idea," Carter fumed. "Why on earth did I assume I could figure this thing out? Sometimes I think too much."

"Be careful, Mr. Carter; please be careful."

He glanced back up at her. "You mean that, don't you?"

"You know I do. In the past few days I've made some plans for the rest of my life, and you are a part of those plans."

"Do you know how good that sounds?"

"I believe I do," she replied.

With gun drawn, Jefferson Carter slipped inside the big metal building.

Bonita tugged the lead lines from Lixie's hands.

"You want to drive some more, do you? I think Daddy's spoiling you."

A wide smile dawned across the girl's face.

It took you four days to learn what Mama meant, but you learned Daddy in one ride?

Bonita sat in Lixie's lap and held the lines, pretending to drive the wagon.

Lixie cuddled the girl. *Lord, this is getting crazy. I was severely melancholy for weeks. Now everything is happening so fast. It's so out of control. Now I long for nothing to do but sit around and talk with a young girl, even though I can't understand a word she says, and a certain Santa Fe lawyer, even though I seem to know what he will say before he speaks it.*

And now I'm sitting here, half hoping that if Hawk is going to kidnap the Fletchers, she's already done that so that the lawyer will not be in danger. Lord, I'm the wrong one to be here. I'm just an army wife. Others fight the battles. I stay at home and worry and pray.

Maybe all those years I was praying for the wrong thing.

Do You see what I'm doing, Lord? I'm still reliving the past. I can't get away from it. I'm hopeless. How difficult for a man to be around me all the time. I'm always looking back. Always reliving every conversation. Always astounded how many times I was too naive to know what was going on. No man should have to go through that.

Run away, Jefferson Carter. Go start a cattle ranch in Montana. Go practice law in Santa Fe. Go be a marshal in Wyoming. But don't hang around the general's depressing widow.

Lord, why can't I forget? Why can't I just be Lixie Miller?

One deep peal, like a bell struck with a dull hammer.

Lixie and Bonita both jumped.

Was that a signal to run? There was no gunshot. No commotion. No shouting. He said gunshot, commotion.

The horses danced as Lixie took the lead lines from Bonita.

The girl pointed to the open door and spoke four brusque words in Apache.

"You think we should check on Daddy? Come on. Maybe he just bumped against a bell."

Lixie tied the lead lines to the hand brake and climbed down. Bonita jumped and landed next to her. Lixie held her finger to her lips. "We must be very, very quiet."

The first room was used for display or storage. There were shipping crates and bells stacked everywhere in no seeming order. Each pile and row offered ample room to hide a person.

When her eyes adjusted to the dimness, Lixie could peek through huge double doors to a shop and furnaces that stood idle. The back side of the huge building opened into a shaded backyard crammed with more bells, scattered like lava rock spewed out randomly from some ancient volcano.

There was no movement, no sounds.

Bonita looked up at her and grinned.

You are a happy girl, but I have no idea why.

Bonita lifted her nose and sniffed and then pointed to the yard out back.

What do you smell? I can't smell anything but charcoal and brass bells and stale smoke. And my own weak and timid perfume.

If he found someone, I would hear voices. If he ran into trouble, there would be shouts or gunfire. If there's nothing, he will amble back this way.

She slipped her right hand into the pocket of Harriet Fletcher's cape; her left hand lay on Bonita's shoulder. They inched their way over to the big door of the shop. "Baby, I hope we know what we're doing," Lixie whispered.

Suddenly she saw a familiar black felt hat.

"There he is!" Lixie called out.

Right behind him strolled Lord and Lady Fletcher.

"Oh, thank You, Lord," Lixie sighed.

Bonita took two steps forward and then bolted behind some bells.

Lixie followed her. "What's the matter, baby?"

She buried her head in Lixie's chest.

"Baby, you're shaking all over. What is it? Is it the *malo* lady?" Lixie guessed. "Where?"

The voice was low, husky, like a woman who drank too much. "Right here, Mrs. Miller!" Chills shot down Lixie's back. She whipped around to face the cocked revolver of Ramona Hawk.

Bonita hid her face.

"Where did you come from?" Lixie gasped.

"From stealing a rig. I planned to take the foundry's mule team, but someone took them first." She stared at Lixie from head to foot. "I thought you'd be down at the station waitin' for the notorious Ramona Hawk. I can't figure out what you're doing here. You should be home knitting doilies and reading Jane Austen. You'll never have what it takes to stop me. No one ever has."

Hawk grabbed the back of Lixie's collar and jerked her behind several stacked wooden crates. Bonita clung to her.

"I've got the general's scorned widow and the Apache girl up here," Hawk shouted toward the back of the foundry. "I want Lord and Lady Fletcher!"

For a moment all Lixie heard was Bonita's muted sobs.

"Lixie," Carter shouted, "is that true?"

"Jefferson, I'm sorry!" Lixie called back.

"Turn her loose, Hawk!" Carter shouted.

"I want the Fletchers, or your girlfriend gets shot. It's as simple as that. You know I'll do it."

"Let them go, and I'll let your partner go," Carter called out.

"Appleby, are you back there?" Hawk called out.

"He's unconscious," Carter admitted.

"Then that isn't much of a trade, is it?" Hawk replied. "That's not the first time he's failed me. You're wastin' time. Send the Fletchers up here, and you stay back there."

"If I fire a shot, the marshal and his deputies will swarm this building before you can get out," Carter threatened.

"You do that, and these two will die."

"I will not be the cause of other people's death," Edwin Fletcher shouted. "My wife stays with Mr. Carter, but I will come forward."

"No good, Fletcher. I want both of you," Hawk yelled. "It'll make a better story in the newspapers."

"Is that what all of this is about? Newspaper publicity?" Lixie asked.

"Attention. Publicity. Money. Power. Proving that I can outsmart them all. It's about winning and losing. That's what life is about, honey," she sneered.

"Not my life," Lixie mumbled.

"Sure it is, and you're a loser." Hawk jammed the gun harder into Lixie's back. "What about it, Mr. Attorney? Send the Fletchers up, and you stay back there. It's the only way no one gets hurt."

"I am *not* a loser," Lixie growled, startled by the strength of her reply.

"Lady, you're the most well-known loser in the entire country. The general's scorned widow." She jerked her head toward the back of the building. "Are you headed this way?" she hollered.

"We're coming," Lord Fletcher called.

"Where's the attorney?"

"He's back there."

"Is Appleby really unconscious?"

"Yes," Lord Fletcher said.

"Good. That will make travel easier."

"You can't carry off two hostages all by yourself," Lixie challenged.

"Three hostages," Hawk sneered.

Lixie's hands began to tremble. "Three?"

"The girl's going with me!"

"No!" Lixie clutched Bonita even tighter.

"You have no idea who she is, do you?"

"What do you mean?"

"She's the granddaughter of Magus Nevadas. He's the Cochise of the Sierra Madres."

"You plan to hold her for ransom too?" Lixie asked.

"No, I plan to use her to find a safe place to hide, after I tell Magus how I rescued his granddaughter from your evil clutches."

Lixie spun around and faced the pointed revolver and the narrow eyes of the woman in the blue gingham dress. "I did nothing but show this girl love! She is a precious dear."

"You're a loser, Mrs. Miller. And you're goin' to lose her too, so get used to it."

"My word, Miss Hawk," Lord Fletcher huffed as he approached, "is there no limit to your evil?"

"There's no such thing as good or evil. It's only winning and losing. That's the way it's always been. Give me the girl," Hawk demanded.

It was as if life slowed down, and everything became crystal clear. Lixie could see right into Hawk's eyes. There was hatred, anger, contempt, and a demonic gleam of triumph. To the right Lord and Lady Fletcher came to a stop by a brass bell that had been polished to a mirrorlike yellow finish. Lixie felt Bonita tremble, could sense her fear, and noted the coldness of her own toes, the sweat in her palms, and the anger rising. She could taste the salt of perspiration on her lower lip and smelled a faint aroma of burnt charcoal.

Lord, I did nothing while a man drained away most of the years of my life. I did nothing while a string of women stole any affection he might have had for me. I have done nothing but mope since his death. I'm tired of doing nothing. I won't stand by and watch anymore.

"I said, hand over the girl!" Hawk waved the gun at the back of the shop. "Stay back there, Mr. Attorney! If you come any closer, I'll shoot your girlfriend. I swear I will. What do I have to lose?"

"Lixie, be careful!" he shouted.

"You do not get my Bonita," Lixie growled.

Hawk raised her dark eyebrows. "I can shoot you."

"I know."

"You wouldn't be the first woman I shot."

"You don't get the girl."

"You're ready to die for her?"

"People have died for much less," Lixie declared.

"You're crazy," Hawk snorted.

"I've been told that for years," Lixie said. "Haven't you been called the same thing?"

Hawk jerked her head back as if she'd been slapped. "Yeah," she mumbled. "I suppose we can agree on that."

Lixie took a step forward. "Give me the gun."

"They might *call* me crazy, but I'm not crazy. I'll shoot you."

"Give me the gun."

"I'll shoot you."

"Yes, I believe you will."

"She's just a little savage."

"She's a precious daughter to me."

"No one dies for some dirty little Indian kid."

"Jesus did."

"This is no time for theology."

"If I'm going to be dead in a few seconds, it's a very good time."

"Lixie, no!" Lord Fletcher took a step, then halted when Hawk turned her revolver on him.

With Hawk distracted, Lixie leaped forward and shoved the barrel of the revolver to the side.

Hawk pulled the trigger.

Flame shot out of the gun barrel.

Acrid gun smoke billowed forth.

The huge bell near the Fletchers rang out. Then a crash sounded near a huge cast-iron bin, and glass shattered in the window by the front door from the ricocheting bullet.

Lixie released the hot barrel.

Hawk spun around toward the sound of the window breaking. Lixie grabbed up a brass clapperless bell the size of an eggplant and slammed it into the back of Ramona Hawk's head. The woman collapsed on the dirt floor.

"My word, Lixie, good show!" Lord Fletcher said.

Lixie squatted down and hugged Bonita tightly as Jefferson Carter ran toward them. "It's okay, baby. . . . It's okay. . . . Mama took care of the *malo* lady."

"Lixie, are you all right?" Carter called out.

"I am now." She stood and took the girl's hand.

"Where are you going?" he asked.

"Home. We haven't had our breakfast."

Marshal Yager and two deputies burst through the door of the foundry. Lixie marched past him without speaking. CS cowboys and other deputies surrounded the foundry as Lixie and Bonita emerged into the daylight.

Paco ran to meet them. "I crawled through the back fence and went and got the marshal."

"Did you shoot Ramona Hawk dead?" Johnny White called out.

"No, I disarmed her with a bell."

"You coldcocked her?"

She put one arm around Bonita and the other around Paco. "Boys, never try to take children away from a mama."

Lixie sat at the kitchen table and watched as Bonita picked up a fried egg with her fingers, rolled it around a slice of bacon, and ate it like a tortilla. Paco stabbed his entire fried egg with a fork and began to nibble around the edges of it. Lixie sipped scalding-hot coffee.

So her grandfather is an important Apache in the Sierra Madres? She has to go back. She has to be a part of her people. She has a place in their lives, in her tribe, perhaps in the history of her people. But it's okay. I knew that. I knew it was just a game. It was sometimes joyous, sometimes frightening, sometimes rather rank . . . but the game is over.

I lost. But I'm not a loser.

The only way to really lose is never to play the game.

Just sit on the patio and rot. For two days I was not rotting.

So . . . so for two days I was a winner. And that might be the only two days I've ever been a winner.

I can't believe I flattened Ramona Hawk with a bell. Now she'll break out of jail and come murder me in my sleep. At least I won't die of boredom. And Bonita won't be with me, so she'll be out of danger.

I actually clobbered Hawk. I know a few others that I wish I had had the nerve to clobber years ago.

"You meditating?"

Lixie crashed her cup down on the saucer at the sound of the man's voice.

"Jefferson! I—I didn't hear you come in."

"I knocked on the door."

"I was just drinking my coffee and . . ."

"Your cup is empty."

"I must have drunk it all. You caught me by surprise."

"Perhaps I should do it more often."

She stared at his eyes, and the creases at the corners accented their warmth. "Yes, perhaps you should."

"I figured you would want a report."

"How is Ramona Hawk?"

"Utterly depressed, but it's not from the blue lump you put on her head. She's depressed because the newspapers are going to report that General Miller's widow got the drop on her. To hear her talk, it's like losing Gettysburg all over again."

"The general's widow? The general's widow didn't stop Ramona Hawk."

"Are you saying you didn't single-handedly flatten her?"

"Of course I did. The newspaper should read: 'Lixie Miller of Lordsburg, New Mexico Territory, apprehended the notorious outlaw queen and Confederate spy, Ramona Hawk.'"

"The editor of the local newspaper said otherwise. You know how they sensationalize a story. I don't reckon you have any choice in the matter."

"We will go to the newspaper office immediately after breakfast. You have never seen the wrath of Lixie Miller."

"I believe I have. Will you carry a bell in your hand?"

Lixie started to laugh. "I believe I will!"

"Do you mind if I tag along as a witness?"

"Be my guest. Would you like some eggs, Mr. Carter?"

He glanced at the two children. "Rolled or stabbed?"

"Either way. We aren't real picky around here."

Lixie stepped over to the woodstove and set the cast-iron frying pan back on it. She reached into a basket and pulled out two brown eggs, then two more.

"Are you going to send Bonita back to Mexico?"

"Of course. She should be with her family."

"How are you going to do that?"

"When Ethan and Langford came by to move Mr. Noble to the hotel, I asked Ethan to telegraph Colonel Banks and have him ask General Crook about the girl. They will know how to do it."

"Can you handle giving her up?"

"Jefferson, I will cry, no doubt, but I'll recover. Life goes on. I will weep no longer over what I don't have or what I didn't have in the past. But I'll make sure I do rejoice over what I have now and in the future."

"You sound more confident than you were yesterday or last night."

"Something changed."

"What?"

"I flattened Ramona Hawk."

"Hmm . . . are you saying anyone suffering from melancholy should go out and clobber someone?"

"Perhaps." She tilted the pan and spooned boiling fat over the sizzling eggs. "Of course, you should only clobber someone who really needs to be clobbered."

"Fortunately, there are plenty around who meet that requirement."

"Perhaps I should carry a bell with me wherever I go."

He laughed. "Like Carrie Nation and her axe?"

"I wonder if saloon keepers would cower when Lixie Miller enters with her bell? What are you staring at, Mr. Carter?"

"At you, Mrs. Miller. I do believe you're the easiest woman in the world to talk to."

"Paco and Bonita, listen to that. Some men will say anything just for a few fried eggs."

"And bacon. And bread. And preserves. And coffee. Seriously, Lixie, you have such a soft, peaceful smile. It's easy to relax around you."

"Keep pourin' it on, counselor. Perhaps you'll get potato cakes and white sausage gravy next time you stop by for breakfast."

"I'll look forward to it. What time are you serving tomorrow?"

"Tomorrow? I thought you would be taking Miss Hawk back to Santa Fe to stand trial."

"The U.S. marshals are on their way to escort her and Appleby back."

"What's his story?"

"He said Ramona Hawk promised to set both guards up with money and señoritas in Mexico. After they broke her out, she told them the money would come from kidnapping the Fletchers."

"So that was her plan all along." Lixie slid the eggs onto a white china plate, forked several strips of bacon beside them, and sliced off a chunk of sourdough bread.

"There was supposed to be an Austrian archduke in El Paso, but when the papers reported that his trip fell through, she settled for the Fletchers."

"She was confident of escaping Santa Fe?"

"I reckon so."

Lixie poured him a cup of coffee. "She does have a rather dramatic flair. Where has Appleby been the last few days?"

"He claims he got in a drunken fight in Socorro and was tossed in jail. She told him when he got out, he was to steal six horses and wait for them in Hachita. But he was only in Hachita two hours before someone stole his stolen horses. He gave up on the whole scheme and came to Lordsburg last night and happened to run into Hawk in an alley. He said he thought she was goin' to shoot him. He's sort of glad he was caught."

"I presume he'll testify?" She poured herself a cup of coffee and sat down across from him.

"Can I have another egg?" Paco asked.

"You didn't eat that one."

"I ate all but the yellow part."

"You have to eat everything."

"That's what my Aunt Julianna says."

Lixie watched Carter fork a big bite of egg. *Lord, all the time I was the general's wife we had a cook. I miss cooking for a hungry man.* "Did you find out what happened to the man up on Bonita Peak?"

"Hawk claims she and Winters—that's his name—were settin' an ambush for the Fletchers when they found our girl running across the desert."

Lixie looked over at Bonita. "By herself?"

"That's what she said. Hawk recognized the girl, and they captured her, figurin' to make points once they reached the Sierra Madres. Only . . ."

Lixie set down her coffee cup. "Only what?"

Carter paused and ran his hand across his chin. "Winters liked to spank and beat on li'l darlin' too much."

"Oh, no." Lixie looked at the girl with egg yoke on her chin and a bruise on her forehead. "Poor baby."

"Remember, this is Hawk's story, so who knows the real truth? But she said when she tried to stop him that mornin', he came swinging at her and ripped her dress, so she shot him. That's when Bonita ran off. She fired a shot or two over her head, but Bonita ran into the Fletchers before Hawk could catch her."

"So she gave up on the kidnap attempt?"

"Just postponed it."

"Until you captured her?"

"To hear her story, she let that happen on purpose."

"On purpose?"

"She'd given up on seeing Appleby again and figured she was on her own. She claims that the only way she could have gotten close to the Fletchers was to be captured and brought in that way."

"She might be right about that."

Carter wiped his mouth on the back of his hand. *Are all men born with that trait?* She slipped a napkin next to his plate.

He gulped the coffee down and then smacked his lips. "She said the women of Lordsburg are crazy."

Lixie reached over with her own linen napkin and wiped off Bonita's chin. "In what way?"

"Hawk said that first it was Grace Denison Parnell. Now you. She thinks you both acted like fools."

"Would you like another egg, Mr. Carter?"

"No, ma'am. Three's plenty for me. Maybe Paco can eat my last one."

"Not until he eats the yoke. What do you think, Mr. Carter? Did we act the fool?"

"I don't know about Mrs. Parnell. She seemed bright enough in Santa Fe."

"And the general's notorious widow?"

"She acted foolishly. She could easily have been killed."

"I considered that. I felt it was worth the risk."

He laid his fork down and ran his tongue around his teeth. "Lixie, did you consider what a hole it would make in my life?"

"Explain yourself."

"I've ridden alone a long, long time. I know there's a beautiful sunset or two still up ahead. Have you ever watched a beautiful sunset all by yourself?"

"I suppose. I haven't really thought about it."

"It's a shallow feeling. A day, a decade, an era is ending. When the sun goes all the way down, I'm still alone. For a couple of days I've been scheming, thinking of ways to keep from having to watch every sunset alone. When she held that gun on you, I kept thinkin' that I'm never goin' to get to share those sunsets."

"That's very poetic, Jefferson."

"It comes from my heart."

"Will you need to go back and prosecute the case against Ramona Hawk?"

"No, I've excused myself. Being a part of her capture makes a conflict of interest. If I'm needed, I'll go testify. But I won't prosecute." When he finished gulping down the coffee, he banged his cup in the saucer.

"What are your intentions then?" she probed.

"Honorable, I assure you." He smiled.

"No, no." Lixie blushed. "I meant, what do you intend to do now? Will you stay in Lordsburg?"

"I know exactly what you meant. I'll stay for a while. Then I intend to follow some leads on little Charley McComas. I think he might still be alive."

"Even if it takes you down to the Sierra Madres of Mexico?"

"I imagine so. It seems like a worthwhile project to follow. But that's not the only reason for staying in Lordsburg."

She raised her eyebrows. "Oh?"

"There's a widow lady I have fifty years of talkin' to catch up on with and a couple of sunsets to share."

"Does that relationship look promising?"

"Like money in the bank." He grinned.

Wearing a fresh navy blue pleated dress and a fashionable straw hat with yellow silk French flowers, her hair perfectly in place, Lixie Miller strolled down the wooden sidewalk toward Railroad Avenue.

Still wearing the dress over her duckings, Bonita ambled hand in hand beside her.

Lord, I like having this girl's hand in mine. You know how depen-dent I have become in just a few days. And I know that at anytime she will need to go home. I could have avoided the pain of separation if I had never taken her to my heart in the first place. But keeping people out makes us shriveled up and bitter on the inside. I won't do that anymore. And I'll never regret these days of playing like I'm a mama.

"Sweet Bonita, I think we should find you some shoes, although I know your soles are as tough as leather." *I wish my soul were as tough as leather.*

From a block away she saw Paco running.

"Guess what?" he yelled.

"They've discovered gold on Fourth Street?"

"They have?" he gasped.

"I was teasing. What's your news?"

"It's not as important as your news."

"That was a joke, Paco. Forgive me. There's no gold on Fourth Street."

"Maybe a little. Madam Drury has two gold front teeth."

"And how do you know that?"

"Someone told me."

"What were you going to say?"

"Oh, the Hernandezes are back. I'm goin' to stay with them tonight. I won't have to sleep in a baby's room, and I won't have to eat the yellow parts of eggs."

"I can see that's a real advantage. However, you do know you are always welcome to stay with us."

"I told Tío Burto all about what happened in the foundry."

"I trust he wasn't too upset."

"He said it was good for business. Ever since the newspaper telegraphed the story back east, he has had a dozen requests from all over the country for a Lixie."

"A Lixie?" she questioned.

"He is calling the bell you clobbered Ramona Hawk with a Lixie."

"What an honor to have a weapon named after me!"

"A weapon?"

"I mean, a bell."

"Where are you and Bonita going?" Paco asked.

Bonita spewed out some Apache words.

"What did she say?" he asked.

Lixie hugged the girl. "She said we're going to buy her some shoes."

"Why?" he pressed.

"Because she doesn't have any."

"I have two pairs, but I never wear them." Paco glanced across the street. "Oh, there they are."

Lixie noticed the pig and duck waddling down the other side of the street. "Buddy and Sylvia?"

"Yeah. I promised Mrs. Sinclair I'd talk to them about those cats."

"What about the cats?"

"Eh, nothing," Paco replied as he ran across the street.

Lixie and Bonita exited the general store and had just turned east on Railroad Street when Johnny White galloped up to them.

"I was headed up to see you!" he called out even before he dismounted. "I was at the depot seeing that Ramona Hawk got loaded up and sent off, and Mr. Holden asked me to run this telegram up to you."

"Who's it from?"

"It's not right to read other people's telegrams."

She unfolded the brown paper.

"It's sad news," White reported.

"Hmmm . . ."

"I only read the first line or two. I didn't know I would find you this soon."

Lixie held it in front of her in the direct sunlight. *Only the U.S. Army can afford long telegrams.*

> *Lixie, dear, the girl you have is named Dylinoo. Yes, she was grand-daughter to Magus Nevadas. However, the Mexican government reported a raid in the Sierra Madres fourteen days ago. The old man and his whole band was wiped out in a fierce battle with the Federales. They reported no survivors. I just interviewed our Apache scouts here at the fort. They said Dylinoo had been staying in San Carlos with an elderly sick aunt. The aunt died, and some in the band were going to take Dylinoo back home. They were on the road when they heard about the battle in Mexico. They explained it to her and then turned around to return to Arizona, but she ran off.*
>
> *It seems they were apprehensive about leaving the reservation any-way and hurried back. Several bands are fighting for control among the Sierra Madre bronco Apaches. They said if she went back to the Sierra Madres, she might be killed.*
>
> *We've notified the San Carlos band where she is. None have offered to take her in. They are afraid such a commitment might make it look as if they are taking sides among the Apaches in the Sierra Madres. It looks like you have an orphan, Lixie.*
>
> *General Crook sends his greetings. He asked you to write to Mary when you have a chance. He will take the girl back with him on his next trip to the Sierra Madres, if that is what you decide.*
>
> *One other thing. The scouts say that Dylinoo went to a mission school at San Carlos. She speaks English quite well.*
>
> *Sincerely, Strat*
Colonel Stratford Banks

"What?" She squatted next to the girl. "Baby, this telegram says you can speak English."

Bonita dropped her head on her chest and stared at her new shoes.

"Your name is Dylinoo, isn't it?"

"My name is Bonita."

Lixie hugged the girl. "Oh, darling, why didn't you tell me?"

"I was scared," Bonita whimpered.

"Were you scared that I would hurt you?"

"I was scared you would send me back."

"Back where, baby? Where is it you don't want to go?"

"Back to San Carlos. They don't like me there."

"Why, darlin'? Why?"

"They say it is my family that makes trouble for all Apaches."

"Is that true?"

"Not anymore. They are all dead."

"Oh, baby . . ." She hugged the girl and began to sob.

"Are you all right, Mrs. Miller?" Johnny White said.

"I don't want to go back. I want to stay with you."

"You and I are both orphans, baby. You can stay with me for as long as you like," Lixie blubbered.

Johnny White tapped on her shoulder. "Mrs. Miller?"

Bonita mumbled something.

"What did you say, darlin'?" Lixie pressed.

"Can I call you Mama?" Bonita asked.

Lixie didn't know if it was five or fifty years of tears flowing down her cheeks.

"Eh, Mrs. Miller," Johnny White asked again, "are you okay?"

"Yes, Johnny. I'm just . . . I'm just fine!" she sobbed. "Everything is wonderful! This is . . ." She tried to talk through the tears, but her sobs were so deep she couldn't get the words out. She finally blurted out, "This is . . . this is . . . the most wonderful day . . . of my life!"

Lixie sucked in a deep breath and glanced across Railroad Avenue at the barren desert on the north side of the tracks. "You are wrong, Ramona Hawk. Lixie Miller is one of the winners!"

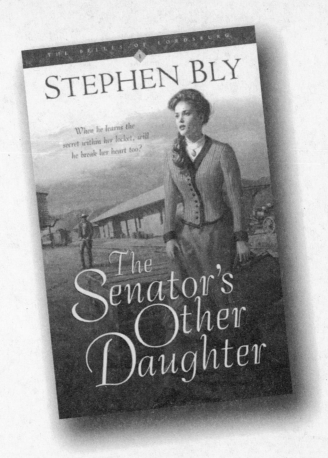

When he learns the
secret within her locket, will
he break her heart too?

STEPHEN BLY

The
Senator's
Other
Daughter

The Belles of Lordsburg

Lordsburg, New Mexico is a dusty little railroad town with few trees, treacherous heat, and no luxuries. But it's perfect. Perfect for black sheep, rebellious sons, and unrepentant outlaws to hide until people stop looking. Perfect for wayward daughters and well-kept secrets to disappear until a father's political career is settled.

At least, that's what Grace Denison thinks. But then she meets a cowboy whose very existence threatens her anonymity and whose questionable ways lead her to a place she's not sure she can—or wants—to go.